NOIR REHAB

Other books in the series:
Fancy Dancer (2020)
Ibizan Run (2023)

NOIR REHAB
A Jake Jakes Mystery

CARL WALDMAN

OUTER CITY PRESS

Outer City Press
PO Box 125, Cherry Valley, NY 13320

Cover art and design by Richard Saba

Paperback ISBN: 9781734529500

For Chloe and Devin ...
As they move through life's mysteries.

CONTENTS

EPILOGUE

PROLOGUE

~

Sam Spade: *"I don't mind a reasonable amount of trouble."*
– Dashiell Hammett, *The Maltese Falcon*

"I'M SORRY, OKAY?"

Jake was dreaming ... or was he? He heard himself apologizing. But to whom?

A man's deep voice interrupted his inner one: "Look at this. What the fuck?"

Jake felt sharp pain.

"Get up, you homeless piece of shit."

Easier said than done after a kick to the kidneys.

"A moment," Jake managed, anger rising up from the pain.

Another voice, this one gravelly, sounded out: "Fucking loser!"

A second kick caught Jake in the side. The kicks hurt but they could have been a lot worse. He saw three sets of legs. They stepped over him and out of the doorway onto the sidewalk. The varying shapes of three men were now silhouetted by the light of a distant streetlamp.

"Don't get too close," the first voice, that of the largest man, said. "He's probably contaminated with some new fucking virus."

Jake pulled himself to one knee, using the doorway to steady himself. Should he attack? Don't be a fool, he told himself.

"You drunk?" the gravelly voice asked.

Jake had been, he remembered, but no longer what with adrenaline and anger churning.

"No," he answered. "No pills either. Just recovering from your kicks, not my own."

He was telling the truth although he probably should have omitted the last part. He couldn't quite make it to upright, leaving his neck exposed. Sure enough, a blow landed right there, sending pain inward, then upward to his brain.

The gravelly voice: "That one was a punch ... for being a wiseass."

1

The blow, as harsh as it was, didn't feel damaging. The assailants were holding back, it seemed.

"I've seen you around here before," the third man said in a cockney accent. "Stay the hell off my block."

Gee, an international crowd, Jake absurdly thought on finding his vertical.

"Understood," he said.

He flinched while stepping past them, expecting another blow. It didn't come and he staggered away, his anger settling into a slow burn.

So much for Vandam Street.

PART I: DOORWAYS AND PARKS

Travis McGee, salvage consultant: *"I get the feeling that this is the last time in history when the offbeats like me will have a chance to live free in the nooks and crannies of the huge and rigid structure of an increasingly codified society."*
– John D. MacDonald, *The Quick Red Fox*

New Calling

THE DIN OF ARRIVING school kids one block over roused Jake all the way from his wakeful dozing on the playground bench. Given the early morning incident and resulting pain, in addition to the ache of the hangover, he'd been in a heightened survival mind, allowing for only half-sleep.

He'd also been in a self-disgusted frame of mind. For three months, he'd been clean other than some beer and weed and way too much tobacco. Living homeless hadn't been a continuation of his self-destructive habits as was the case with so many other street denizens. His circumstances had served as a daily reminder of where polydrug abuse had led him and had helped foster avoidance.

That was one way to resist altering consciousness, he'd resolved: cultivate shame and poverty to the point of near-starvation. Always an excuse to drink, he'd scolded his alcoholic mother ad nauseum. But last night he hadn't listened to his refrain.

He remembered eating a slice of pizza on Spring Street, although nothing after that. A blackout and all-too familiar hangover like this had to be from hard stuff, not beer. Bourbon, he would lay odds. A liquor store near the pizzeria had to be the dealer supplying this jumping-off-the-wagon fix. Jake reached into his pocket. Just eleven bills and a few coins left of the hard-earned eighteen dollars.

What had prompted the relapse? He'd walked past liquor stores without succumbing these past months. Had he spotted someone he knew? That is, had someone he knew spotted him – one woman or another – an expression on her face undermining his resolve?

What a fuckup he was, putting himself at risk in a random doorway like that. While living on the street, his fuzzy brain reasoned, the survival trick is fostering invisibility. People take notice when you panhandle. You also get noticed when you rant, a telltale sign of street insanity. And when people have to step over you, they see an obstacle – and probably someone contaminated – as the recent incident had painfully corroborated.

The gray day only encouraged self-flagellation. Jake decided to set out on a survival mission: He would reconnoiter a new sleeping place for the coming night. He left the Playground of the Americas. The small park, its name taken from Sixth Avenue's alternate name, Avenue of the Americas, had become his home base. After the assault, he'd kept watch for the park's gatekeeper from across the avenue. After the man had unlocked the gate and departed, Jake had entered the playground and peed in the bushes behind his favorite bench, something to be avoided since the odor of urine persisted and might lead to complaints. Being attacked had served as his rationalization for the convenience of relieving himself there. Then he'd tried to calm down enough to doze. Had he, even for a moment?

He crossed Sixth Avenue and angled up Bedford Street. A block and a half to the northwest up the narrow street, he observed a couple with what seemed like overnight bags exiting a brownstone and departing in a taxi. Leaving town? No one left behind? A safe bet for a doorway on loan?

Before returning to the playground, Jake stopped at the corner delicatessen on Sixth and Bedford and bought a coffee. The cashier knew him as a regular, but Jake inevitably felt self-conscious because of street grime and odors.

The playground was still empty. Always a good thing since adults, except those accompanied by children, weren't supposed to be there. Jake kept a functioning broom he'd found in someone's garbage hidden in the bushes behind his bench of choice, and sometimes he would sweep the small park as if he had an official role. At the very least, he was demonstrating a sense of responsibility for the shared space. Sweep today after the coffee?

No, he would head up to the public restroom at Washington Square Park.

A man wearing a skullcap, incongruous with his expensive-looking suit, walked northward along Sixth Avenue. In the short time it took him to reach the corner and cross Houston Street, he looked over his shoulder three times. Worried about being followed? Maybe he'd been with a woman and was checking for a husband in pursuit. Or maybe he was a gangster returning from a hit, a not-so-unlikely scenario in the Big Noir Apple. Jake had the urge to follow Mr. Skullcap and try to solve the mystery.

A notion formed in Jake's now caffeinated brain. Why not keep his attention on the twists and turns of other people's lives rather than on his own? To get out of his own head, he could make a point of observing and even following others. Mystery novels and movies, especially film noir, had been his mother's third favorite escape from reality after alcohol and pills. Why not roleplay being a private eye this morning? A sober, focused P.I. at that.

Behind and along part of the playground's rear chainlink fence was a wooden one, delineating a backyard belonging to a rundown brownstone facing MacDougal Street. Because of the rare human appearance, the tunneling rats, and the detritus visible through the gaps between the fence's slats, Jake knew the backyard got little use. On the fourth day of his homelessness – starting ironically on Independence Day – he'd devised a makeshift locker out of an extra heavy-duty black plastic bag. He'd used a knot at the top of the bag to secure it between the pointed tops of the fence's slats, dangling it over into the yard and out of sight of the playground and sidewalks beyond.

Other than his pen knife, his passport, his New York State Driver's License, and his vaccine certificate, Jake kept all his possessions in the plastic bag, including a blanket for cooler weather. No need for it on these early October warm nights. The pavement, stone, and brick retained just enough of the day's heat – for now anyway. The bitter cold would come all too soon. Winter was the deadline he'd set for his return to Shaleville if no other lodging presented itself. There, he wouldn't be homeless thanks to his sister. And by then hopefully, after the self-help lesson of living like this, he would manage to spare her his demons.

5

When no one walked alongside the park, Jake retrieved his bag, removed the toothbrush he kept in a second smaller bag inside the big black one, and used the trickle of the water fountain in the far corner of the playground for a discreet brushing. He also scrubbed his hands, trying to eliminate the grime imbedded in his flesh, the freebie tattoo of the street, and any viruses. He needed a shave, but that was no small deal at a slow-running water fountain and with a plastic disposable razor in a condition beyond disposing. He would take it with him to the public restroom in spite of shaving there being frowned upon.

Jake decided he would disguise himself as a jogger for his newly hatched plan. Once again waiting for the right moment, without passersby possibly observing, he changed from his stained jeans into equally stained sweatpants. He then replaced his ragged tan suede jacket for an equally ragged hoodie. A black New York Giants cap with orange lettering – not the football team, rather the baseball team that had moved to San Francisco more than half a century ago – helped with the jock look. He'd cleaned it recently with soap and water, making it look decent enough. The black Converse sneakers he donned, although tattered, could even pass for a fashion statement in this town. Now, to the Washington Square restroom and new opportunities the big city offered.

Jake crossed Houston and walked eastward along the big open paved park, utilized for a variety of sports, then took a left at MacDougal. This was downtime on the commercially developed street – its storefronts, restaurants, cafes, bars, and clubs recovering from the previous night – and he maintained a sense of near-invisibility.

On reaching Washington Square four blocks to the north, he angled toward the men's room. It was empty and he shaved quickly. Afterwards, somewhat refreshed, he chose a bench, an eastern-facing one for the best chance of some morning sunlight. From there he watched the focal point of the park – not the commemorative arch but rather the fountain. Buskers often performed around it. None did so yet today. But people were out and about – a continuing reaffirmation of post-pandemic return to normalcy – although keeping a reasonable distance from one another. Two men tossed a frisbee on a nearby lawn, making a dramatized performance out of that.

Jake visually tracked the flow of pedestrians, now with what he imagined a detective's perceptions. He hoped to run into Ricky, a homeless regular at the park and a good person to talk to about coping with life on street. Jake hadn't seen him in weeks and was worried. He and Ricky had met here when Jake still had an apartment, and they'd quickly bonded over their art. Originally from North Carolina, Ricky – or Ricky Rad – had been a well-known graffiti artist who favored subway tunnels for his work. Jake once had followed him into a subway station to see one of his pieces on the side of a tiled wall. It featured block lettering – *RADICAL 1* – shaped like a cityscape with a remarkable gamut of grays.

When Jake had informed him in July that he also was living homeless, Ricky had said, "Welcome to the club. How's about Jake Soho as your new handle?"

Jake had thought a street typically follows the first name or initial in tags. Soho or SoHo had come to refer to blocks south of Houston Street.

"What, I get a whole neighborhood?"

Ricky had responded with, "I know you spend lots of time here in the West Village. But Jake Soho sounds better than Jake Greenwich Village, right? Your first show was on Prince Street and you hang out in that playground on the south side of Houston. Own it!"

Jake Soho had a nice ring to it, Jake had mused. A break from the name his mother had bestowed on him – Jake Jakes. People inevitably commented about the double Jake thing, and he'd explained time and again that he was born in 1990, the year the neo-noir film *The Two Jakes*, the sequel to *Chinatown*, was released.

Since last spending time with Ricky, Jake had asked other street friends – Tenor and Mackerel – about their mutual friend more than once, but they hadn't seen him for a while either.

"Hey, Jake Soho ..."

As if summoned by Jake's thoughts, Tenor was barking his street handle from a location near the Washington Arch. He approached along the row of benches, pushing his shopping cart loaded with his life's possessions. Other folks on benches watched him pass by with what Jake interpreted as disdain. Tenor had earned his street name from his busking with his saxophone before hocking it. He looked serious today, revealing inner tautness, or was it just his skull showing through?

"Got any goodies today?" he asked.

Tenor, unlike many on the street, was as equally obsessed with food as stimulants. At least he still had an appetite and might survive longer that his gaunt appearance indicated.

"Not a damn thing."

"So why you ain't working?"

I *am* working, Jake thought – at private detection. To Tenor he said, "I saw a loaf of bread being passed around at the chessboards … Wonder Bread over yonder."

"Righto. Time to go kibitz. A bottle, too?"

"Sorry, Tenor, you'll have to reconnoiter that yourself."

Jake watched Tenor shuffle off. He seemed mostly bone with little remaining sinew and flesh. His body was ravaged by crystal meth starvation – a mirror of what might have been Jake's future if he'd kept using that particular drug. At least, as far as Jake knew, Tenor had gotten a Covid-19 vaccine. It had become Ricky Rad's personal mission to make sure his friends got one when they qualified. Ricky had accompanied many folks, including Jake.

"Good luck!" Jake called after Tenor.

Jake watched the world pass him by for a while longer, then decided it was time to look elsewhere for a mark. He stood up and headed south out of the park across West 4th Street and along Thompson toward Soho … in honor of Ricky Rad.

Jake eyed pedestrians as he walked. A long block into Soho, at the corner of Thompson and Prince Streets, he saw a woman pass by in a dramatic forties-style hat, like one a movie femme fatale might wear. Not surprisingly, within minutes, the cinematic fashionista led him to a clothing boutique farther south.

A young well-to-do couple caught his eye because they wore matching sleek shiny suits. Jake sauntered after them. They led him to a jewelry store on Spring Street.

He began to feel as if he were again shopping with auburn-haired Gillian on the Upper East Side, following her to one store after another and resisting the growing pressure to be trapped. Theirs had been a short relationship. A mutual breakup came quickly, not long after she'd proclaimed that she didn't like his version of "downtown artsy wild," and he'd responded he didn't like hers of "uptown shallow materialism."

Soho, with a number of art galleries, had seemed more appropriate to downtown Samantha than to uptown Gillian – Samantha, full of dreams of art and dressed in a mishmash of multilayered clothing that worked well with her tawny hair.

Women and shared neighborhoods. Let the past and his failures go, Jake told himself. Hard to do without depressants or stimulants, he well knew.

Rallying around his new purpose, he next tailed a disheveled middle-aged man with an unopened package wrapped in newspapers under his arm. This mark sat down on a bench at Spring and Thompson, closed his eyes, and turned his head toward the sun.

Jake lingered. A woman in a floral dress soon passed by, heading north up Thompson while talking loudly into her phone. It was amazing how public people were with their private lives. But cellphones sure made the task of extracting information on the street easier. Jake followed, staying in earshot.

"I played him for a change. It felt great." Pause. "No, his obnoxious mother and sister." Pause. "I don't care anymore. His taste's up his ass." Pause. "You sure?" Pause. "Okay, I'll do it if you come along. Just to piss them all off." Pause. "And their little *dog*, too!"

A *Wizard of Oz* reference? Jake inferred as such from the intonation. Caitlyn, his sister, would like that.

After a half-block the cellphone talker entered a sunglasses boutique. Yet another Soho shopper.

Jake seized on the last bit of phone dialogue as a cue to follow dogwalkers. The first was a tiny woman leading an overweight corgi, its stomach nearly touching the ground. She ended up at an apartment building. So did a tall tattooed muscular man with two dogs – a Doberman and a Rottweiler. A macho trio, they appeared to be, regardless of the dogs' genders. Another man walked a Labrador retriever to an SUV with New Jersey plates. A sly one, he was, to be driving in from New Jersey to walk his Labrador retriever on a Manhattan street to troll for hookups, or so Jake deduced.

Maybe he should have his family dog Cracker with him in order to meet women. Caitlyn had found the animal as a stray and brought it home. Their mother Grace had refused to get a dog for years and had insisted Caitlyn take it to the pound. Jake had backed up his sister about keeping it, browbeating their mother to relent.

As he remembered it, he'd told her, "You can't settle on one man to keep. If there's a male stray around here, let's make it a dog, okay?"

His support had meant a lot to his sister, who still held out hope that their mother could clean up and stay that way. Watching the Billy Wilder film, *The Lost Weekend*, ironically chosen by Grace as family entertainment, and seeing the character Don Birnam, played by Ray Milland, spiral downward had helped young Caitlyn catch on to the concept and challenges – and, too often, the hopelessness – of alcoholism.

Jake's gaze stayed inward as he again mentally drudged through how he himself had failed his sister because of his own downward substance-abuse spiral. She'd understood why he'd moved to New York. She knew about his fascination with this city that had started during a high school freshman trip, when he'd been taken with its energy and edginess, even as he resented that day's force-fed, scripted sightseeing. During her school trip three years later, she'd been turned off by the city's disconnect with nature and had proclaimed that she was forever a small-town girl. Even so, she'd expressed wanting to visit him in his new life and he hadn't made it happen. Indeed, what a fuckup he was.

One tall woman with a Boston terrier looked vaguely familiar. Jake tailed her west along Prince Street, then north on Sullivan. Who was she? He racked his brain as he followed her from the opposite side of the street – a trick even a greenhorn private dick could come up with. She led him all the way back to Washington Square Park, where she entered the dog run.

Others present turned their heads at the tall lady and her small dog. Did they recognize her, too? Jake used to pride himself on his visual memory. Not at the moment. A sign of drug-induced memory loss? But then it came to him. He'd seen her face and long limbs on magazine covers. Model/actress. A foreign-sounding name. He remembered that much at least. Whatever her name was, he wouldn't try to follow her home. No stalking celebrities, he decided. He was making up detection rules as he went along. Maintain some dignity, he told himself. Avoid the pathetic.

The day had heated up – more than during September even, more fittingly like the dog days of August – and Jake was sweating under his sweatshirt. He headed for the row of benches opposite the fountain, where he'd sat earlier. He'd completed a giant circle from this point and had gotten nowhere in his new calling.

A middle-aged, well-dressed woman sitting nearby stood up and, shooting a glance at him, moved away. How bad did he smell today? He should have given himself a sponge bath rather than shave. Brooklyn Aki (Japan Aki by way of Brooklyn) would have berated him. She was by far the most odor-conscious woman he'd ever met and claimed he stunk, even when he showered daily. He thought that was just another one of her obsessive-compulsive traits, although maybe he did smell back then, oozing drugs.

Obsessive-compulsive was one label that sure wouldn't stick to him as it did to Aki. His coping with street life confirmed that. He'd been called ADHD as a pre-adolescent and also once as having a "mild bipolar disorder, with some mixed episodes" – episodes in which symptoms of both depression and mania were present. Labels galore. "Prone to anger" was another one attached to him. One label that sure fit him snugly, as it did his mother, was "self-medicator."

Speaking of depression, remembering the language of lunacy was carrying him into it. Daytime drowsiness thankfully seeped in, washing away self-reflection ...

~

"Where are you Jake? Are you dead? Why do this to me?"

A female voice out of his past followed by a myoclonic jerk. Now, a male voice in the distance, pulling him back to wakefulness. This one had nothing to do with him. It was just some stranger in the park, shouting. But who had been the imploring female voice from his subconscious?

Caitlyn of course.

After a stop at the now-busy restroom, Jake left the park and walked back southward along MacDougal, then westward along

11

West 3rd Street to its corner with Sixth Avenue. Before and since living on the street, he often came to the block along the avenue between 3rd and 4th Streets to watch games in the "Cage" of the West 4th Street Courts, known for high-quality basketball. Today, however, he took up position along the park's chainlink fence from where he could discreetly watch people move in and out of one of the four entrances to the West 4th Street subway station.

No one grabbed his attention until a slender brunette, wearing a brown blazer, tan slacks, and white sneakers, ascended the stairs onto the street, crying. She paused to wipe her eyes with her sleeve, then turned the corner from Sixth and headed east on West 3rd. Jake followed.

Walking briskly, she led him past the intersecting north-south MacDougal, Sullivan, and Thompson Streets. At LaGuardia Place, as the light turned yellow, she hastened her slightly pigeon-toed stride to cross, leaving him at the red. Vehicles came from both directions so he couldn't jaywalk. He watched her turn right, heading south on LaGuardia. She then crossed Bleecker and turned left onto it, heading east again.

The light changed. Jake, sucking in the pain from the early morning blows, jogged across the wide street and down LaGuardia. On reaching the corner with Bleecker, he saw the brunette turn right from that street into Washington Square Village, the apartment complex owned by New York University and housing faculty and staff. The blue, yellow, red, and silver buildings, considered cutting edge in the fifties, someone had told him, now looked as dated to him as fins on cars.

Jake wasn't surprised at this destination. The woman seemed an academic type. In her thirties probably, she could be a professor or a professor's wife, or even a graduate assistant working toward a Ph.D. But don't get ahead of yourself, he told himself. She might be traversing the complex to Houston Street along its southern limits.

The brunette reminded Jake of Nan, she of his first relationship on moving to the city. She'd been a grad student in Art History at NYU. They'd met at the gallery that hosted his first show. They'd broken up some months later after she'd heard the owner scold him for being drunk at someone else's opening. That had started the fight with her anyway; it had soon evolved into a dispute about seemingly every issue big or small from their first day together. NYU Nan was long gone from these parts, teaching somewhere in the Midwest, he'd found out, on phoning her in a drunken, weak moment.

Jake entered the complex just in time to see the woman angle toward the entrance of one of the buildings. A doorman in a big-buttoned overcoat and general's hat opened the door for her, nodding in recognition.

Jake felt validation in his competent sleuthing. The woman apparently had some connection to academia. Stake out the apartment building in the morning? It would be interesting to see how this evidently brainy woman, who had a reason to cry in public, spent her days.

Maybe not validation after all, he admitted to himself, when he saw her glancing back through the glass entranceway at him, a look of concern on her face. Had she been aware of him all along? He fought back irritation going on anger. At her for being wise to him? Or at himself for deluding himself? Or maybe at himself for very likely creeping out a tearful woman. At least she hadn't appeared to pause long enough to inform the doorman of his suspicious presence.

Jake kept moving toward Houston Street, exiting the complex. What now? Being hungry, he decided to keep moving and forage like a hunter-gatherer of old, looking for returnables in corner trash bins or in clear garbage bags ready for pickup in front of homes and businesses. He wasn't desperate enough today to rummage through mixed garbage.

A decent enough harvest – $1.35 worth – and he fed the bottle-and-can-eating machines at the supermarket on LaGuardia. After cashing out his receipts, he headed back west.

At the northeast corner of Houston, he crossed Sixth Avenue and entered the corner deli for the second time that day. He bought a meager lunch – a pint of milk and a buttered roll. Outside again, he made his way to the Playground of the Americas. He sat down and began slowly eating.

Hunger under control, Jake pulled from his pocket one of several partly smoked cigarettes he'd scrounged up the day before, along with a full book of matches offered as promotional freebies in a restaurant vestibule. Pride mattered little when it came to nicotine, a readily available and affordable drug by way of foraging.

The hours ticked by. Jake remained motionless, ruminating, recovering. He'd bungled his roleplaying that day. Yet, while tailing people, he'd experienced the illusion of purpose and sometimes even a hint of exhilaration. Playing detective forced him out of his circular thoughts and away from stubborn drug cravings. He'd learned from his initiation as a P.I. and would try again tomorrow.

An elderly man entered the playground but didn't glance his way. Two mothers with small children soon arrived but also seemed oblivious to his presence. The playground's closing time approached, and the other visitors didn't stay long. For now, his sought-after invisibility felt real.

The gatekeeper would be arriving soon to lock up. Jake retrieved his suede jacket from his makeshift locker and exited the playground. He crossed Sixth Avenue, proceeding up Bedford Street toward the house he'd scouted that morning. To reaffirm that it was empty, he sat down on a stoop on the opposite side of the street and settled in to wait.

Dusk morphed into darkness. No lights came on in the house, and Jake crossed Bedford and tucked himself into the shadows of the hopefully safe doorway, using his jacket as a pillow.

Greenwich Village streets, true to form, buzzed with sounds of nightlife. Jake could rationalize the activity as either increasing or decreasing vulnerability. If no harm came to him ... on a personal or apocalyptic scale ... daylight would break for him once more.

Inertia

DAYLIGHT DID RETURN, Jake's side of the Earth spinning toward sunlight. Remarkable that nothing bad happened, given humanity's ways. On cue, reminding him of human waste, came the sounds of a garbage truck – the shrill birdlike beeping as it backed up, the wheeze of hydraulics moving its innards, and the grinding of garbage being chewed up.

Unnoticed as far as he knew, Jake rose to his feet and stepped out of the doorway onto the sidewalk. First stop, the corner deli

14

where he bought a coffee, a mini-chocolate bar, a banana, and, even though his funds were getting low, a newspaper. Second stop, the bench in the small playground.

Jake ate and read. Since he'd lost his cellphone, discarded printed news served as his primary link to the world at large – sometimes purchased, sometimes taken from the corner freebie publications bins, and sometimes retrieved from the city's corner trash containers. He absorbed the news good or bad as an outsider, one psychological benefit of homelessness, at least for him. He could feel distanced from the ludicrous goings-on. Better that, he'd decided, than seizing on one news report or another as an excuse for his plight.

But his normal routine didn't offset his morning doubts. What had he been thinking? His homelessness crashed back down on him with a vengeance. New calling? New purpose? Following people around like he was onto something important?

Jake saw some movement out of the corner of his eye. He turned to see a rat scurrying along the bottom of the fence behind him, then disappear into the backyard of the brownstone. How appropriate. He himself had become a scurrier between safe havens.

Fear of beatings and sickness washed through him. And shame mixed with the fear for living like this. Part of his state of mind, he figured, was a delayed psychological crash after his binge. He first resisted the self-loathing. But why not just wallow in it? Didn't he deserve to?

To that end, he envisioned himself in his former apartment on Charleton Street and allowed himself to long for it. Although railroad-style, with the bathtub in the kitchen and a single window offering just a view of the neighboring building's brick wall, Jake now remembered it as luxurious. He'd certainly worked hard to make it more so, spackling and painting the cracked plaster walls. His eventual eviction had been the start of his phase of leeching off women.

Living on the street had been the next phase. He'd considered homeless shelters but was scared off by what he'd heard about them. Soup kitchens and missions made him nervous enough. Word had it that for those willing to be on file to accept some counseling, drop-in centers, as run by the NYC Department of

Homeless Services with support of nonprofits, helped street denizens cope. Spend time talking to someone for a shower sure seemed a worthwhile tradeoff. But he'd procrastinated.

Sounds of the city momentarily distracted him from depressing thoughts – the drone of traffic and the whoop-whoop crescendo and decrescendo of sirens.

A middle-aged woman, who he assumed to be homeless because of her laundry cart filled with sundry items, entered the playground, further distracting him. Seeing her led to thoughts about his street friend Manic Mary. She'd been a certifiable paranoid schizophrenic – talk about a heavy label to carry around – so paranoid that she was afraid of the medications that might have helped her. She'd fled the normal life others kept trying to surround her with, wandering from city to city. Her journey through homelessness had begun in Seattle after a breakup with her girlfriend. But she'd been a survivor. She'd moved along the precipice but never quite over the edge, fleeing before the latest city swallowed her up. She'd told Jake about stints in Seattle, San Francisco, Albuquerque, and Atlanta, and regularly sleeping in cardboard boxes over heating vents. In New York City she'd finally found a home.

"I'm not homeless anymore, Jake … just houseless!" she'd affirmed.

Labels used to include "bums," "tramps," "vagrants," and "hobos." "Homeless" was the PC term but that even pissed off Mary.

Jake had accompanied her to her home once. He'd had no idea until then the degree to which some people on hard times used abandoned train tunnels and their connecting chambers or nooks and crannies as shelter – those part of the subway system as well as those under and branching out from the Grand Central and Penn Station Amtrak lines. For decades, the authorities had made sporadic efforts to drive out the "mole people," as they'd come to be known. But some inevitably had returned underground, especially in wintertime. Hierarchal communities had even developed. Mary's community had turned a passageway once connecting two buildings into a home. Rats, roaches, foul odors, and too many people – itchy people, indicating head lice and / or scabies – hadn't offset that concept.

When in Mary's presence, listening to her stories – however scattered and piecemeal – Jake had felt better about humanity. A female friend, like Aki. Jake should be blogging about Manic Mary and Ricky Rad. Who had told him that? Rainy had, a friend who had become a lover and then an ex.

Jake stood up, approached the woman, and handed her a dollar.

"In case you're hungry," he told her.

She looked at him, barely seeming to register him, then quickly stood up and left, pushing her cart with considerable effort.

Jake sat back down. A bus's brakes squealed up to a Sixth Avenue stoplight. He longed for the comfort of even that. When first living on the street, he used to scrounge up fares. He liked riding a bus all the way to its last stop on the other end of Manhattan Island. The return trip required a second fare. With subways he could work out a route through the maze of tunnels, riding interminably on a one-trip MetroCard. But why take another ride to nowhere? He couldn't even rouse himself to search for a cigarette butt.

When Jake couldn't bear to watch the movement around him any longer, resenting the passersby for their seemingly competent lives, he leaned back and looked upward at the tops of buildings – chimneys, water towers, add-ons – and the grayish-pinkish polluted sky above. Visions of New York disintegrating – collapsing into itself like the Twin Towers had time and again on repeated news broadcasts – seemed as real to him as the flow of people and vehicles.

A woman with a toddler entered the park. She glanced over at Jake in the way women nervously glance at men on lonely city streets before looking away. This was a mother, looking at a shabbily dressed adult man in a kids' playground.

Jake had to act on this loss of near-invisibility. Not just for his state of mind but also for that of others, changing locations enough to keep the world around him unthreatened. A restroom beckoned anyway. He stood up and moved out, fighting back anger as he walked. That woman had a kid, he reasoned with himself. Forgive her if she judged him out of fear. She might very well have empathy for the less fortunate who occupy park benches. He mentally absolved her, shifting anger toward self-serving hatemongers who generalized their blame, looking down on all the home-have-nots as an undesirable class unto themselves – this society's untouchables – regardless of their individual stories.

~

A performer worked a small crowd near the fountain. From his bench perch in Washington Square, Jake heard a male voice and reserved laughter, followed by interludes of silence. No music so not a dancer and probably not a gymnast or a juggler either. A magician more likely than a comic. Before the pandemic, Jake had spent many hours as a front-row audience member to street theater. Not today in his jaded state.

Some teens broke off from the crowd, heading north through the Washington Arch, and Jake found just enough motivation to follow them. Other than the typical drug bazaar, nothing was going on at the arch's base, not even a solitary soul offering black-market drugs. Jake moved past the two gargantuan marble George Washingtons keeping guard – George as general and president both – and proceeded along this southernmost block of Fifth Avenue.

Why tail these particular teens? Partly because of the skateboards the two boys had under their arms, reminding Jake of his own past efforts at wheelies, pivots, ollies, and slides; partly because one wore a SUNY Albany T-shirt, a reminder of upstate New York; and probably most of all because one of the two girls reminded him of Rainy, a younger version, granted, but also with brunette hair in a ponytail.

Universal Rainy, who worked a wide variety of jobs – from tutoring to waiting on tables to dog-walking to house-painting – and desired women as much as men. She'd been the last woman with whom Jake had been romantically involved before homelessness.

"Christ, Jake, you can't listen for a moment," she'd told him. "You're all over the place."

"I keep getting back to you."

"Yeah, and then you drift off again."

She'd then broke it to him that she didn't want to be with someone who couldn't be with her without being on something.

18

He'd used pushing her out of his head as an excuse to be on even more somethings. That had lasted until his resolution of cleaning up his addictive behavior – his recently compromised resolution, he reminded himself, like too many other such resolutions these past years.

Jake deduced where the teens were headed when they made a right on 8th Street and a left on University Place. They were on their way to Union Square Park, he felt certain. The park's southern end on 14th Street – considered the northern boundary of the neighborhood delineated as Greenwich Village – had become a favorite destination for skateboarding.

A solid deduction, it turned out, cheering Jake up a bit. At the park the two teens with the boards – one gangly and the other compact – went right to the back of the line and waited. When their turns came, they began acing railslides, earning exclamations from the spectators. The shorter, compact fellow was more precise in his motions, sliding down the curved steel railing as if he were a smart bomb. Jake, however, preferred the tricks of the gangly one, who on each attempt seemed on the verge of toppling, hair and arms at wild angles, but who always managed to pull out a smooth landing. One other skater did fall and, without helmet or elbow or knee pads, the crash landing was ugly, all of him seeming to scrape. The crowd gasped. Jake remembered a few of his own falls as a middle-schooler on Main Street, Shaleville – not from railslides certainly since he'd never graduated beyond curbs.

Jake glanced one more time at surrogate Rainy, then climbed the stone steps past the skateboarders in search of a bench in the shade. He was feeling shaky and needed to sit. Union Square Park was even more crowded than Washington Square today, and finding an empty seat that didn't violate the new social distancing etiquette necessitated some wandering.

He finally sat down along a row of mostly empty seats near the Marquis de Lafayette statue. Across from him was a slouching probably twenty-something woman, moving a felt-tip pen over an open sketchpad in her lap. A southpaw, like Jake. She had on earbuds and her head bobbed slightly to whatever was playing from the cellphone on the bench next to her. She had hennaed red hair that just reached her neck. Translucent blue-frame glasses matched her blue eyes. A gray artist's smock, splattered with

19

paint, partly covered a white t-shirt and blue jeans with holes. Her leather boots were faded. Based on her body language, Jake projected that she was in the park because she didn't want to be somewhere else. But what did he know?

The woman put down the pen, picked up the phone, and swiped the screen.

She held it near her mouth and spoke into it, just loud enough for Jake to hear.

"Yeah?" Pause. "It figures. When?" Pause. "No problem. I'll goddamn do it … and with no questions from little obedient me. I'm checking out where it'll happen right now in fact. But you know I'll need an explanation for what kind of shit you're into." Pause. "Okay, right, whatever. But you have to convince him who *he* can trust." Pause. "Protect me? That's bullshit. It's just a control thing. Tell him he's acting like a loser with a little power." She laughed sarcastically, then another pause. "Stop worrying and appreciate what I do for you." Pause. "Will I see you tonight?" Pause. "Fuck you, Ned."

She stood up and moved quickly away. Jake had the urge to follow but felt trapped in inertia. Was that phone conversation enough of a rationale to tail her? Or would he just be acting like a creepy stalker of an attractive woman?

Clouds had formed. Thunder sounded out in the distance.

He needed a drink and then some. He stood up and walked in a different direction from the woman. But not to a deli for beer or a liquor store for something stronger. He would resist.

Rain soon came. The scaffolding erected around a building under repairs served as shelter from the wet. Jake stood there in the growing storm, propped up against a corrugated metal wall, watching the water drip down the iron poles to the sidewalk's concrete.

The rain finally slowed to a sprinkle. Jake walked to a restaurant where he trusted the leftovers tossed out after dinner. Some restaurants throw ammonia on their garbage to drive away the homeless. Others, word on the street had it, put rat poison in their garbage to prevent foraging. At least one street death he'd heard about was blamed on that. Inside a small plastic bag in one of the big garbage bags, he turned up a doggie pouch of curried rice. He checked for bugs. He didn't see any but just the thought of them caused him to gag and he discarded his find.

Jake continued downtown, passing a hulking shape tucked against a building out of the rain – a man sleeping. He wore a puffy powder-blue faded and frayed coat and reminded Jake of a discarded mattress, all used-up, ready to be picked up by the Grim Reaper's sanitation engineers. Body odor intermingled with the stink of stale alcohol, making even olfactory-weary Jake gag again.

He lingered long enough to make sure the man's breathing was regular. It was. The hovering Specter of Death would have to wait.

Boroughing

THE NEXT MORNING, Jake returned to Union Square with the Greenmarket in mind, its produce cheaper than at a deli. He walked slowly along the park's western edge, stretching out the minutes because after something to eat … what?

Jake bought the biggest apple he could scope out on two different fruit stands. After his purchase, he still had enough to buy a forty-ounce malt liquor with a decent alcohol count. Don't do it, he told himself. Concentrate on the apple.

Chewing on it, he ambled back to 14th Street and then eastward. Skateboarders had again gathered at the railing. No surrogate Rainy among them today. He entered the park, wondering if he should sit or simply keep walking.

The henna-haired woman with the blue eyes and matching blue-frame glasses sat along the same walkway near the same bench as the day before. She again wore the artist's smock, now over a red skirt and clashing purple tights, and again had the sketchpad across her thighs and felt-tip pen in her left hand.

Jake's gumshoe persona was revived by the serendipity of seeing her again. Take the empty seat next to her? The sketching would give him an opening for conversation. He could talk art world with her. And drive her away? He decided to keep to the private part of private eye and just observe. He chose a bench on the opposite side of the walkway. A number of people were present; hopefully he didn't stand out.

He slowly finished his apple, keeping a side glance on her. When she looked up through her glasses, it was in the direction of a tree behind him to the right, so he could study her unnoticed. Her artist's focus attracted him, as did her insouciance.

The woman eventually closed her sketchpad and looked around. Her eyes ran over him. What did she think on seeing him? No apparent recognition from the day before. He was after all one of the used-up, surplus people, just this side of invisible.

Time passed. She now sat motionless, eyes closed as if in meditation.

With clouds now blocking the sun and a slight chill in the air, the benches started emptying. The faux redhead stayed on. Jake stood out more and more on his side of the walkway. He decided to feign dozing. He could nestle in and watch her through half-closed eyes, like a reptile seemingly oblivious to its prey yet ever ready.

A man sat down beside her. Probably in his thirties, wearing a brown leather coat – the kind of shiny leather that looks like imitation plastic – creased chinos, and black suede shoes with rubber soles. Muscular build. Short brown hair. His clothes and shovel-face made him look foreign. Slavic? He carried a small black canvas *I Love New York* bag over his shoulder. Was this the Ned from her conversation the day before?

Apparently not. She didn't greet him and the man didn't speak to her. Why sit so close then? A come on? The woman seemed okay with it. The man yawned, looked around, then sat up as abruptly as he'd sat down and headed north.

The woman pulled out her phone. Jake strained to hear, hoping for enough of a lull in the city background noise to make out her words. Other than "Done, done, okay?" he couldn't hear anything she said. She put away her phone, moved out, rangy but graceful, heading south toward 14th Street.

It was then Jake noticed she had the *I Love New York* bag strung from her shoulder. Mr. Shiny Leather had passed a bag to Ms. Faux Redhead. Cash, drugs, stolen DVDs – whatever it involved, a mystery of some kind to pursue. He stood up to follow.

On exiting the park, the woman walked toward the subway entrance on Park Avenue, disappearing down the stairs. Jake had guessed she lived or worked in the neighborhood. Perhaps not. If she wanted a secret meeting place with easy access to public transportation, she might very well choose this park since a lot of trains converge at Union Square Station with a number of entrances to the platforms and tracks below.

Jake hurried down the stairs and saw the woman heading for the platform servicing the eastward-bound L train to Brooklyn. She had her MetroCard ready and, swiping it, pushed on through the turnstile. He had to rush over to a MetroCard vending machine and follow the instructions, touching the appropriate boxes on the screen. He slipped in his dollar bills. The machine gave back a one-ride card. He hurried to a turnstile, swiped the card, and moved onto the platform. Lots of people waited there. Jake kept several of them between him and his mark.

A train soon clattered to a halt. Its doors gasped open. Passengers exited and new passengers stepped aboard, the wannabe redhead among them. Jake entered at the far end of the same car she had and again positioned himself behind people. He had a clear visual line on her hand, first gripping on a pole, then holding the horizontal metal tubing above the seats. No leather straps to cling to anymore. Riders were still sometimes called "straphangers," as in the black-and-white movies his mother had fed him like popcorn itself.

"This is the Brooklyn bound L train," a soothing recorded female voice announced. "The next stop is Third Avenue."

"Stand clear of the closing door, please." A recorded male voice now spoke, a little more authoritatively.

Jake felt the pull of the train as it gathered speed. The electricity of the live third rail seemed to course through veins and arteries.

A lot of young people rode the L train, also called the Canarsie Local after the Brooklyn neighborhood at its other end. He'd often ridden it himself to get to bars, parties, friends' apartments, and a dealer's crib before he began using the delivery services.

The woman with the bag announcing *I Love New York* – did she really? – stayed aboard as the train made stops at Third then First Avenue. The train cut through the bedrock under the East

River into another borough, Brooklyn, and onto another island, Long Island.

Until recently, Jake had barely registered the borough of Manhattan as an island and the boroughs of Brooklyn and Queens as part of the much larger Long Island. No doubt about the geographical designation of Staten Island, the smallest borough. He'd finally caught on to the Bronx being the only New York City borough on the North American mainland. In his new life he had to give thought to where he might best cope and how to best get there cheaply. Homelessness as Geography 101.

The other passengers gave Jake space – more space than even they were giving one another. Because of his odor and all that it implied, no doubt. He had a psychological antidote for that angry thought. Aki, his OCD germaphobic photographer friend of the sensitive nose, had kept her distance from him even before the pandemic. Having escaped a conservative village and family in Japan, she accepted and embraced varying lifestyles, just not the odors that came with them, her face often tight with disgust. He'd accepted that behavior from a friend so why not accept it from strangers?

Passengers came and went through the first stops in Brooklyn – Bedford Avenue, Lorimer Street, Graham Avenue, and Grand Street, all names with a history bigger than his own, he reminded himself, trying not to take himself too seriously despite being energized.

After the Montrose Avenue stop, she walked over to a now-empty seat. At the Grand Street stop, through the window, he saw a sloppy tag on the tile wall: *ROGUE 123*. A tagger must have written that from between cars while the train was stopped, or had spray-painted it from the tracks, risking the dangerous electrified third rail in addition to oncoming trains, perhaps with a friend to act as a ladder. Given how driven taggers were to do their thing, either seemed likely. The only tags Jake saw on the interior of the subway car itself were some barely legible writing scratched in stainless steel or in glass windows.

Ricky Rad came to mind again. He'd carried on the tradition of earlier taggers, he'd explained in detail to Jake. Once upon a time in New York City – from the late nineteen-sixties well into the eighties – the outsides and sometimes insides of subway cars had been the galleries of choice for graffiti artists, or "writers" as they were called because much of their work involved lettering. The trains, sometimes every inch of every car decorated, had become moving art galleries traversing the city, making the represented tagger/artist/writer "all city" in street lingo.

Jake's mother had visited a high-school friend in Queens and had brought him along as a small boy and his sister Caitlyn as a toddler. Jake had a vague memory of the somewhat even scarier wonderland the subways had been at that time. Tagging in subways had waned when the city began cracking down, making it hard for artists/writers to reach the parked subway cars. Razor wire and dogs had been used to protect the railway yards. Cleaning solvents had been improved. The trains themselves had eventually been engineered to resist paints. City hardware stores had started locking up "rusto" (Rust-Oleum) and other spray paints, just as they did knives.

Graffiti art had continued to grow. A subculture had developed around the practice, often associated with rapping and break-dancing. Young artist/writers carried their "black books" in which they drafted their work before going public with it. They sometimes formed "crews" to collaborate on works, organized like art street gangs. They created remarkably detailed "pieces" – the term on the street for "masterpieces" – on walls and other parts of the city's infrastructure. The most elaborate pieces earned the name "burners," seeming to burn out of walls. Those pieces in high-up dangerous places came to be called "heavens" or "giraffiti." "Throw-ups" became the term for graffiti somewhere between a tag and a piece, and artists were said to "bomb" surfaces with them, covering as much of an area as possible. Sometimes one artist painted over another's work as if a territorial thing. Some of the works were politically and socially relevant. Some, like those of Ricky Rad, although done in spray paint, were as detailed as those of commercial illustrators.

Tagging in all its variations, condemned by city officials and passengers seeking order, had come to be embraced by proponents of artistic self-expression. Asking and getting permission to do walls had become a thing. Ricky had told Jake he and some other taggers he knew refused to ask permission.

On seeing his mark open the black bag and peer inside, Jake's attention returned from reminiscing to the task at hand. She reached inside the bag for a moment but didn't remove anything. It wasn't until four stops after Montrose – Myrtle-Wyckoff – that she stood up to exit. So did a bunch of other passengers and, after the train jerked to a stop and the doors slid open, Jake was able to follow her onto the platform unnoticed. Or so it seemed since she didn't glance back. He bet other passengers noticed as his odor went with him through the sliding doors.

At the top of the stairs the woman exited the new-looking station and turned onto Palmetto Street, the third street sharing the busy intersection with Myrtle and Wyckoff Avenues. Street activity buzzed in this part of the neighborhood known as Bushwick.

Things quieted down along Palmetto, this part of it residential with small rowhouses. Following his mark from the opposite side of the street, Jake stayed just close enough that if she quickly disappeared inside a house, he could see where she'd gone. She still seemed oblivious to what was behind her, moving deliberately in her long fluid strides.

After passing Ridgewood Place that entered Palmetto from the left, the woman continued to Irving Avenue and crossed it. About two-thirds the way down Palmetto's next block, she stopped in front of what looked like a one-story warehouse. Three concrete steps led to a metal door with peeling green paint. Off to one side was a concrete ramp leading to a larger metal door for loading and unloading, this one painted gray. The building had no windows.

The woman pulled out her phone. A car rounded the corner of Knickerbocker Avenue and headed along one-way Palmetto toward her and Jake. It slowed down near her, music blasting. The passenger yelled something at her over the music. She ignored the harassment, keeping her back to the car as it accelerated away, concentrating on her cellphone. Only when the car neared Irving Avenue did she glance its way.

While all that was happening, Jake had angled past where she stood and crossed the street to the doorway of a storefront. Plywood covered the window and a big padlock dangled from the weatherworn door. He caught his breath in the doorway's shadows, hoping she hadn't spotted him.

"I'm outside," Jake could hear her say – into her phone, he presumed. "I want in." Pause. "Whattya you worried about?" Pause. "Well, tell Marcus a little trust would be a good fucking thing. I'll be meeting him eventually, won't I?" Pause. "I know, I know." Pause. "But from here on out I refuse to be the good little errand girl without knowing what the fuck is going on." Pause. "To hell with you, Ned."

Silence, except street sounds. A honking sounded out in the distance, like an angry goose. Jake waited. She also was waiting, probably no more than fifteen feet from him. He wanted to catch a glimpse of anyone appearing from the building but didn't dare stick his head out.

He heard a moan-like sound, a door opening apparently, and a male voice: "Great. Thanks."

"That's it?" the woman asked.

"For now."

"Fuck you, Ned."

She said that a lot.

"Come on, Leandra, don't take it personally," Ned told her. "We're just following instructions. You did good. We're underway."

"I looked in the bag," she said. "What's with the Mickey Mouse doll? This some kind of fucking joke?"

He shushed her. Then, in a quieter voice: "I can't say … and you promised not to look."

"I should know what you're getting me into, shouldn't I?"

"You will, you will, when we get the okay. Marcus agrees you should be involved, but word hasn't come yet. They're probably waiting to see if the doll works out."

Drugs, it had to be drugs, Jake surmised.

"Who? That creep who passed this to me?" she asked sarcastically. "Where'd Marcus dig him up?"

"It's a long story."

"Must be. So that's all you have to say after I did you this favor?"

"Look. This will be the end of the world as they know it. Talk about occupying. Occupy their brains. You'll love it. It's perfect. That's all I'm saying for now. Be patient. I gotta go."

"You returning to the East Village tonight?"

"Probably not. Stuff to do here."

"Goodbye, asshole."

Taking a chance, Jake glanced around the edge of the doorway just in time to catch sight of the man – Ned, she'd called him – who had been talking to her. Tall and thin with brown dreadlocks sticking out from a beanie cap. He wore a woolen sweater and blue jeans. Probably Jake's age. He reentered the green door. Jake pulled his head back as he heard the door moan shut.

His thoughts bounced about. Something bizarre was going on here. Whatever it was, it sure sounded big. That "end of the world" bit and "occupy their brains." Maybe this crew planned to release some new designer drug on the street that would shake things up. Another thought came to him that these were just hardcore rock musicians who thought they were onto something and were being all secretive about it. Maybe the name of their band was the Mickey Mouses. Wouldn't that be a great solution to the mystery? Jake could go watch the faux redhead with the loping walk perform. Leandra was her name, he now knew. Leandra and the Occupiers. Now there was a band name.

Jake glanced around the edge of the doorway again. No more shadowing Leandra since he'd hesitated too long when she headed off. Not that it mattered, he told himself. She would probably take a subway back to her home and he didn't have any more money for a fare. He would have to collect a lot of empties, panhandle, or take the long walk.

Jake decided to stay and see if anyone exited the cinderblock warehouse. To get a better view, he crossed back over to the west side of Palmetto and leaned against a building a little way down the block. Just a homeless guy killing time.

A young man in the black uniform of punk rockers, enhanced by facial piercings, walked by. He had a guitar in a clear plastic bag, the instrument's head sticking out. It would have been a timely confirmation of Jake's band theory if the fellow had headed for the warehouse. Although he passed it by, the sight of him confirmed Jake's take on New York City's facile identity thing. Buy a guitar, learn to play three chords, and proclaim yourself a musician. Buy some tights and become a dancer. Carry a pen and pad and you're a poet; a brush and pad, and you're a painter. It hadn't taken Jake long to find an identity after having migrated here from upstate without even a college stopover. He'd started doing odd handyman jobs for cash as he'd done in his hometown, but he'd also begun using throwaway materials to make sculptures. Jake the sculptor, an identity that had carried him through a series of relationships until his alcoholic, druggy behavior won out. And now?

A private detective? Still some kind of all-too-easy New York fantasy?

After an interminable hour or so, two men exited the warehouse – Ned with the dreads along with a shorter, compact, owl-faced fellow about the same age, with close-cropped yellowish hair under a black leather short-brimmed hat and a light stubble on his weak chin. He wore a green New York Jets jacket, tan carpenter pants covered in paint, and black leather boots. This was Marcus, Jake assumed. Both he and Ned wore small backpacks. The contents of the *I Love New York* bag – a Mickey Mouse doll for real? – might now be in either one. The two nodded self-importantly and headed in opposite directions.

Jake had to make up his mind whom to follow and chose the taller Ned, easier to spot in a crowd. Would he go join Leandra? Wait, she'd been angry she wouldn't see him that night. Separate lodgings? Ned walked briskly along Palmetto toward Myrtle. To the subway station?

No, he stopped at a corner bus stop. Jake stood, watching and resenting his latest mark. What, for not making the task easier of figuring out what was going on?

A bus arrived. Ned boarded it. So much for today's adventure. Jake would sleep on what to do about this mystery. It was late afternoon and he had a long trek back to Manhattan.

He walked along Myrtle, knowing that heading west under the tracks of the aboveground M train would get him closer to the Williamsburg Bridge to Manhattan. He stopped from time to time to poke in some corner and residential trash containers for returnables but found none. A group of teens commented on him and laughed, profiling him as one of the garbage-pickers.

Anger surged. Jake envisioned himself going into what had once been his own teenage brawling mode, taking them all out. He asked himself the absurd question whether boiling anger was hardboiled, like the heroes he extolled. Being chill – a shamus concept as well – worked better here since they were just stupid teens. In other words, he told himself, let it go.

He walked on. Beginning to doubt his geography, Jake was relieved to reach Broadway – Brooklyn's Broadway, not Manhattan's Great White Way – and since he knew where it was in relation to the bridge, he followed it northwestward. He also knew that Broadway met Penn Street where Aki lived.

Jake had made the walk between Manhattan and Brooklyn to his friend's apartment a number of times, when he had drug energy and found the subway too confining. He'd crossed both the Manhattan Bridge and Brooklyn Bridge farther to the south in addition to the Williamsburg, but he'd never mastered the maze of Brooklyn streets near them and, more than once, had had to ask for directions. It probably had made people nervous when he did, drunk or drugged up, probably talking too fast and with wild eyes.

Now, without the drug buffer and with darkness falling, Jake felt increasingly vulnerable. As an antidote, he took in the chiaroscuro of the cityscape, this one with lower and softer edges than his turf back across the Hudson. While doing so in the fading sunlight and growing artificial light, he had the thought that New York City looked best in black and white, the way he'd been introduced to it watching old movies.

Jake reached Penn Street. It angled southward. This stretch of Penn he knew as relatively safe, a number of businesses mixed in with the residences, most of them operated by Orthodox Jews. He needed rest so he detoured along it.

Why Penn? He certainly didn't want Aki to see him like this. But the comfort zone of a known block was motivation enough.

Moving quickly on the side of the block opposite her building, he made his way to a doorway of a closed business, a plumbing store. The nearest streetlamp illuminated a portion of it but, when he stepped inside, shadows enveloped him. He sat down, his back against the metal and glass door, and closed his eyes. He would nap in this familiar neighborhood, then make his way to Manhattan. At least he hadn't lost the ability to fall asleep anywhere in spite of his having wreaked havoc with his sleep cycle.

A car alarm briefly sounded out in the distance. Jake felt the weight of his head pushing his chin to his chest ...

Visuals flicker behind his closed eyelids ... paint-splattered smock, henna red hair, blue-framed glasses, peeling green paint on a door ... and then the images begin to break up, becoming abstract ...

Domesticity

"FUCK!" JAKE VOCALIZED, his rage boiling over as cold water hit his head.

What a miserable way to awaken. He'd heard of the homeless getting doused but had managed to avoid that experience until now. He wiped his eyes and looked up, expecting a beefy plumbing store proprietor. No, it was skinny little Aki who had emptied a water bottle on him, camera hanging from her neck, camera bag dangling from one shoulder, and a tote bag from the other. She wore an orange scarf, black jeans, and a purple polo shirt. Always something orange. He'd once given her an international orange safety vest he'd picked up in a hardware store. For her it had been a major fashion statement. At least she hadn't dyed her black hair orange.

"Jake. Whatcha doing here? Waiting for me?"

He wiped his face with his sleeve. "Huh? No."

"You heard I tried to find you?"

"Huh?"

"Stop it with the 'huhs'? And what's with your skanky clothing?" She retreated a few steps. "You know you really stink."

Jake sat up, collecting scattered thoughts. "I was just trying to take a nap and, no, I wasn't waiting for you. I know better than to bother you when I'm like this. I was on my way back to Manhattan and I just felt safe here on this block. Safe from water being thrown on me for one thing."

"I thought about taking a picture of this guy sleeping in a doorway and saw it was you. You strung out? What're you on?"

"Nothing."

31

"Then what's your problem?"

"I'm homeless."

"Mother-fucking shit!"

Aki sounded like a native New Yorker even though she was born and raised in Japan. She'd told him she'd improved her English and learned American slang as a teenager by watching hundreds of American movies. Captivated by the global rock scene, by age sixteen she'd become a photographer of visiting foreign bands – a rock celebrity stalker, she'd admitted.

"Don't worry," he reassured her. "Homelessness is working for me as a kind of rehab. The shame of it all plays a part. So does the fear. I have to stay sober and alert."

She was still scowling. "Yeah right, alert like a log."

"Really," he insisted. "I'm getting it together."

"Whatever. If you're gonna sleep outside on my block, why not just call me and at least beg for a shower and a couch?"

"Lost my phone."

She stared at him like she might a foolish child. "You're pathetic."

"And you're as bluntly honest as ever. Anyway, I wanted to spare you the agita."

"Yeah, why the hell am I even talking to you out here? Oh, right, I owe you."

"Say what?"

"Rainy tell you I was trying to reach you?"

"You talked to Rainy?"

"She said she had no idea where you were. I thought about tracking down your sister's number and calling her, but I didn't want to freak her out."

"I'm glad you didn't."

She stared at him another long moment, expressionless. Knowing her, he assumed she was coming to some decision.

She finally spoke: "Come on. I'll explain upstairs. First, I decontaminate you. You take a long bath ... a shower first, then you can soak. I'll launder your clothes while you do. Then we'll talk. I can feed you, too. You hungry?"

"I haven't stopped being hungry in a long time."

"But you can't stay over. No way! Promise me you'll leave without an argument?"

"Didn't I clear out whenever you asked me to?"

"Yeah, but people get weird when they're down and out. Promise?"

"Yes, Aki."

"Wait ... did you finally get the vaccine?"

"Yes, even though I'm pretty sure I'd already caught and survived the disease."

She sighed. "Yeah, me too." She thought another moment. Then:

"Okay, pay attention. I'll prop open the doors with my bags. Don't touch them. You walk on through and wait at the far end of the hall. I'll go up the stairs first, then you follow, keeping your distance. Ten feet, not six! And don't touch the banister."

Jake watched her cross the street. She stepped lightly, her lithe body almost seeming to float. She set up the entranceway as planned. He crossed the street and passed through the propped-open doors – the outer door to the vestibule and the inner one to the hallway – while she waited outside. Despite its dilapidated condition, the hallway was welcoming – at least to him. While he waited beyond the staircase, she reentered and climbed the stairs to the second-story. He held back, taking up position probably fifteen feet away from her door while she used three keys in the three locks to open it.

"Stay out here," she ordered. "I'll get the bathroom ready. Man oh man. I better have enough bleach to wipe down the whole freaking apartment after this."

"I bet you have a two-year supply."

She ignored that and disappeared inside. Jake stared down the hall at the familiar door, feeling gross and awkward. Too late for pride now. He'd already swallowed it on being discovered like that, sleeping on her block, stinking.

He shifted on weary feet. He marveled at the hallway's walls and ceiling – shelter! – despite a hint of claustrophobia.

The door opened. Aki, wearing a mask and gloves, propped the door open with a trash can, then retreated farther inside.

"Okay, come on in," she called out.

Jake stepped into her apartment fortress. She was standing on the opposite side of the narrow hall, its walls covered with her photographs. She pointed to the bathroom door.

"Okay, listen up good. There's a garbage bag in there. Put your dirty clothes in it … even your sneakers … and toss them through the door. It'll take me like an hour to launder them. I'll put them in a clean bag and shove them back in. Use that bag to put the towel in after you're all done. I'll launder that, too. Got that?"

"Got it."

"Remember, shower first before soaking in my tub. Use lots of soap. In your hair, too. Afterwards, throw out the bar. Don't close the window and don't touch anything you don't have to. And don't bother looking for pills in the medicine cabinet. I removed them."

"Understood."

"I'll prepare some eats," she added, a little more gently.

"Great."

Jake stepped into the bathroom. As Aki had indicated, there was a garbage bag on the toilet seat. The exhaust fan was on; the window, open. The shower curtain of the fiberglass combined bath-and-shower unit was pulled back. A new big green bar of soap called out to him from the built-in soap dish. He followed her instructions, undressing and bagging his foul clothes. He wondered what exactly she planned to do with his old Converse sneakers. No matter. He'd given up all control. He opened the door and tossed the bag on the hall floor. He turned on the tub water – as hot as he thought he could endure – stepped inside, drew the curtain behind him, and changed the faucet setting to shower.

The streaming water felt great. He could have been under a natural hot spring in a luxury spa. After he'd lathered and rinsed several times, he ran a bath and lowered himself into the water. It was a little cold at first since he'd already used so much hot water. After a while, he ran the hot again and the water temperature climbed. Aki's Spa. Comfortable enough to slip toward sleep. He ran the water from time to time to stay awake. He soaked at least an hour.

"Here's your excuse for clothing. No sneakers yet."

A skinny arm threw a garbage bag through a door. Jake removed the stopper; the water emptied slowly as he dried off with the towel. It was a reassuring sound – water gurgling in a bathtub drain. He dumped out the clean clothes and put on his underwear and slacks. They smelled a little too much of bleach.

Jake rubbed his longish hair one more time with the towel, thinking she'd probably removed her hair dryer from the bathroom so as not to risk its being contaminated by him. Per instructions, he put the towel in the now-empty garbage bag and passed it through the door.

"Take these," Aki spoke from the hall.

Her hand appeared again, placing a pink plastic razor, a small plastic comb, a travel-size bottle of mouthwash, a plastic spray bottle of disinfectant, and a pile of paper towels torn off from a roll and neatly stacked.

"After you shave, comb your hair, rinse and gargle, spray all over the room with disinfectant, using the paper towels to wipe. Wash the spray bottle with soap and water afterwards for twenty seconds. Throw out everything else and tie the garbage bag at the top."

He dressed halfway, leaving his shirt off, and studied his reflection in the mirror. He was seeing himself in a new way, kind of like Humphrey Bogart playing Vincent Parry in the film *Dark Passage*, part of his mother's extensive VHS collection. Jake had also read the novel by David Goodis. Being on the run even though he's innocent, Parry gets his face done over by a disbarred plastic surgeon. The pre-operation part of the movie uses the subjective camera technique, showing the point of view of the character himself. When the bandages come off, Parry sees his new face for the first time, and the audience sees Bogie.

Jake was similarly rediscovering himself after months of street grime: skinnier; a little nicked up from the shaving; his skin ashen, despite time sitting in the sun; his black hair and brown eyes also seemingly faded. Near-starvation and polluted air were bad enough; added to that were years of partying way too hard.

His eyes drifted down to the reflection of his chest and the powerful reminder of past recklessness – a small letter X he'd carved over his heart when just out of high school. Over a girl? Which girl? Surprisingly, or maybe not because he'd been so wasted at the time, he didn't remember. Crossing out his feelings perhaps. That had been his only experience with self-cutting. He'd never even gotten a tattoo or piercings for body jewelry. Nor had he punctured his veins with needles. He'd drawn the line at needles in his drug use. One doesn't need needles for self-abuse, he well knew.

Jake lathering up his face with the bar of soap, then set about trying to shave with the undersized razor. The stubble resisted but he did a passable job. He put on the rest of his clothing, combed his hair, and rinsed and gargled with the mouthwash. He then threw out everything as instructed and tied the garbage shut. He exited the bathroom and moved along the hallway past Aki's bedroom door – shut tight as always – into the living room. This part of the small apartment used to serve as a studio for shoots. There was no backdrop as before, however, nor lighting equipment – just the same wooden stools, couch, coffee table, drafting table, desk, and chair.

The apartment smelled of bleach, rubbing alcohol, and incense. Aki, still wearing the mask, stood at the far corner of the room. She pointed with a gloved finger to the counter that separated the kitchenette from the living room/office. It held a plate, with a sandwich, a pickle, chips, and a bottle of Orangina.

"All yours," she said. "Eat, then move your stool away from the counter. Afterwards, we smoke and talk."

Jake sat on the nearest of the two stools and dug in. Rye and pastrami with a dill pickle. Indeed, Aki was all New Yorker now, diet included.

She must have already put the towel in the washer that lined the side kitchen wall because, keeping her distance from him, she started filling it with a hose from the kitchen sink before turning it on. She'd originally bought the washer/drier stack, even though she didn't have a proper hookup, in order to wash models' outfits before shoots. Good thing for him, because he doubted she would have let him inside without being able to launder his clothes.

Even though Jake was ravenous, he forced himself to eat slowly. When he'd finished and moved the stool away from the counter, Aki walked back around it, cleared the dish and bottle, put them in the sink already filled with soapy water, then sprayed and wiped the countertop.

"I hope you didn't wash and dry my sneakers," Jake said. "They'd probably disintegrate. Then I'll be homeless *and* barefoot."

"Not funny. They're soaking in rubbing alcohol. I'll dry them with a fan."

She returned to the living room and the open window. Jake could make out a bucket on the fire escape. Using the towels, she reached inside the bucket, pulled out his sneakers, and placed them on the windowsill. She propped a fan on a stand opposite the sill and turned it on.

"You're sure resourceful when it comes to odors and germs," he jabbed, feeling a little more his old self, clean and fed.

"Yeah, well, you're testing my limits."

Jake marveled at how powerful she came across despite her slender frame. One tough little dame. He'd met her at a gig in the East Village. They were both having relationship issues and they'd become phone confidants. She'd even let him stay on her couch a couple of nights after his eviction – despite Covid 19 still obsessing her – and only because she'd had some of the symptoms during the outbreak and had recovered.

Of all Jake's close female friends these past years, Aki was the best to have met up with like this. They'd never been romantic and, after his stint living with Rainy, he hadn't resorted to asking for her couch again – even for just one night – knowing what an ordeal anyone in her apartment was for her.

She removed her mask and gloves and, pointing to the couch, now with a newspaper spread out on one of its cushions, she said, "Sit there."

Jake did so. She sat in her office chair and rolled it all of an inch toward the couch. She wanted to get to what was on her mind and for him to hurry up and leave, he assumed.

She opened a desk drawer, pulled out a joint, broke it in two, and, using a folded newspaper as an arm extension, passed half of it to him. She also passed him his own book of matches and a small aluminum ashtray.

"There's some tobacco mixed in. You know the way I roll."

That he did, literally and otherwise. "Good. I was craving a cigarette."

They both lit their half-joints and smoked together in silence. The shelter, the bath, the food, the joint. He hadn't had it this good in a while.

37

After putting her half-joint down, Aki placed a photo on the end of the newspaper and passed it to him.

"Remember your own work?"

He looked. The photo's subject was a sculpture he'd made using BX electrical cable – a spiderweb kind of thing. It had been on exhibit in a tiny Soho gallery for a couple of months. She then passed him a postcard.

"You can keep both," she said.

She'd taken a photo of the original photo to create the postcard. She'd kept the sculpture's outline but had used camera settings and color to make it seem abstract. He turned the card over and saw Japanese writing along with *Infinite Web by Aki Sato*.

"Yeah, I remember that piece. I don't remember you taking a photo of it, then interpreting it like that. My work made better by your work."

"No B.S., please. Not better but different. I won a competition in Japan with my adaptation. I got it published in a Tokyo art magazine. Get it? My art photo based on my photo of your work got me noticed on Instagram. I now have a ton of followers, a lot of them successful Japanese who buy art. People from all over go to my website as well. Corbis picked up the rights to a good portion of my images and they're getting used. As of a month ago, I don't have to rent studio space. I have my own on Lafayette Street."

He tried to get his mind around all this. "This is great. You sure deserve it, Aki. I was wondering where all your equipment went. So it's in a nice big studio?"

"Yup. I'll be giving up this place soon and moving over there to live. I'm waiting for the kitchen to be finished. The point is, I'm doing great. And it all started with a photo of that weird-ass sculpture of yours. I've been feeling guilty. I want to keep the fates happy so they keep looking after me. Now do you get it? I owe you. I pay my debts. I want to buy that piece for my studio if possible. You deserve it for helping me by creating that piece. What was it selling for?"

He remembered the amount because in his arrogance back then he'd wanted the gallery to charge more. Even at the low price though, it hadn't sold, contributing to his self-doubt and malaise.

"Six hundred."

"I'll give you three times that ... eighteen hundred. What the hell, round it up to two grand."

"Say what? Really?"

"Just another business expense. I'm paying a helluva lot more for the new kitchen."

He fell silent, trying to fathom this good news. "That'd be awesome," he finally declared.

"When can you deliver it?"

How long would it take him to make another if he couldn't locate the original? Where would he make it? Would Aki catch on? Or would she accept a reconstruction if necessary? BX cable was BX cable. He knew where the original used to be. In Rainy's aunt's building – one of the storage rooms at the apartment complex known as Stuyvesant Town.

"Rainy has all my pieces," he said. "She didn't tell you?"

"I didn't say why I was calling."

"Give me at least a week or so to set up getting it from her. Where do I deliver it? Here?"

"No, the studio."

She reached over to her desk again, then passed a business card to him. It had one of her photos on it – a touched-up cloudscape – as a background to her info. Her loft was on Lafayette Street.

"I'll give you something up front ... five hundred in cash," she told him. "On good faith. That way if you fuck up and can't produce it at least I made the effort. You'll get the rest when I get the piece. And you can't show up at my studio looking like you did today. You have to get some new clothes. Promise?"

"I promise."

"I'll have my bank wire yours the balance. Less chance of a screw-up. What's your bank?"

"Citibank."

"You have your account info on you?"

"Yeah. Up here." He pointed to his head.

"A bleeping miracle."

She reached for a pad and pen and he recited the numbers.

"You never use a middle name or initial, right?" she asked.

"It's 'J' for another Jake," he joked.

"No way."

"You're right. No middle name. There were only two Jakes in the film."

"Real funny. So Rainy kicked you out?"

"She told you?"

"All she said was that you two broke up and she had no idea where you were. How long ago that happen?"

"About four months."

She scrunched up her face, as if in thought. Then: "So you lived with her at least two months."

"Something like that."

"A relationship record for you."

Jake gave a self-deprecating laugh. "Could be."

"That's when you went homeless?"

"I was more of a mess than usual."

She sighed. "But the street? Can't you stay drugfree long enough in the day to work on people's houses? You got construction skills, right? And find something cheap to rent where you can start sculpting again."

"Where's cheap? I read that prices have been going back up since the pandemic. Anyway, like I said, living like this has helped me stay clean … most of the time anyway. I've slipped up a couple times."

"You're not gonna spend all this money on booze and drugs, are you? I saw what you used to spend on top shelf shots and under-the-counter pills. You better spend wisely now."

"You're right. And you've given me a fresh start."

"You better follow through so I know there's hope for you." She sighed again, standing up. "Okay, let's finish this."

She went to the drawer again, took out an envelope and a small black leather bag. She moved around to the kitchen side of the counter, where she counted out the cash into a perfect pile of two hundreds, four fifties, five twenties, and three singles – the last for the subway, she said. She then produced a cellphone from the leather bag along with a charger.

"And take this."

"Really?"

"I keep all my old phones. It's a relic, so limited battery time and memory and no Siri or GPS. But it should work. The camera, too. Call me the minute you activate it."

"It's wiped?"

"You bet. Okay, I'm tired ... now please go away now."

Jake stood up. Aki backed farther into the kitchen as he approached the counter to gather up his bounty.

"Thanks for everything, Aki."

"Wait a second," she said.

She reached under the counter and pulled out a plastic cylindrical jar. From it she pulled out a disinfectant wipe and put it on the counter.

"Use it to turn the doorknob and also on the downstairs doors."

She backed away again as Jake returned for it.

"Will do. Again, Aki, thanks for everything. Keep on believing in me, so I can."

Her nod was noncommittal.

PART II: CROSSROADS

Philip Marlowe, P.I.: *"You can have a hangover from other things
than alcohol. I had one from women."*
– Raymond Chandler, *The Big Sleep*

New Normal

BEFORE HIS ENCOUNTER WITH AKI, Jake had found some kind
of balance on the street. He had to find a new balance and not
relapse again. It was all about how to spend the money now in his
pocket, with more to come if things worked out.

The subway ride on the M train from the Hewes Street Station
in Brooklyn back to Manhattan had been the first expenditure.
On returning to Jake Soho territory, he'd again slept in that same
Bedford Street doorway despite his windfall. He'd enjoyed a feast
for breakfast in a diner – eggs, bacon, OJ, and an English muffin.
After purchasing a small backpack and gym bag, he'd bought
new clothes – black jeans, three plain T-shirts, dark green hooded
sweatshirt with pockets, pants, baseball cap (a black one with no
logo), black canvas sneakers, underwear, and socks. All for $75
from some store on Broadway going out of business. And he'd
purchased a new five-dollar wallet and a ten-dollar watch from a
street stand, tools of a respectable citizen.

Jake, after changing into his new clothes at a coffee shop, had
gone to the Verizon Center on Broadway to reactivate the gifted
cellphone. Since he still owed for two months on his past account,
he'd had to make good on that bill. He'd also sprung for unlimited
data, a smart phone being a tool of a modern detective.

He'd called Aki as promised and left a message. She
hadn't answered but eventually texted, "Welcome back to
Planet Earth."

Heading back to his home base just before 5:00 that afternoon,
Jake had additional confirmation that his world had changed
when a woman with two kids in tow had asked him for directions
to Vandam Street. It had been a long time since anyone had
approached him like that. And he certainly knew how to get to

Vandam Street. On remembering the pain from the attack, he almost played dumb.

"Keep going south along Sixth Avenue. Two-and-a-half blocks. Cross the avenue. You'll see it."

"Thank you."

How normal was that?

At his bench in the Playground of the Americas, Jake sorted his possessions. No need to keep the clothes that were in tatters and he started a throwaway pile. He separated out one old pair of pants, a fairly intact sweater his sister had knit him, his Giants cap, his portfolio with photos of his sculptures, and some of the new clothes, then put them in the gym bag. He kept the new sweats and a change of underwear and socks to carry with him in the backpack. Before too long, he would buy cold weather clothing – just the basics, a lined coat, a pair of insulated boots, and a woolen cap.

The train and bus stations used to have storage lockers, Jake mused. In the movie *The Maltese Falcon* – directed by John Huston and based on the Dashiell Hammett novel – prototypical P.I. Sam Spade, played by Humphrey Bogart, checks the falcon statuette at the fictional Union Bus Terminal in San Francisco. He then mails the claim ticket to himself at "Box 589, P.O. Station C., City" – a detail Jake remembered from his mother's playful quizzes. Since public storage like that had been mostly phased out in the age of terrorism, he again resorted to his own personal storage facility. He put the gym bag in a sturdy new garbage bag and, when no one was looking, he hung it over the fence. He then gathered up and tossed his discarded garments in a nearby trash can, wondering if some other homeless person would discover them.

After his first purchases, he felt conflicted regarding others. Get a hotel room? He would then probably want a 12-pack, a joint, and even some pills. No, he wouldn't waste money on hotel rooms or even SROs and risk the temptation of private substance abuse until he had more confidence in himself. Staying on park benches and in doorways felt the right thing to do for the time being. By stopping at several public restrooms throughout a day and discreetly using a sponge or washcloth, he could stay clean enough. When he felt confident in his new normal, he would splurge on a room.

For now, he would treat himself to Italian food at Arturo's at Houston and Thompson … and make use of the restroom.

Kitchen Utensil Holder

JAKE ATE BREAKFAST on a bench – coffee, an everything bagel with cream cheese, and an orange – but did so on one of the few benches in the large park at Houston Street and Sixth Avenue. He was a clean and respectably dressed spectator watching hockey on rollerblades. The skaters turned the dented metal trash cans on their sides and used them as goals, shooting special street pucks mounted on rollers. They were skilled, making for a good game.

Watching street hockey was a way of procrastinating. He had a pressing responsibility: to get Aki the "BX Web," as he'd called it. Aki had played to the cosmic with her photo, naming it "Infinite Web." Accomplishing the task meant contacting Rainy. Jake again took psychological refuge in his assumed profession. Locating the artwork would be a new case. John D. MacDonald's series of books presents the protagonist Travis McGee as a "salvage consultant," who helps people retrieve what they've lost. And so it would be for Jake. Find the lost sculpture and, in the process, perhaps shed the past and find a new self.

But how? Go to Stuyvesant Town? To do what? Ring the bell in the hope Rainy would appear at the door. If her aunt answered, do what? Schmooze her until Rainy showed up? Would Rainy even talk to him after the alcohol-fueled scene he'd made in response to the breakup? If she did talk, would he end up on another bender?

Get to it, he finally resolved. He pulled out his phone and entered Rainy's number. He remembered it, the last number that had stuck in his memory before he'd gone incommunicado on the street.

Leave a message if she didn't pick up? Let her call him? Would she?

"Hello." A man's voice.

"Is this still Rainy's number?" Jake asked.

"One moment."

Sharing her phone? At least the man didn't ask who was phoning. She might have declined the call.

"Hello." Her throaty voice.

"Hi, Rainy. It's Jake."

"Jesus Christ," she said.

"At least I warrant a 'Jesus Christ.'"

She ignored that. "Where are you?"

"West Village. You in the city?"

A disconcerting thing about cellphones was that you had to ask to know where people were when talking, unlike with landlines.

"In striking distance."

"Not to worry, Rainy … I have no emotional agenda. I'm calling for a practical reason."

A bit softer: "You sure you can separate the two? Where've you been?"

Jake lied: "Couch surfing. Trying to stay clean."

That was enough. Why should he divulge the rest? If they ever again were to sit across from each other, maybe he would fill her in on his time on the street.

"Well, that's good. Is it working?"

"For now. If I keep the present clean, the future seems to follow."

"Sounds like the way to go for you. Me, it's about keeping it together for a regular job. I'm working for an outreach group … advocacy for the homeless."

Jake almost choked on air.

"Oh," he managed.

"So what's the practical reason?" she asked.

Jake rallied. "Aki said she called you, trying to find me."

"Right."

"The reason why is she wants to buy that spiderweb thing I did with electrical cable. She's had success with a photo of it and wants the piece for a new studio. Is it still in your aunt's basement with the rest?"

"No."

"Where then?"

"Here," she replied.

"There?"

"In my kitchen. I live in Hoboken now. Commute to work on the Path train. I have my own apartment. I don't know what you'll make of this ... all six of your pieces are on display. I had little else when I moved in so I decorated with them. I actually added some hooks to the web and I hung pots and pans on it." She let out a small laugh. "Is that okay?"

Jake didn't care about the pots and pans. He had to digest the idea that Rainy actually lived with his art, not to mention her working on behalf of the homeless.

"I guess you want them all back now," she said when he didn't reply.

"No, no. Just the one for Aki."

"You know, in that last argument we had, you did say keep them. I wasn't sure you meant it. I think you thought you were punishing me with the burden of them. But I did see them as a gift and they've helped me remember the good times."

It was starting to feel like former conversations with her ... meaningful. Jake imagined her looking up at him, nodding earnestly, her ponytail bobbing slightly.

"I'm honored and a bit shocked you're showing them," he told her. "But can you part with the one for Aki? How about if I make you another one for your kitchen stuff?"

"Sure, Jake, that would be great. A smaller version would work better anyway."

"Why don't I call you when I've finished a new one? We can arrange a switch. How big do you want it?"

"Wait. Let me look."

Jake imagined her walking across an apartment – probably not in a high-rise; perhaps in a townhouse converted into multiple units.

Her voice returned: "I'd say about a foot smaller from side to side, and the same from top to bottom."

Did he remember the original's specs? He did – a good sign, indicating a relatively intact memory.

"So about two links less both across and up and down."

"Yeah, perfect. You doing much sculpture these days?" she asked.

"No."

"That's too bad." She sounded sincere.

"Maybe this will get me focused again."

"I hope so."

He had a question for her. Risk it? He did: "Is your friend a roommate or more?"

It took her a moment to answer. "More. You seeing anyone?" She'd turned the question back on him.

"Not really. Too busy looking inward, I guess." It was high time to wrap up this call. "Thanks, Rainy. I'll be in touch."

"Right. Good talking to you, Jake. Call me when you're ready."

Then, cellphone silence … just like that.

~

Jake walked to an electrical supply store on Canal Street and bought a twenty-five-foot roll of 12/2 BX cable along with three dozen connectors. Having hocked the tools he'd brought to the city from upstate, he also picked up a wire cutter, screwdriver, measuring tape, and construction bags.

He needed a place to work on the what … he didn't even want to call it a sculpture … how about kitchen utensil holder? He decided to sit on the grass in Washington Square, where people engage in all kinds of activities – from sunning to reading to yoga to painting – and where his project might go unnoticed.

Wrong. A young couple who had been necking nearby decided to make his work their freebie show, fixating on him. Or so it felt.

He could have told the voyeurs off but managed to tune them out while he slowly measured, snipped, and attached. Art as therapy? It did feel good, reliving a past creative spark, and he lost himself in it. He took only one break. Carrying the tools in his backpack and the half-finished piece over his shoulder, he went to the restroom and then a deli for an iced tea and power bar. Refreshed, he returned to the park to finish up before darkness fell. At least the audience departed as the gloom descended. Finally, with the last connector screwed in place, the five-by-three-foot piece was ready for Rainy's kitchen wall.

Jake stopped at Mamoun's on MacDougal Street on the way back to his home base and ordered a falafel to go. He made it to the small playground before its closing and discreetly stashed the web along with his backpack and tools over the backyard fence. He continued down Sixth Avenue to Prince Street, bought a coffee at the corner deli, and sat on a nearby public bench to sip it between bites of his falafel, all the while pondering his options.

Once underway, his making the web, even in a public place, had proved a welcome escape from his thoughts. Making a decision on how to deliver it presented a new conundrum. He didn't want to see Rainy at all again, especially considering her new job. Nor did he want to see his sculptures representing his former self on display at her house. All too much.

Simple: Drop the new piece off at Aki's studio, then have Rainy go there herself to make the swap. Rainy would probably be wary of seeing him anyway.

He texted Aki: "I've created a new BX Web for Rainy to replace the original I gave her. She's fine with that. Ok if I drop it off at the studio tomorrow and have her set up coming by to make the exchange? That way she and I won't have to see each other. I'll phone before I make the delivery."

"Sounds like an adult plan," she texted back.

He wandered the neighborhood to work off restlessness. Along Bleecker Street he stopped in front of a window with three mannequins. They seemed to look at him with contempt. Women out of his past frozen behind glass. Best to revisit them in his dreams.

After seeing lights on in the house on Bedford Street, Jake needed a new place to sleep. What he found was a first for him. Scaffolding at King and MacDougal had been poorly assembled, like something out of a shantytown. Missing pieces left a convenient hole within the overhang through which he could wiggle to find refuge on top.

Moving up in life? In more ways than one, he hoped.

Deliveries

JAKE STARTED HIS DAY with a visit to two public restrooms – Washington Square and Barnes & Noble – and did his best to clean up. Back in the Playground of the Americas, he phoned Aki.

She answered with "Jake Jakes … the reformed one, I hope."

"I'm doing much better. You at the studio now?" he asked, hoping she was in Brooklyn.

"No."

"Is there a doorman?"

"No, a super."

"Can I leave the piece for Rainy with him? Like in an hour or so?"

"What shape are you in?"

"Presentable by most standards," he said lightly.

"Good enough. He's borderline himself. I'll make sure he's around. His buzzer says 'superintendent.' If you don't hear otherwise, it's a go. Text me when it's done. I'll confirm."

"Okay. Then, I'll call Rainy and let her know. You two can set up a time for the exchange." Jake had an additional thought: "I'd appreciate if she doesn't know my recent history. She's been working with the homeless and I don't want her to feel she has to offer advice."

"Not a peep from me. You're showing some pride. That's a good thing. You still living on the street?"

"No," he lied, "an Airbnb."

"Good." She paused, then: "Listen up ... unless you get it together, I don't want to hear from you. I'll be your friend like before but not if you end up wasted and half-frozen in doorways. You were beginning to rot from inside."

"Deal."

"After the transfer, I'll wire the rest of your dollars."

"Okay. Thanks, Aki."

"Take care of yourself, Jake," she said, her voice signing off with atypical warmth.

After his conversation, he bought supplies in a nearby stationery store and returned to the playground, where he retrieved the new BX Web from his makeshift locker and wrapped it in brown paper, writing Aki's name and address on it. He walked the blocks to Lafayette and dropped the package off with the super of her new building as arranged. Despite Aki's description of the super as "borderline," he seemed scrubbed and sanitary in new-looking work clothes. Not particularly friendly though. Sullen in demeanor, he accepted the package from Jake without a word.

Jake texted Aki about the successful delivery, then phoned Rainy. Via voicemail he informed her the replacement piece was ready and in Aki's possession and gave her Aki's phone number – which she must have anyway from Aki's recent call to her – and the studio's address. He also told her that if she wanted to sell any of his other pieces at whatever amount within reason, he would split the take fifty-fifty just as if she were an art gallery owner.

To make sure all was okay with his Citibank account, he then headed to the branch on LaGuardia Place, where he'd opened it on arrival in the city.

"Hey, Mr. Soho … nice threads! Is that really you?"

Jake's street friend Mackerel had taken up position outside the bank door, acting as a doorman for customers. Jake was relieved to see him alive and typically smiling. He'd grown up in New Mexico and Jake was reminded of that whenever he saw him. Ricky had compared Mackerel's ruddy complexion to reddish earth; his premature lines, to dirt-filled canyons; and the spotty stubble, to juniper trees. Jake had mixed feelings about this kind of doorman endeavor, assuming that fresh banking money in the wallets and purses of the non-homeless made them even more leery of society's rejects.

"I made a score. How's it going for you, Mack?"

"It's barely going. A slow day … no question it's a recession. No trickle-down effect, except my leg."

He tilted his head back in laughter, revealing yellow teeth that matched his yellow eyes. The abstract tat climbing up his neck looked like oversize veins. He sure appeared crazy, the effects of alcohol saturation and accompanying malnourishment undoing what had once been a strong body and fine mind. His torso was still round but, like lanky Tenor, he had a pallid, ghostly look. Homeless people come in all shapes and sizes but end up with that same gray cast of the street.

"No flying a sign today?" Jake asked.

"I got squat the last time."

"What'd the sign say?"

"'Homeless, not helpless, so help!'"

"Maybe a little too clever."

"Yeah, I outsmarted myself."

50

Jake passed his friend a twenty, saying, "Take the rest of the day off."

Mackerel gave a big smile. "I'll stay here and catch you on the way out."

"I should've kept ten back. Where's your cart?"

"I traded it for a bottle."

Another sign of Mackerel's decline, Jake thought as he entered the bank. Like Tenor, Mackerel had pilfered a shopping cart. He'd kept it well-organized with plastic bags for separate kinds of discoveries – cans, bottles, and miscellaneous objects – along with plastic gloves and paper towels he would buy to fight back filth.

The last time Jake had used his bankcard – eons ago, it seemed – the account had only twenty-something dollars remaining. He'd left that untouched to keep the account from going to zero. Good planning, it turned out. He deposited fifty dollars from Aki's advance funds to ascertain all was still in order. All went smoothly. The teller had an abnormally big smile. Abnormal in a good way.

Jake exited the bank. Mackerel had left his spot, the twenty no doubt burning a hole in his pocket.

Jake felt competent. He'd completed a series of tasks. This feeling of self-satisfaction would soon pass, he knew. But now he would reward himself for all his practical achievements with a meal at a Polish-American restaurant on Second Avenue he used to frequent. He would take a leisurely walk there and have a leisurely meal before deciding the rest of the day ... if not the rest of his life.

~

On arrival at the brick-and-tiled diner, Jake didn't recognize any of the wait staff, not having eaten there since before the pandemic. A thin, attractive waitress – very Slavic-looking with straight blond hair, fine features, and sharp blue eyes – arrived at his booth with a menu and glass of water. Jake already knew what he wanted: pierogis – two of them potato and three sauerkraut – with onions and sour cream on the side, plus coffee. Expressionless and with minimal words in a strong Polish accent, she took his order, writing with long slender fingers. She moved away quickly, saying nothing more.

The restaurant was sotto voce and calming compared to the street. The waitress soon returned with the coffee.

Jake was ready: "Are you from Poland? Been in New York a while?"

"Yes. Five months," she replied matter-of-factly.

"I'm Jake. I used to be a regular here but I've been away. What's your name?"

Her eyes were active. She was smart, he could tell … certainly about men. And seemingly wound a little tight.

"Gisela."

He kept the conversation going: "Did you come to New York to study?"

"Yes."

"To study what?"

"Filmmaking."

"That's great. Where?"

She hesitated, still trying to read his intent. Or knowing it all too well? "School of Visual Arts."

"That's great," he repeated.

He would have to do better than that.

But she asked a question: "What do you do?"

He'd gotten her interest. A triumph of sorts, at least for recently downtrodden him. But along with it came pressure, since he had to decide how to answer.

He went with honesty. "I'm reevaluating. I used to sculpt."

She nodded knowingly, then hurried off. He headed for the men's room. It was reserved for customers and, yes, he qualified as one. Imagine that.

Back at his booth, Jake succumbed to soul-searching. This neighborhood place brought back his art period and, along with that, his drug abuse. When young, he began experimenting with lots of substances, starting with alcohol and nicotine, followed by marijuana. He'd had his psychedelics phase his teen years, both mushrooms and laboratory stuff, especially acid. He'd done MDMA – a.k.a. ecstasy – at clubs and raves. Expensive cocaine was an occasional thing. He'd taken all kinds of black-market prescription pills, both ingesting and snorting them.

In the city, when he had money enough from selling some of his artwork, he'd snorted way too much cocaine as well as different amphetamines, including Adderall, Dexedrine, and Ritalin - all prescribed for treatment of narcolepsy and ADHD - and even the especially nasty methamphetamine family of drugs. His brain seemed lucid on the uppers with tight parallel and perpendicular planes forming compartments to sort out onrushing thoughts and bombarding stimuli. He didn't get tired. He could crisscross the city all day on missions that in normal consciousness might seem trivial and a hassle, but in his altered state seemingly of existential importance. Inhibitions about promoting himself as an artist faded. The crashes followed the good times, however. When he came down from the heavy-duty uppers, he turned into a washed-out, short-fused creep, even more so then when hungover from alcohol.

Well, maybe a toss-up.

A childhood fear of needles had helped him maintain some kind of limit all these years. That and the balance cannabis offered countering alcohol-binging and hard-drug cravings. Of the two upstate friends that he'd seen shoot up, as Jake had last heard, one had cleaned up and was doing just fine as a husband, father, and auto mechanic, and the other had OD'd. Jake had never found out what drug or combination of drugs had killed him. He'd also been a binge drinker, that much Jake knew. The synthetic opioid fentanyl, killing so many on its own or when mixed with other drugs, hadn't hit his hometown by then.

Reviewing past risky behavior helped Jake resist the ever-present urges. Hopefully, anyway. He was at a crossroads. The best way to stay on the path to recovery was to keep busy. He still hadn't made up his mind where he would go or what he would do upon receiving the big check from Aki. Return to the Brooklyn warehouse? Why even stay in the city? He would certainly have to face up to his sister. On becoming homeless, he'd stopped calling her and didn't answer her calls either. Then, two-and-a-half weeks into his new life, he'd lost his phone. He knew she would offer to take him in, but he didn't want to burden her until he was self-sufficient and psychologically beyond the heavy drinking and hard drugs.

Gisela carried the plate of pierogis over to his table. Not wanting to come on too strong, he didn't try to draw her into conversation this time around. When she returned a little while later to pour more coffee and ask if everything were okay, he had food in his mouth and just nodded.

Jake took his time with his meal, glancing at the waitress from time to time. What angle might he pursue on her next approach? Maybe none at all; maybe it would be better to leave a big tip and a warm "thank you" today, then return another time for more conversation, proving he was a regular. Or maybe he should just avoid women altogether for now. Kick that addiction, too.

On signaling for the check, he glanced through the restaurant window as a couple walked by. It was the Mickey Mouse duo. He might have failed to recognize them if it hadn't been for the sketchpad Leandra carried. Ned wore a hoodie with the hood up, not a beanie as before. Leandra's hair was no longer red, but rather blue, like her glasses. Jake processed that, wondering what her natural hair looked like. The two walked quickly, heading uptown.

Gisela wasn't ready with the bill. Jake walked over to her at another booth.

"Excuse me," he said.

She turned.

He handed her a twenty. "That cover it?" he said, trying to sound meaningful.

She took the bill and nodded with a big smile.

"I saw some friends pass by," big spender, smile-inducing Jake explained, then hurried toward the door.

His guess was that Leandra and Ned were heading for the L train on 14th Street to take to Brooklyn as usual. He had a few blocks to decide whether he wanted to tail them into the subway. To Jake's surprise, they crossed the wide 14th Street and continued to 15th, where they turned right. They walked the long block eastward to First Avenue, then turned north again. Jake caught the green light and darted across the avenue to its east side.

Although he now tailed them from across the avenue, Jake stayed as far back as he could without losing sight of them. He didn't want to blow this opportunity. They weren't just out for a relaxed stroll, he was convinced. They walked block after block at a determined pace, moving uptown with the one-way traffic. At times, they dashed through red lights, beating the traffic on the cross streets, forcing him to wait unless traffic cleared enough to jaywalk. He jogged when he had to.

He followed them across 23rd Street – like 14th Street, a two-way street. He hadn't been on this part of First Avenue in a long time. Being a functional neighborhood with hospitals and medical centers, it didn't seem a likely place for a walk without some practical purpose. Exercise? The duo didn't come off as candidates for that.

They crossed 34th, another two-way street. Just north of 40th Street, Jake saw Ned check his phone and say something to Leandra. They then slowed down. At 36th Street Jake crossed to the east side of the avenue.

On reaching the two-way busy 42nd Street, Jake remembered what brought a lot of people to this neighborhood – United Nations Headquarters. The duo crossed on the west side of the avenue, known along this stretch as United Nations Plaza; Jake crossed on the east side and walked along the UN complex. He remembered its layout from earlier wanderings: four buildings and a park beginning just north of 42nd Street and extending to 48th Street, with the visitors' entrance on 46th.

The couple entered Ralph Bunche Park, a tiny park directly opposite the UN complex. Jake slowed his pace enough to see whether they would sit down on a bench. When they did, he kept walking northward beyond them. Numerous pedestrians strolled the plaza under the colorful display of international flags, and he was able to use them as shields as he walked as far as 45th Street before crossing to the west side and heading back downtown.

Jake knew something of the little park because during one of the let's-play-tourist days with Rainy, the two of them had decided to visit the UN. On witnessing a demonstration for Puerto Rican independence going on in the park, they'd walked up the stairs to observe. He remembered her saying that the steel obelisk in the park reminded her of the monolith in *2001: A Space Odyssey*. He also remembered her being moved by the biblical quotation on the Isaiah Wall that flanked the steps: "They shall beat their swords into plowshares, and their spears into pruning hooks; nation shall not lift up sword against nation, neither shall they learn war any more."

Rainy had also loved the sculpture of the handgun with the barrel tied in a knot located in the UN visitors' area – the "pretzel pistol," she'd called it. The UN flag – sky blue with a globe and two olive branches – she'd seen as hopeful. Jake had seen it as neglected. She'd even later researched Ralph Bunche – an African-American who had become a UN diplomat and had won the Nobel Peace Prize – and had told Jake all about him.

That memorable day, Rainy had given Jake a fresh and positive take on New York, something he sure had needed at that time, as jaded as he'd become. His city right now strangely related to some strangers who had led him back to this memory-inducing location.

Jake took the park's curved stone steps, angling upward behind the benches to the park's upper level, the dead end of 43rd Street. As he passed under the Isaiah quotation, he saw another recognizable person descending. It was the man who had joined Ned outside the warehouse, the shorter one with the round owl face; Ned had referred to him as Marcus. He was dressed the same as before, in a green Jets jacket and carpenters pants, black leather cap and boots, and small backpack. He looked up at the quotation just as Jake crossed paths with him. Jake continued up the steps and positioned himself behind the painted black iron fence and looked below in time to see Marcus sit down next to the other two. Why not meet downtown, like at Union Square Park where Jake had first seen Leandra?

The three didn't talk as far as he could tell. Jake remembered Leandra saying she wanted to meet Marcus. She must have already done so because Jake saw no sign of an introduction. He could imagine all sorts of scary scenarios related to the United Nations for the three being here. Or was it just a random rendezvous location related to a drugs-for-profit scheme?

He looked over at the Secretariat tower and General Assembly building across the way – male and female symbols, Rainy had described them. Eyes back on the trio, Jake saw that Marcus had a Sharpie in hand and was writing on the bench.

Two men walked toward the trio from the north. Jake recognized one of them. He was the foreign-looking, muscular man who had delivered the bag to Leandra at Union Square Park. He wore the same tight-fitting leather jacket. The other man –

tall, slender, intense aquiline face, and with a groomed ponytail – wore a well-tailored suit. With no noticeable greeting they sat down on the bench – Leather Jacket next to Ned, Business Suit next to Marcus, and Leandra in the middle of all of them.

They talked for several minutes. From time to time, Leather Jacket looked around them as if checking for anyone in earshot. At one point, he looked upward, but Jake saw the glance coming as the man's head started to turn and looked over at two young women near him at the railing. They were speaking a foreign language – Italian, he thought.

Jake spoke: "Let the world be united."

They just looked at him uncomfortably. That was okay because he turned his attention back downward. Business Suit now also glanced around, apparently surveilling. He reached into his jacket pocket and pulled out an envelope. He handed it to Marcus. Marcus, who had his backpack in his lap, quickly placed the envelope inside.

The two men stood up and, without even nods goodbye, moved to the corner of 43rd Street and crossed United Nations Plaza. They headed uptown – perhaps for the visitors' entrance? – but Jake couldn't be sure from where he stood.

Marcus also stood up. Leandra and Ned followed his lead. The three left the park and headed southward. Jake waited about half a minute then followed down the steps. Passing the bench, he looked for what Marcus had written and saw *M. Palmetto* inscribed in black ink. Palmetto, the street in Brooklyn. With an "M." It had to be Marcus's tag, following the custom of writing a name or initial and the street where the tagger lives.

By the time Jake stepped onto First Avenue, his three marks were out of sight. They must have taken a right on 42nd Street. Jake hurried to catch up, soon reaching the corner. He saw them walking westward down the long block. Toward the subway on Lexington? They moved at a leisurely pace. He followed some distance behind. They crossed Second Avenue. The light turned red before Jake arrived there, but he could see them continuing toward Third Avenue. They stopped suddenly, turned, and disappeared into a storefront.

The light changed to green and Jake crossed. He checked to see if they'd entered a shop offering tobacco, magazines, and newspapers.

They weren't there.

He came to a small shop with touristy items … targeting UN visitors, the window display indicated. The three weren't there either. That left the diner just beyond this shop.

Jake entered the tourist shop and asked the man behind the counter how much the cheapest Yankees hats were.

"Ten dollars."

"Tax, too?"

The shopkeeper smiled conspiratorially. "For you, no."

Jake handed over a ten. The hat was a one-size-fits-all cheapie. Jake stuffed his other hat – the plain black one – in the pocket of his sweatshirt, adjusted the plastic band of the Yankees one, curved its brim downward at the edges, and put it on, pulling it down low. Then he removed the sweatshirt and slung it over his arm. He exited and returned to the newsstand, buying a *Daily News*.

Entering the diner, he had the thought that if any of the three had spotted him before, changing hats might very well call attention to him rather than the opposite. But he'd made his move and he'd become a hat-wearing Yankee fan, betraying his childhood allegiance to the Mets.

He cased the room. The three sat at a booth toward the far rear corner. Leandra and Ned sat next to each other on one side, with Marcus facing them, the back of his head toward Jake and the front door. They all had menus in hand. Two other booths along the side wall had customers, leaving just one in the corner. Without waiting for someone to direct him where to sit, he hurried to the empty booth and slid onto the vinyl seat, his back opposite Leandra's and Ned's.

Jake opened the newspaper and buried himself in it, playacting just another preoccupied New Yorker. The waiter approached his booth, handed him a menu, and moved on.

He heard Marcus and Ned order deluxe burgers, one with fries and one with onion rings. Leandra ordered dolmades and a Greek salad without the feta cheese.

"Don't touch my salad with any utensil used for cheese, eggs, fish, or meat."

A vegan.

The waiter returned to Jake's booth. What to order after that big lunch?

"I'll have a vanilla malted," he said.

Jake kept reading the paper, or at least his eyes moved over the pages. Some of the pictures registered but not the words. He was too busy straining to hear. He could make out some of what they were saying as long as the other customers didn't break into laughter or the waiters didn't call out an order.

Leandra: "What's with his sleazy aide playing the heavy and all? He could at least say hello."

Ned: "He looks ex-military."

Marcus: "Probably a bodyguard."

Ned: "Five grand expense money isn't too shabby … talk at McGill … wants us there …"

Leandra: "Educating the functionaries … the mules?"

Marcus: "… celebrity in France … website."

Leandra seemed to know now what their efforts were about, but not from the beginning, Jake knew, and it made sense that she would be the skeptical one. Marcus, responding to their questions, kept his voice down.

Ned: "We can't just act. We have to believe. I believe. It's genius."

Leandra: "When's the talk?"

Marcus: "… November."

Ned, reassuringly to Leandra: "You can sketch Montreal."

Marcus, a little louder: "Remember, no paper trail, no email, no social media bullshit. You've shut all your sites down, right?"

Jake heard matching "yeahs."

His malted arrived before their food did. Jake drank slowly, the newspaper still open in front of him. He'd already decided not to follow them when they departed. Too obvious.

After the waiter brought them their check, Jake ordered a slice of apple pie and coffee. He kept pretending to read as they headed for the door, folding shut the paper after they'd exited.

The pie and coffee came. While eating and sipping, Jake analyzed what they'd discussed. He'd heard "mules." That sure could relate to drugs. But a lecture at McGill? They must have meant the university in Montreal, Quebec, indicated by the mention of France. Ned had said that he "believed." In what? A successful deal?

On his minicomputer referred to far and wide as a cellphone, Jake did a search for "McGill," and a link to the McGill University website appeared at the top. He clicked on and reached the homepage. He then clicked on "Events." Listings came up and he scrolled down to November. A lecture by a Paul-Louis Boucher entitled, "Beyond Big Mac and Mickey Mouse: Cultural Survivalism in the 21st Century," was scheduled on November 1st at 7:30 p.m., sponsored by the Department of Sociology, and held at the Centre Mont Royal. Jake searched that and learned it was a private conference center near the McGill campus.

He then searched Boucher's name and found an article in French with a picture. The well-dressed man on the bench with the pointy face and ponytail had indeed been this Boucher. Jake clicked on "Translate this page." The article covered a talk Boucher had given in Belgium last year. Jake learned that he was a professor at the Sorbonne in Paris and the author of *Astérix et les Romaines culturelles*.

Jake searched for the title of the book but couldn't find it. Other searches convinced him it hadn't been translated into English. He tried a general search and found it listed in two French bibliographies. Astérix, he learned with further searches, is a French comic book character, an ancient Gaul who resists Roman occupation. He has superhuman strength by drinking a magic potion prepared by a Druid, sort of like Popeye with his spinach and just as endearing.

Boucher. November 1, 7:30 p.m. McGill. Mickey Mouse. The doll. Boucher's talk. For some reason this Boucher fellow wanted Marcus, Ned, and Leandra at his lecture in Montreal. Transport something out of Canada into the U.S.? Boucher as an international drug dealer? Drugs as revolution? Was he somehow duping these three young people for his own profit? Marcus had mentioned "five grand expense money." The contents of the envelope, no doubt.

Maybe Boucher had been at a UN conference or given a talk there. Jake could possibly find out more about him if he went over to the UN Public Concourse and inquired about him at an information desk, but it was getting late. Not today.

Just a bit more virtual searching, Jake decided. Leandra was an artist. Probably an unknown one. But unknown artists promote themselves online. Jake had done so himself through social media but, one drunken night when his life was unraveling, he'd deactivated his accounts. This bunch apparently had stopped using social media themselves. But a general search for a Leandra, an unusual name, might turn something up and so he tried. He was led to information about several other Leandras of some renown. Nothing, however, about the one on his mind.

After settling his bill with the waiter, Jake stood up to leave. As he passed the booth where the three of them had been sitting, on a hunch he looked to the right. Sure enough, on the wall just above the seat was fancy writing in black Sharpie – *M. Palmetto*.

Once again, the tag. Marcus was carrying on the tagging vandalism thing, even during and after some suspicious rendezvous. Hubris of a sort, it sure seemed, especially since he was the one barking out orders to shut down attention-getting acts.

Enough of midtown. Walk another block and a half to Lexington. Take the Shuttle across town to the Times Square Station. Take the Broadway Local downtown to the Houston Street station, walk one block west to his favorite little park, sit down on his thinking bench, and cogitate over what he was going to do about all this.

Default Destiny

DESTINY? WHAT DOES THAT MEAN? That, if we survive, we live and what we experience after the fact seems so ordained? Destiny only seems to work in hindsight. When looking forward, one still has to make choices. So, destiny … interpreting the past as meaningful and making choices accordingly?

Jake had recognized the crossroads the day before. Money in his pocket. A chance at some kind of path other than street life? Homelessness had led him to roleplaying detective, which had led him to Leandra and the behind-the-green-door boys, which had led him to Aki's apartment and money in his pocket, making it possible for him to keep going with this mystery he'd stumbled

61

upon. Wanting pierogis in the East Village had led him to the UN and an awareness of a Frenchman named Paul-Louis Boucher and his aide. It all sure seemed writ. Sure, destiny, what the hell.

Okay then, what next?

He saw three options. One: Hang around the Brooklyn building and trail any of the three and find out where Leandra and Ned lived. Marcus, the Sharpie evidence indicated, lived in the warehouse or nearby on Palmetto Street. But what more would knowing where the others lived tell him about their plans?

Two: Break into the Brooklyn building and look for clues. A tempting idea and he knew they'd be away soon for the lecture. But what if someone else used the place. Risk breaking and entering? He hadn't even done that as a strung-out druggie.

Or three: Leave New York and go to Montreal. There were side benefits to that: Get off these streets; stay on the move; keep one step ahead of his drug demons. Yes, he would go to Boucher's lecture and try to determine his agenda.

It was destiny, right? By default, anyway.

PART III: ALMOST EUROPE

Frank Chambers, drifter: *"Except for the shape, she really wasn't any raving beauty, but she had a sulky look to her, and her lips stuck out in a way that made me want to mash them in for her."*
– James M. Cain, *The Postman Always Rings Twice*

Northern Passage

JAKE SAT IN A BIG METAL BOX on wheels, watching city streets pass by through tinted glass. Within minutes, the Greyhound bus entered Lincoln Tunnel, at first traveling downward into the bedrock under the Hudson River, then back upward into the township of Weehawken, New Jersey. As it did, the movie title *Escape from New York* reverberated in Jake's brain.

He'd decided to take a bus out of the city because it seemed the easiest way to escape the concrete, steel, and glass canyons that had so engulfed him – no need to find a car rental company and no need to drive on city streets. Compared to trains, buses were cheaper and had more frequent departures. Just take a subway to Port Authority, locate the right window, and buy a ticket for the next bus to Albany. After those tasks, his wait had been under an hour. Because of the midweek departure, after the rush hour travelers had moved on, he even had a seat all to himself, critical for his peace of mind. The nearest person was across the isle – a young, shaggy man listening to music on earphones.

On arrival in Albany, Jake would take a taxi to the airport, a convenient location outside the city to rent a car. He'd decided to spend money on a rental car rather than a bus all the way to Montreal. A car would enable him to make quick travel decisions while on the case if need be. He also hoped to use it to detour to Shaleville to see his sister.

While waiting for Aki's check, Jake had saved money by continuing to sleep in the scaffolding, which had worked out okay during the run of relatively warm and clear days and nights.

He'd eaten regularly, building up health and strength. He'd also visited the UN and learned that Paul-Louis Boucher had been part of the French delegation at a conference on cultural colonialism. Jake had also spent time in bookstores and online, reading up on Boucher's career arc and on Montreal.

The driver – a big gray-haired, gray-shirted man – handled the bus like a giant toy, maneuvering it without any wasted braking along winding New Jersey roads. He eventually crossed back into New York State and merged onto Route 87, this part of it known as the Thruway. Once on the open road north, he smoothly took the bus up to the speed it seemed to crave.

As Jake moved out of his precarious past into an uncertain future, he tried not to obsess about what might lie ahead but simply feel the bus's vibrating motion. Having endured restless sleep the night before and waking up early in anticipation of his trip, he was exhausted and let himself go, the bus now like one big rolling bedroom. He climbed back to a semi-wakeful state from time to time, as the driver changed lanes and speed, then slid back down into all-embracing sleep and a mixed salad of dreams …

~

On being pulled back to wakefulness in the third hour of his journey, Jake saw the New York State capital buildings in the distance. Albany, already – at the other end of the Hudson River from Manhattan, with a bold skyline seeming to announce "state capital." Within minutes, he saw the Albany Bus Station, his first destination, one that evoked his past as it led to his future. He blinked himself into readiness, resisting scratching his increasingly itchy new beard that he hoped would keep any of the suspect trio – or rather quintet – from recognizing him.

The driver angled the bus next to the station and shut down the engine. He reached over to his left to release the door. It opened, emitting what sounded like a big sigh of relief. Jake waited until all the other passengers, fourteen of them, exited. With his two pieces of luggage – the backpack and the gym bag – he made his way along the aisle and down the steps and continued through the glass door into the station. The big room was quiet, just a few people on the benches – semi-comatose, it seemed. The antiseptic smell of mopped tile floors was in the air. The floors, however, still looked dirty.

He remembered a period of trips to and from here. His mother had regularly caught a bus from Albany to Pittsfield, Massachusetts, to visit some guy she'd met in a mall movie theater. Jake's senior year of high school, he'd dropped her off and picked her up way too many times because she'd lost her license after getting a DWI – or Dee-Wee as she called it – along with a charge of reckless driving for ignoring the tailing cop car's flashing lights and speeding up as if to get away. She'd claimed she'd had no idea he was behind her. Not likely, but she'd stuck to her story. Jake had hated the trips to the bus station, in large part because he disliked that particular boyfriend – cold, arrogant, and a bit scary – even more so than the others, as did his sister. The relationship had unfortunately lasted longer than many of his mother's – five months or so.

Jake exited the station and lit a cigarette. After smoking it halfway down, he headed for a waiting taxi. A bald but full-bearded man opened the door for him then climbed inside. After announcing he wanted Budget Car Rental at the airport, Jake leaned his head against his bunched-up sweatshirt and the taxi's window frame. He just couldn't call up small talk. Too many memories.

Jake retained this remote state of mind right through paying the driver and exiting the cab, then moved like a sleepwalker into the Budget Rental building and to the counter. He followed instructions and produced his driver's license and bankcard and gave the necessary info, his lassitude serving as buffer to everything around him.

Rally, Jake told himself as he opened the door of the rental. It was a blue Honda, only 6,000-plus miles old and all his for the time being thanks to Aki's funds. He cautiously pulled out of the airport. It had been a long while since he'd driven anything, so he decided to delay turning on the radio, avoiding any distraction. Knowing these roads well, he soon relaxed behind the wheel and allowed himself the luxury of streaming music.

~

The Adirondacks loomed large, appearing to Jake like big feisty teenagers compared to the more eroded adult Catskills. Route 87 north of Albany had been designated as the Northway rather than the Thruway. Despite some winding, with the road laid out along the path of least geological resistance, the Northway did carry Jake ever northward through the mountains. The bright blue of the cloudless sky struck him as nature's bluescreen for the green forested slopes mixed with exposed black and gray rock. Driving along the stunning mountain corridor reminded urban-weary Jake in vivid color that other worlds had continued to exist even as he'd been engulfed by another one these past years. He stopped only once, pulling off the highway for gas and coffee in a small Adirondacks town.

He used cigarettes as a marker for progress. Every sixty miles he allowed himself one. He wished he had bought something better than this generic brand. They were beginning to taste foul.

The four-hour bucolic drive came to an end at the Canadian border. The signs, the buildings, the uniformed personnel at the crossing – blights on the natural landscape – were a reminder of humanity's self-importance. Nature would exact its revenge. It already was doing so, Jake couldn't help think on nearing the customs booth ahead, the temperature being unnaturally warm this far north. Where he came from, they called it Indian summer when a warm, sunny day came about in October or November. Now, it felt like yet another apocalypse in the making. He should have rented an electric car.

Vehicles ahead of him inched forward toward the dreaded booth. Jake prepared himself mentally for an interrogation. He even tried to influence the agent telepathically as he neared the window. "Be friendly," he broadcast.

The thirty-something woman looked snappy and efficient in her uniform as she leaned slightly toward him, saying, "Welcome to Canada. Passport, license, and health certificate, please." Slight French accent. Neutral tone at least.

Jake handed her proof of his existence and his responsible nature. She took them with gloved hands and looked them over. The passport and license had old pictures, showing him without a beard. Why did he feel guilty? He wasn't carrying anything illicit. Could she read his past on him?

"Where are you going?"

"Montreal."

"What is the purpose of your visit?"

Jake was having a hard time explaining that one to himself. "I'll be attending a talk at McGill University tomorrow." That was true. "Also, good food."

"When will you be leaving Canada?"

"In four days."

That was just a guess. He'd rented the car for at least a week. The woman studied him. If she had any suspicions, she could have the car searched.

"Enjoy your stay in Canada."

She actually smiled as she waved Jake past, and he felt like a little kid who had just won approval from an adult. Accepted by a foreign country even. He pulled away from the complex of the squat official buildings of the international border, heading north to his destiny in Montreal and beyond.

The road had become Route 15, the Canadian continuation of Route 87. He had about forty miles to go to Montreal – up here, notated as sixty kilometers. The Adirondacks had receded to the south, and he now drove over flatlands, with scattered signs of industry and mostly one-story houses dotting the landscape, some of them part of developments offering up sameness.

Jake had traveled this road once before. He didn't know his father. His mother had told him he was probably either a Canadian Mohawk she'd met at a Santana concert at the Saratoga Performing Arts Center, or a part-Greek, part-Italian guy she'd met at the Saratoga Race Course. After graduating high school, while working in construction around Shaleville, Jake had decided to cope with growing restlessness by taking a possible roots journey. He'd driven a big circle, visiting the Six Nations Reserve in Ontario west of Lake Ontario, then Akwesasne straddling the Ontario-New York border on the St. Lawrence River, and finally Kahnawake just south of Montreal. He'd also visited Montreal itself, returning to the United States on Route 15.

The highway eventually made a loop and merged with Route 10. Following the flow of traffic, Jake drove onto Pont Champlain across the wide St. Lawrence and reached the small Île des Soeurs (Nuns' Island). Rather than stay on 15 heading northwest over another bridge, he exited right and followed 10 north along the river. He knew from studying online maps that the island that makes up Montreal tilts slightly to the northeast and sits at the confluence of three rivers – the St. Lawrence, the Rivière des Prairies, and the Ottawa – much like Manhattan Island touches upon the Hudson, East, and Harlem Rivers.

Before long, Route 10 became Rue University, leading him into downtown Montreal. It had been a long day. His thoughts moved ahead of him. Darkness would descend soon. Where to sleep … in the car to save money?

His mind had moved too far ahead. He slammed on the breaks. His vehicle – unintentionally weaponized – had come within inches of a woman crossing the street. Her eyes looked at him through big glasses. She pounded his car hood, shouting "*Arrêt!*," then pointed to a nearby sign.

Jake knew that particular French word and gave her a sheepish nod. He realized as he clenched the wheel harder that his mind had just been made up for him about the car. He would use it as little as possible while in the city.

Continuing northwestward, he crossed more streets, some of them busy thoroughfares, until he reached Rue Sherbrooke from where he could see the McGill University complex. No convenient parking here, however. In addition to the many metered streets – filled up at this time of day – he saw signs announcing *réservé*, *défense de stationer*, *détenteur de permit de residents*. He didn't have to be bilingual to be warned off.

Rather than take a left on Sherbrooke to pass by the entranceway to the McGill campus, Jake made a right, hoping he could find parking on a quieter street. He drove a number of blocks until he came to Rue Saint-Dominique and took another right, heading back southeastward. After a block and a half on the sloping street, he came upon an Econo Lodge. Its red-and-white sign looked out of place in this relatively old part of the city but at least matched the flanking red-and white Canadian flag with its handsome maple leaf. A good location, in reasonable walking distance to McGill. Beyond the hotel he even found unmetered parking.

The hotel had available, reasonably priced rooms. A lanky, dark-complexioned concierge greeted him, his accent revealing he was a francophone, someone speaking French as a first language. Even so, he communicated in perfect English. Carrying his backpack and gym bag, Jake rode the elevator to the second floor and Room 202.

The room was small, with minimal floor space around the one double bed, but it struck recently homeless Jake as haut monde, with Cable TV *and* free shampoo. He unpacked, making use of dresser drawers and the small closet with fixed hangers. He washed up, using all the soap and towels he wanted. He then turned on the TV and, remote in hand, lay down on the throne of a bed.

He surfed up and down, checking out shows in both French and English. The unfamiliar channels and unfamiliar language on most of them affirmed the notion that he'd come a long, long way. He recognized a familiar face, that of Steve McQueen. The voice didn't sound like him though. *The Getaway*, a crime movie that he knew well – directed by Sam Pekinpah and based on a novel by Jim Thompson – had been dubbed in French. Yet Doc McCoy was one cool character in any language, and so was his French-dubbed wife Carol McCoy, played by Ali MacGraw.

Jake felt keyed up and didn't expect to sleep so soon … and he loved the film in any and all languages. The gentle French vowels must have had a lullaby effect. In this foreign land, here so unexpectedly, he wanted to cross over to his own sense of noir. He felt himself drifting into the imaginary …

Neon lights flashing outside his window … music swelling with suspicions and emotions … a haunting saxophone riff … and a femme fatale knocking on the door …

Psycho-Grid

DESPITE ONLINE RESEARCH, Jake had a long way to go sorting out a mental Montreal map. He would do some scouting today in advance of the lecture. After a long shower and the hotel's continental breakfast served at a side table in the lobby – croissants, juice, and coffee – he set out.

The morning sun burned off the nighttime cold. Jake walked along Saint-Dominique to Sherbrooke, then made a right, passing in front of centuries-old and modern buildings both. He came to Boulevard Saint-Laurent, his goal, a helpful point of reference for his psycho-grid. The Main – its old popular name – had been a historical demarcation line, with French-speaking people generally having settled roughly to the northeast, and English-speaking people, to the southwest. Like Fifth Avenue in New York City, he'd read, Saint-Laurent serves as the point zero in house numbering, starting at One East and One West, and so on.

Saint-Laurent is also useful as a directional marker. To the northwest, Jake knew, it extends to Plateau Mont-Royal, Montreal's most densely populated area, with small, winding streets and supposedly a Parisian feel. That neighborhood borders Parc du Mont Royal – the large park extending northwestward of McGill – sort of Montreal's version of New York City's Central Park. Southeastward from where he was staying, Saint-Laurent passes by the Quartier Chinois (Chinatown), then continues on to the cobblestone streets of Vieux-Montréal (Old Montreal) and the wharfs of Vieux Port (Old Port), where French explorers staked their claim in the 17th century and built fortifications.

Jake entered the Saint-Laurent metro station to preview the system. He'd read that each of the sixty-two metro stations are unique, designed by a different architect. From what he could see from the entrance area, this one was bright and clean, a stark contrast to all-too-often deteriorating New York City subway stations. He studied the map display. The various routes and color coding seemed a lot more rational than New York's equivalent. A smaller system certainly. No machines here; you had to pay a human being at the booth.

He resurfaced and headed back southwest on Sherbrooke, passing Saint-Dominique, the street where his hotel was located. He came upon a pawn shop offering money exchange. The elderly man spoke broken English and worked out the math with Jake, who asked for a total of fifty dollars Canadian. He got a twenty, two tens, and a five of the large, colorful bills. He also got a two-dollar copper-and-silver coin, a one-dollar copper coin, and the rest in quarters, dimes, nickels, and pennies, these resembling the equivalent U.S. varieties. He gave the two-dollar coin back for a used French-English dictionary and returned outside.

Signs on buildings were mostly in French. When a sign had both languages, the French lettering was larger as mandated by law. Jake used the English-French dictionary to translate some of the French words he encountered: *ouvert*, "open," *fermé*, "closed," e*space à louer*, "space for rent."

He crossed Rue University and continued on Sherbrooke parallel to the McGill campus. Several blocks later at Rue Mansfield, he reached the Centre Mont Royal, the privately run multimedia conference center, where Boucher would give his talk. Some event was underway inside the multistoried modern building, and people milled about the steps at its two entrances, one on each of the connecting streets.

Jake continued southwestward on Sherbrooke. His goal now was Rue Crescent, a center of activity for anglophones. After some more hoofing, he reached it and turned left. As expected, he soon passed numerous restaurants and bars. He felt stabs of hunger and chose a Thai restaurant for lunch, walking up a metal staircase that extended out onto the sidewalk – an architectural trait typical of Montreal buildings, he'd noticed.

He sat down and settled in, still marveling at the ease of such things when one has the means. The waitress, a middle-aged Thai woman – he assumed she was Thai – spoke perfect English. Not that he needed to communicate much beyond ordering pad thai and green tea. He watched the street life from his window seat. A lot of young people noisily passed – students between classes? He fought the urge to shovel down the food, instead eating slowly, savoring the spices. From a coffee and roll in the Playground of the Americas to Thai food in a restaurant in a foreign city. He'd come a long way.

Back on Crescent, Jake walked toward another center of activity, Rue Sainte-Catherine. At its corner he stopped to smoke a cigarette and watch two musicians on alto sax and upright bass. Busking permits clipped to their belts, they performed a Thelonious Monk tune. An elderly woman stopped to give them some coins. Thinking of Tenor from another city's streets, Jake emptied his pockets of American coins into the sax case.

He headed back northeastward along Saint-Catherine, passing stores, fast food joints, and strip clubs advertising *danse contact*. He could figure that phrase out without using his dictionary. He sat down to rest on the steps of St. James United Church. Urban contrast – a church near strip clubs.

Walking on, Jake encountered some seedy-looking youth, dressed in varied styles – hippie, goth, and punk – milling about or sitting on the sidewalk, many with backpacks. Runaways? He'd read that more than half of homeless youth run away from home because of conflicts with parents (Rainy, now Ms. Advocate-for-the-Homeless, could no doubt verify that statistic) – street life as a rebellion and lifestyle thing rather than as a result of poverty, mental illness, or drug addiction. Hadn't his own homelessness in effect been a lifestyle choice, given the fact that he'd always had a last resort for shelter – his sister's house?

Some of the youth sure did look wild-eyed and strung out, maybe the result of running away rather than the cause of it. One of the goth boys glared at Jake through hostility glasses – or was he projecting? He fought back resentment, remembering his looking at people from the homeless perspective. So easy to cop attitudes. One needs the shield of non-reaction whatever the circumstances, his shamus alter ego advised.

He followed Sainte-Catherine all the way to Rue Saint-Denis – a long way, taking him beyond Saint-Laurent. He wanted to check out the scene in this supposed center of francophone activity known as the Quartier Latin, named after the neighborhood in Paris. The abundance of cafés and boutiques seemed a confirmation of that. But he was just skimming the surface, like a tourist. A different state of mind, that, and one detracting from his self-image of doing something purposeful beyond sightseeing.

Exhaustion was getting the better of him. He had the urge to energize himself with a shot and a chaser. He walked steadfastly along Saint-Denis, past two bars beckoning him. At Sherbrooke he made a left, following it back toward his hotel. On again reaching the Saint-Laurent metro station, he descended its stairs and, with some of his fresh Canadian money, purchased two one-time ticket cards to have on hand for tailing people.

Back outside, he continued on Sherbrooke to Saint-Dominique and his hotel room. His introduction to Montreal by foot had been one big circle.

He now had the luxury of a private nap. Yet the good life still felt weird and Jake had a hard time falling asleep. His mind's eye kept returning to the faces of street people from his walk … along with faces from the other city he'd just left.

The haves and the have nots. He well knew he could revert to the latter PDQ.

Boucher and Congregation

JAKE STAYED MOST of the next day – the day of Boucher's scheduled talk – at the hotel, only venturing out to check on the rental car and to buy sandwich materials, chips, fruit, and bottled water at a nearby épicerie. He absorbed French Canadian culture via TV. He also gazed at the ceiling while talking heads conversed in French. Not something to take for granted, a ceiling.

The day wore on and the event that had brought Jake all this way was approaching. He took a long shower – another luxury – and ate a second sandwich. He set out at 6:30 p.m., allowing plenty of time to walk across town to the 7:30 lecture.

Jake followed a trickle of people through glass doors into the Centre Mont Royal at its Rue Mansfield entrance. The event was to take place in Le Grand Salon, the auditorium on the first level. The trickle led him there. The early birds were predominantly young people – McGill students assigned to the lecture by a professor perhaps. Just a few older folks dotted the big room.

He'd arrived early enough to get a seat near the stage, choosing one in the third row to the far left to have a good angle for viewing audience faces, in particular those of Leandra, Ned, and Marcus.

No problem: As soon as he'd taken a cushioned seat and glanced over at those already situated in the front rows, he saw their profiles. Ringleader Marcus's round head was now completely shaved; Ned of the dreads wore his beanie; and chameleon Leandra now had jet black hair streaked ever so slightly with silver. They sat in the first row and, like good little students, they all seemed intent on the business at hand.

No one had taken the seats to their left yet. A man and a woman about their age sat to their right, talking to each other. The man wore a red, white, and blue Montreal Expos baseball hat, with long stringy brown hair showing. The Expos had moved and the franchise had become the Washington Nationals, making the cap a throwback like Jake's New York Giants one. The woman to his right had black hair, hers without streaks, cut short in a retro cut, popularized by the iconic actress and dancer Louise Brooks. No sign of the muscular fellow who had passed Leandra the canvas bag in Union Square Park and who had arrived with Boucher at Ralph Bunche Park.

The retro woman leaned partly forward and spoke to the others. They must have all come together. Co-conspirators? With the seats directly behind them still empty, Jake thought about moving there to try to overhear conversation as he had managed to do at the Manhattan diner. He had his nearly two-week beard and he wore a knitted cap resembling Ned's rather than his preferred baseball-style hats, so he felt confident they wouldn't recognize him from three-hundred-plus miles south. But they might take note of him in the audience, ruining tailing them.

People kept filing into the hall. The front row and most others filled up. Jake could see why the McGill sociology department had lined up such a large auditorium for this event. Boucher apparently was a draw. Like a rock star. No, like a preacher … and this was his congregation. The podium at the center of the stage did strike Jake as church-like.

A middle-aged man and a young woman walked on stage. The audience hushed immediately, then offered scattered applause. The man had a groomed mustache and beard and wore the uniform of an academic – tweed jacket and wire-rimmed glasses. The woman wore a dark blue pantsuit.

The man spoke: "Good evening, my dear friends. Welcome to the Centre Mont-Royal. I'm Dr. Damon Huntington of McGill's Department of Sociology. I'm delighted to see each and every one of you … my students, other McGill students, students from other schools, and members of the community at large, some of whom I understand have traveled from far and wide for this event. You all know why you're here. Paul-Louis Boucher is renowned beyond his own institution, the Sorbonne. He is a key thinker in sociology, communication, and cultural studies. His talks and writings have served notice on America that their cultural exports only skim the surface of consciousness … that there are deep-rooted ways of thinking that cannot be undone by the facile and the trivial."

Applause.

The host smiled. "I see that we are in agreement. Anyway, I won't waste any more of your time. Next to me is Natalie Beaubien of McGill's English department. She'll be translating for Monsieur Boucher. Some of you of course won't need a translation. McGill is officially an English-language university, but I certainly wish all of you here can learn French well enough to someday understand our friend Paul-Louis Boucher in his native tongue. Now, my good friends, let's show our friend how happy we are that he has come to Montreal!"

Cue more applause, this time raucous. Many people rose to their feet, including the five in the front row. Jake now saw that dedicated artist Leandra had her sketchpad under one arm.

Boucher glided onto the stage. He looked exactly as Jake remembered him – same gray, well-cut suit on the lean body and same perfectly groomed ponytail. Huntington stayed onstage long enough to join in on the applause. Boucher nodded to his translator and moved to a central microphone, she to a side one. The applause subsided.

"*Bon soir, tous mes amis.*"

Some cheering. Then, expectant silence.

Boucher's deep voice projected well and had a gentle urgency to it. His pauses, as he waited for the translation, added to the dramatic effect. Even his aquiline good looks along with his precise gestures seemed to bolster his message, as if his entire being were cutting through meaning. Natalie Beaubien's delivery and tone were a good match for his. She came across as more than just a translator; she seemed a true believer.

What was the message? Jake at first didn't hang on every translated word. He found himself caught up in the cadence of Boucher's French and he was intrigued by the audience's reaction. But he quickly got the gist of his premise, pretty much what he'd expected based on his online research. The sociologist had a bone to pick with American domination of world culture. The globalization of mass media culture was certainly not a new gripe among the French.

Boucher's angle, as presented in his book *Astérix et les Romaines culturelles* (i.e., *Astérix and the Cultural Romans*), which he cited several times, was that every individual of every foreign land must defend his own culture against usurpation by global corporations that promote their visions for profit. Each individual must become like the little comic book Gaul character of ancient times, Astérix, who resists Roman occupation in his homeland. What did that mean in the 21st century? Not taking up the sword, but rather resisting through one's own art and writings. American culture, Boucher said, is the stuff of ridicule, a goldmine of parody. Don't wallow in defeatism over the American-spawned shopping malls, theme parks, theme towns, and fast foods even if they reach France or Quebec. Rise to the challenges and counter them with the arrows of art and parody, as the creators of Astérix had done – the writer René Goscinny and illustrator Albert Uderzo. Jake had found enough about Astérix's world online in English to know that it includes the character Toon who resembles Mickey Mouse. The name of the alien race that Toon represents – the Tadilsweny – is even an anagram of Walt Disney. Disney for Boucher represented an invading alien force. Defeat popular culture with a higher esthetic.

Boucher and Beaubien were eloquent, cogent, and even beguiling. Yet some of the concepts and translated phrases, although powerful, started to feel a bit too clever to Jake: "the historical simulacra of Walt Disney," "turn the kitschy back on the peddlers of kitsch," "bring hyperreality, the reality of simulations, back to the real," "redefine the referents," "occupy the occupiers," "defeat mall mediocrity and burger tack with a higher esthetic," and one that was way over the top but that got a cheer from the audience ... "soak yourself in semiotics and sink the floating signifiers with your own symbolic torpedoes." Maybe Boucher himself helped translate that last one. Or maybe Beaubien just couldn't resist alliteration.

Attendees seemed spellbound and responded with a standing ovation. Jake played along, standing with the crowd. Boucher beamed and waved, remaining center stage until the room calmed down. When Boucher exited stage left, Jake spotted his muscular assistant, aide, cohort, bodyguard, lover – whatever! – stepping out from the wings to greet and hug him. Jake also saw that the five, now standing in the front row, applauded longer than most around them.

Now what? Tail the New York City trio to find out if their trip here was anything more than just idol worship? It all seemed so on-the-up-and-up. Jake reminded himself of the items changing hands and the mysterious conversation back in the Big Apple about payment and being mules. As if to confirm Jake's thoughts, while people filed out of the auditorium, Marcus walked along the front row to a side door and, after a word with a man posted there, disappeared inside. The other four moved to now-empty seats at the corner of the row and sat back down.

Jake made his way to the back of the Grand Salon to avoid being noticed, but from where he could keep an eye on the front row and the side door. Thankfully, other audience members lingered to talk, concealing his presence. His eyes kept returning to Leandra. She'd donned a blue woolen cap. She wore no smock as in New York but rather a frayed denim blue jacket, with added patchwork of varying materials, hanging part way over torn jeans.

After several minutes, Marcus reemerged carrying a drum – a djembe with straps – a big black leather photographer's bag, and a blue vinyl suitcase. The others stood up and angled over through the rows of seats to meet him. Marcus passed the drum to Leandra, who slung it over her shoulder, and the suitcase to Ned. He kept the photographer's bag. Jake turned away from them as they walked to the rear of the big room and exited, then followed.

Outside, the woman with the Louise Brooks-like haircut and the man with the Expos cap joined the trio, then walked alongside them. She stood about, five-three, Jake guessed. He was about as tall as Ned. Both French Canadian? The woman's clothing matched her raven hair – black sweater, skirt, leggings, and leather boots – and contrasted her pale skin. The man, wearing a brown suede jacket and black leather jeans, had a sallow face. They both smoked cigarettes as they walked.

No one talked. The five crossed Sherbrooke and followed it, eventually passing the McGill campus. At Rue University they turned left at the corner and followed the campus to the northwest, then took a right onto Rue Prince-Arthur. At Rue Clark, a narrow street, they made a left to head northwestward again. This was the Plateau Mont-Royal neighborhood, Jake knew, or "little Paris" after Paris's Left Bank.

Jake stayed a good distance back and on the opposite side of the street as much as possible. He remained unnoticed, he felt certain. The more people one is tailing, the easier it is, he found. They distract one another and also have a feeling of security and pay less attention to goings-on around them. His marks never even looked over their shoulders. Did that mean they had nothing to hide? What was with the Mickey Mouse doll in Brooklyn, the envelope at the United Nations Plaza, and now a drum, a suitcase, and a photographer's bag?

Still on Rue Clark, beyond Rue Marie-Anne, they stopped and climbed metal steps to a second-floor apartment on the left. Jake hung in the shadows on the opposite corner, waiting to confirm that the three out-of-towners were probably sleeping there. Even if they had a hotel, he now knew at least where two of their friends apparently lived. Or were they better described as contacts? He would stay at least one hour, he decided, and if no one reappeared, return early the next day for more of the same.

After exactly one hour in the cold, jiggling to stay warm, Jake set out on the long walk back to his hotel. It wasn't until he'd reached Sherbrooke that he realized that Rue Clark was just two blocks from Saint-Dominique, with Boulevard Saint-Laurent – The Main – between them. That would make it easy to get his bearings in the a.m.

Shadow Man

WIND OFF THE ST. LAWRENCE RIVER bit at him, and Jake was glad to have worn layers. His disguise today was a Toronto Blue Jays hat he'd purchased. He regretted it since the knitted cap would have been better to cover his ears in this morning cold.

He'd had no problem again locating the apartment on Rue Clark. The greater challenge had been finding a discreet observation point since the building was on a residential block. He'd decided to watch the metal stairs and second-story door from a short distance up Rue Marie-Anne.

He'd changed his location once – moving across Clark but still on Rue Marie-Anne – because a woman had been staring at him from a window opposite, wondering no doubt why this stranger was lurking about. At such times, Jake couldn't help but wonder that himself. Watching the apartment from his rental car would be more comfortable certainly, but perhaps even more conspicuous on a block like this with reserved parking.

Seconds became minutes … minutes, an hour. Just one cigarette so far. He absorbed the city around him. Some walls along these streets had graffiti art – a lot of big block writing in bold colors. In his online searches Jake had read that Montreal, especially here on the Plateau, was a living museum with artists celebrated and sponsored. Legal tagging. Ricky Rad could have done his art aboveground in this city.

Jake looked more than once one at a piece on a brick wall down the block toward Parc Jeanne Mance, an extension of Parc du Mont-Royal. At first, he saw it as abstract but then he discerned humans and finally letters – *MISHMASH*, they said. He'd solved that little mystery, but what about the big one that had led him to a foreign city? He turned his attention back to the apartment.

One more cigarette later, Leandra appeared, wearing the same denim jacket, jeans, and blue woolen cap as the evening before. No sketchpad today. She descended the metal staircase without glancing Jake's way. Still without looking toward him, she angled across Clark and headed in the opposite direction along Marie-Anne. She walked fast, disappearing south around the corner on Boulevard Saint-Laurent. Jake hurried to catch up, glad to warm up through motion.

He reached the corner and saw Leandra entering a doorway, a *pâtisserie*. She reemerged a few minutes later with a takeout coffee and a croissant in a napkin and proceeded southeastward. Sipping and taking bites slowed her down a bit. Jake crossed Saint-Laurent, now tailing her from the opposite side of the street.

On finishing her breakfast to go, Leandra quickened her pace again. Wherever she was heading, she was doing so with purpose. She continued all the way to Sherbrooke, then took a left, continuing as far as Saint-Denis, then southeastward again through the Quartier Latin.

At Boulevard de Maisonneuve she made a left. After crossing Rue Berri, she disappeared into a big building. Jake hurried his pace to see where she'd gone. The Voyageur Terminus, Montreal's main bus station, he soon discovered. Taking a side trip without her cohorts? And without luggage?

He entered the stately building. He scanned those gathered, finally spotting Leandra again, her blue cap bobbing ahead of him. She stopped opposite a row of ticket windows and waited in line. When it was her turn, Jake moved forward as if considering to stand in line to buy a ticket or not. Yet he couldn't overhear what she said to the lady at the counter. He did see that she paid money and received a ticket. It looked like one ticket, no more. Was she the mule on a bus while the boys drove?

Jake turned sideways. He waited a long moment, then looked for her again. She'd reached the station door and exited. He hurried after her and also exited, expecting to see her heading back along Boulevard de Maisonneuve. He hustled in that direction, first looking up and down Rue Berri, then the same on Rue Saint-Denis. No Leandra. She must have gone in the other direction or perhaps into another building. To shake him? In any case, he'd lost her.

Fuck it. He would return to the hotel, change his clothes to make himself less recognizable – although it could be too late for that – then eat something and once again stake out the apartment.

~

Jake now wore sweatpants, hoody, and knitted cap – his attempt at looking like a cold weather jogger. He was in no shape to jog but he could at least power walk to stay warm. Take a metro? There was no direct route, the online map indicated. Hoofing it made the most sense.

Toward the end of his long walk along Saint-Laurent toward Rue Clark, while crossing Avenue des Pins, Jake saw Ned and Marcus exiting a storefront. With slightly different timing, they might have passed within feet of him, dashing his hope of anonymity. They fortunately headed in the same direction he was walking. Jake reached the store they'd just exited. The sign said *Horlogerie – Réparations*. In the window were clocks of various shapes and sizes. Watch repair?

He followed the duo two and a half more blocks – past Avenue Duluth and Rue Rachel – and wasn't surprised to see them turn left on Rue Marie-Anne. On reaching the corner of Marie-Anne himself, he saw them turn right onto Clark. By the time he'd reached the next corner, there was no sign of them along the block, only a man waxing his car. They'd apparently climbed the metal stairs and reentered the building.

Dumb luck, finding out where they'd been like that. One thing puzzled Jake about this affair. All that he knew about them from New York and Montreal struck him as strange and suspicious. Yet he saw no sign of vigilance. No looking over their collective shoulder to see if they were being followed. Activists, perhaps, but amateurish ones.

Whatever. Jake knew his mission. Time for another stakeout in the cold, with gnawing questions and crawling moments.

~

The raven-haired woman from the night before appeared fifty-three minutes later. No all-black outfit this time; just a black skirt, with a violet sweater and matching tights and woolen hat. She appeared to be dressed up for a social event or even some kind of meeting.

After stopping to light a cigarette, she walked up Clark away from Rue Marie-Anne. Jake followed, jogging as he passed the apartment's metal stairs in case one of the others might be looking out onto the street. At the corner she took a right on Avenue du Mont-Royal and proceeded northeastward, one block after another. Her compact walk was a lot different from loping Leandra's. Her hips seemed to lock in with every step, her upper body moving relatively little.

One block beyond Saint-Denis she reached Rue Rivard and the Mont-Royal metro station. Thanks to his earlier gumshoe planning, he had a ticket ready. Keeping a good distance behind her, he passed through the turnstile and followed her to the southbound Orange Line.

Jake stayed at the back of the platform. She stood at the platform's edge some thirty feet away. He'd hated witnessing that in New York City subways. Too many stories of crazies coming up behind people and pushing them onto the tracks. Raven, as he now thought of her, stepped back a few feet when a train approached. A clean blue car with big windows and a big white stripe pulled up in front of him. It was a lot quieter than the New York version. Jake felt a hint of nostalgia for the dirtier, clattering Metropolitan Transit Authority line.

He entered the car at the far end from her. She didn't sit down even though seats were available. He tried not to fix on her too much in case she looked his way. He glanced over as the train neared the first station – Sherbrooke. Her attention was elsewhere. At the ensuing stop, Berri-UQUAM, beneath the bus station where Jake had been earlier that day, she exited. He held back a few seconds, then also stepped onto the platform. He stayed well behind her but kept her in sight as she made her way to another platform – the Green Line westward. This train took a little longer to arrive. From afar he could see that Raven seemed to be moving to music inside her head, gently swaying. Her eyes were even closed. He took a photo of her.

The train pulled up and Jake again entered at the opposite end of the same car as she did. This time, his mark sat down and rode three stops, exiting at the McGill station. He followed her through the turnstiles and along winding subterranean passageways.

It seemed like a mall down here, the passageway leading past boutiques, banks, and restaurants. He realized he must be in the Underground City, the vast commercial and even partly residential network below a large section of Montreal, including most of the downtown region – an underworld that felt to him like an off-world. The future of humankind?

Raven was window shopping. That made it hard to follow her since she often turned sideways to take in the storefronts. At one point she glanced to the right into a window while moving forward – for a little too long over her shoulder – making Jake wonder if she were checking reflections to see if anyone tailed her. He stood out down here in his sweats, a lot of the other subterraneans dressed for business as she seemed to be.

She entered a clothing store. Jake retreated to the far side of the adjoining business – a crêperie – and waited. The odors soon got to him and he stepped inside to purchase a basic crêpe with powdered sugar. He took up position at a side counter on a stool from where, sitting at an angle, he could watch the doorway of the store. He ate slowly, waiting.

Raven reappeared after about twenty minutes, a blue plastic bag in hand. Jake left the stool to follow. She moved more quickly now, no longer pausing to look in windows. After passing a dozen or so stores, she approached an escalator and stepped onto it. He held back, letting a man and a woman go ahead of him before following behind them. Looking between the heads of the couple, he could see Raven halfway up the escalator. She pulled a white woolen scarf out of the bag and wrapped it around her neck. Her purchase. But then she quickly glanced over her shoulder, reached under her sweater, and pulled out another sweater stuffed in there. It looked expensive, like cashmere. She placed it in the bag.

A shoplifter. Knowing what he now knew about her, Jake hung back farther in case she looked over her shoulder again. Given what she was up to, he was fortunate she hadn't spotted him yet … if indeed she hadn't.

Raven headed for a flight of stairs. He followed moments later into the open air. He found himself at Boulevard de Maisonneuve and Rue University and saw his mark walking northward on the west side of the latter. A lot of pedestrians were out and about this late afternoon, and he had good cover to proceed after her.

She crossed Avenue du President-Kennedy, continuing northward to Sherbrooke and across it, then westward to the McGill campus entranceway. She followed a pathway angling to the right, then left it to sit down on the groomed lawn and light a cigarette. Jake hurried to catch up with a couple walking in the same direction, timing his movements so that when he did pass Raven, he was on their far side. He kept going a good distance to another lawn area from where he could observe her at a distance. He sat on a bench and, like her, lit a cigarette.

He was exhausted from this day of shadowing people, not just from the walking but also from the concentration it entailed trying to go unnoticed. He was ready for his hotel bed and TV. What more could he accomplish waiting here on this woman? He now knew what prompted her excursion to the Underground City. Shopping in her outlaw way. While following her, Jake might have missed an opportunity to follow Leandra, Ned, or Marcus.

He saw that Raven was talking on a cellphone and was reminded of the first day he'd come upon Leandra on a bench in Union Square Park and, the second time, when Boucher's righthand man showed up. Jake imagined Boucher's gopher suddenly showing up to pass Raven a black canvas bag with a Mickey Mouse doll inside it. In his vision this bag announced *J'aime Montreal* rather than *I Love New York*.

She was after a bag, but not from Boucher. Raven had been facing a group of students playing Frisbee on the lawn opposite her, their possessions lying on the grass nearby. She suddenly stood up and looked around. Jake quickly lowered his head as if dozing. When he looked up again, he saw her grab a briefcase and move quickly away toward a side walkway to Rue University.

She was good. She was quick. She'd made another score. She would probably go home now with her pickings.

Jake was spent. He had the sniffles from so much standing in the cold. He followed Sherbrooke back to Rue Saint-Dominique and the hotel and reached the refuge of his room. It was only dusk, but he shed his clothes and crawled under the covers. Sights of the city above and underground – and of Leandra and Raven moving through it – led him first away from, then into sleep.

Raven by Any Other Name

JAKE STOOD NEAR the same corner of Clark and Marie-Anne. He played the tourist today. Ordinary clothes. Map and notebook in hand. Studying Montreal architecture. Befuddled look on his face. Cellphone camera in hand.

No sign of Leandra, Ned, and Marcus. At least, unlike yesterday, it was sunny and warm, offering some relief to his head cold. He allowed himself a quick break, purchasing a jambon-beurre sandwich to go at a nearby café with a restroom, then rushed back to his stakeout.

Almost another hour passed before he saw recognizable faces. Raven and he of the Expos cap and stringy brown hair had exited the building. Today, like at the Boucher talk, she was decked out in black. Contrasting her powder-enhanced skin was bright red lipstick, matching a red shoulder bag. He again wore the brown suede jacket and black leather pants, and now a black leather hat. The cinematic pair walked arm-in-arm. He looked like a modern

84

gangster on the rise in Montreal's underworld. Klepto Raven now seemed a gun moll to Jake.

Still playing the tourist, glancing at the map, Jake turned his back to them. After a few moments, he turned to see where they were going. They walked northeastward on Marie-Anne. Should he follow them? If he did, he might miss the New York City trio. But he needed action.

They crossed Saint-Laurent and made a right. Jake stayed on the opposite side of the boulevard to follow. They stopped at a café – Café Pi (the *pi* sign, that is) – advertising chess. They hugged and he entered. A chess-playing gangster or was this establishment just a front?

Jake reigned in his movie fantasies as he watched her turn around and walk back along The Main. His marks, just innocent young people who'd been on a stroll? She entered the small park at the corner of Marie-Anne and Saint-Laurent – *Parc du Portugal*, the sign said – and sat down on a bench. Seeking another score? Wasn't this a little too close to home for thievery?

She took a cigarette out of a blue pack – Gauloises, Jake saw – and lit it. Should he return to his regular observation point and keep an eye out for Leandra, Ned, and Marcus? He decided to stick with Raven a little longer, not sure what he intended by doing so, other than satisfying his curiosity how she might pull off another pinch. He also wanted to sit down and rest, fighting fatigue. He entered the park at the far corner from her, chose a bench out of her direct view, and settled in.

Jake scanned the park's gazebo, tiled lion's-head fountain, wooden benches, squirrels, pigeons, and foliage. New York had been renovating its parks to counter its cranky self but had a long way to go before catching up to Montreal with its abundant well-groomed parks, both large and small. He glanced over at the boulevard to see a passing police car. It was familiar-looking, reminding him of a NYC cop car, but this one with more white than blue.

He turned his attention back to the park and saw Raven approaching. No question about her noticing him now. Her dark brown eyes were locked on him as she walked right up to him and spoke.

"Qu'est-ce que vous voulez? What is it you want?" Her English had a slight French accent.

"What do I want?" Jake feebly echoed. "I'd settle for a Gauloise." He showed her his pack of generics.

She ignored that.

"Why are you following me?" she asked again, fingering her coat buttons, her eyes narrow and fiery. "I saw you at McGill yesterday. Today, you followed me here from my home. What do you want?"

"Sit down and I'll tell you," he said, buying time.

"Why don't I go get my boyfriend so you can tell him? I know you know he's nearby."

"Right, he'd rather play chess than go to a park with you."

Jake wondered if he'd gone too far with that comment, but then he saw what he thought was a flicker of a smile, as if she might actually be enjoying this.

"You're American," she said with some contempt.

"Good ear. Yes."

"You speak French?"

"I understand a little. I'm trying to learn more while here." He pulled out his pocket dictionary and held it up.

"Typical of Americans not to know other people's languages. What do you want besides a French cigarette?"

"I'll tell you if you sit down. It's not bad."

Jake still didn't know what he was going to tell her. She studied him a moment longer, then shrugged and sat down next to him. She smelled slightly of garlic, mixed with perfume.

"Just make it quick ... and no *merde*," she said.

Jake had found his angle: "I've been following you longer than you know. Ever since the Boucher talk. I followed you from there with the others to be able to find you again if I wanted. And I wanted. I followed you from your house to the metro yesterday. I saw you steal clothing in the Underground City and the bag at McGill. But I don't care about any of that."

That gave her pause. Then: "Who are you?"

"Just a tourist from New York. Really."

"What do you want with me?"

If at all shaken, she was doing a good job concealing it.

"Just to watch you."

"What is this? Spit it out." Only she said "*spee-it*."

"Okay, I'll confess. I'm an artist who no longer paints. Why don't I paint? Because a woman who looks like you broke my stupid heart. I was working on a series of paintings of her two months ago. It was better than making love. Not for her, I guess. She preferred making love with someone else when I wasn't looking. I destroyed the paintings and moved out, ending up on the street. I've been living homeless. When one of my sculptures sold, I decided to use some of the money to get out of New York. I've always wanted to visit Montreal and so I did and rented a hotel." Jake paused for effect. "Then I see you."

"I look like her. *Et alors?*"

"Too much so. Same raven-colored hair and dark eyes. Smart eyes. Even your style is the same. She wore black a lot of the time."

"And the rest of me?"

"Your exact height to the half-inch. Ha, ha. Just joking. Maybe she's two inches taller."

She let out a small smile, saying, "*Tu es un idiot, tu sais.*"

"I caught the idiot part of that," Jake said, smiling back.

"*Attends!* Are you stalking me or her?"

"I'm not stalking anyone, but I will say I'm already seeing a lot less of her in you now. I'm seeing you as you."

She absorbed that, then said, "Where do you stay? What hotel?"

"The Econo Lodge … on Saint-Dominique."

"Show me the keycard."

He pulled it out of his coat's upper pocket.

"What's your name?"

"Jake."

"Show me your driver's license or passport."

He didn't want to give up his full name but had little choice if he wanted to keep her talking. He produced both.

She reached for them and studied them a good while before returning them, with no comment about the double Jake thing.

She stood up. "Let's go tell your story to my boyfriend."

Jake also stood up. "Sure. Why not? I'm not crazy. I'm a painter who made the mistake of getting too involved with a face from my past. But I won't tell him how much I find myself enjoying your company"

"*Assieds-toi*," she said as she sat back down. "Let's not bother his chess game. Here's your Gauloise."

Jake sat down again, accepting the cigarette and lighting it with his pocket lighter. She lit one herself.

"What's your name?" he asked.

"You can have my cigarettes, you can have some of my time, but you can't have my name."

"Can I call you Raven since you're raven-haired."

"*Pourquoi pas?* Why not."

"Okay. Raven, want to go for coffee?"

~

They sat opposite each other in a wine bar on The Main, over red wine, cheese, and a baguette. His treat, Jake had told her.

"Is shoplifting and stealing people's bags your only income?" he asked.

"Do you judge me for that?"

"Now that I'm getting to know you as more than a face, I can't help but wonder about it. The shoplifting is easier to accept because it's not so personal. But some student had a miserable day because you stole his briefcase."

"That was the first time, going onto a campus like that to steal. I kept the iPod and some change but left everything else in one of the buildings."

"Taking that kind of risk for an iPod?"

"I wanted to see if I could do it. I could tell they were Americans and saw how expensive their clothes were, so I decided to try for whatever. And I succeeded." She made it sound all so logical.

"One of these times you'll get caught and that'll cost you a lot more than what you keep."

"It's not about the money. I have enough money."

"Lucky you. How's that?"

"My parents send me enough money. I pay the rent and buy all the food for me and Raphael."

"Okay. So why steal?"

"Something to do. I only steal from American stores and from Americans. My next challenge is pickpocketing. I want to see if I can get an American tourist's wallet. But I might forget the whole thing."

"I say forget it. Risky behavior. And not nice."

"See? You do judge me."

"Where do your parents live?" he asked.

"Florida."

"On vacation?"

"No, permanently. That was their stupid dream. To live like Americans."

"Americans, the bad guys to you. Is that why you went to hear Boucher?"

"*Les québécois* need that message as much as *les français*."

"Didn't you go there with the enemy … weren't those three there with you and Raphael Americans?" Had he revealed too much? "I heard them talking when I followed you," he added.

"Some Americans understand that the whole world shouldn't be American in culture," she asserted.

"I'm one of them. That's why I went to the lecture. I like what he has to say. I was looking to do something non-touristy. I'm glad I did. I learned some stuff. And I saw you."

"You followed me because of a sick fantasy. I am not your model, your ex-lover. I'm better than she is." She laughed along with that declaration.

"Maybe you are. I see now that I'd have to paint you much differently."

"Draw me on the napkin." She reached in her bag and pulled out a pen, handing it to him.

Executing any kind of portrait was something Jake hadn't done in a long time. Yet he had to deliver if he wanted to keep whatever he had going with Raven. Funny about lying. How it begins to feel like the truth. He'd included enough of the truth to believe the rest himself … on some strange level at least. He set to work.

He did the best he could. He got the shape of the hair right anyway. To capture something more of her, he made the eyes big and piercing.

She reached for the napkin and studied his work.

"*Pas mal.* Sign it," she instructed, handing it back to him.

He did so and passed it back. She put it in her bag.

"You have my drawing. Can I take a photo of you in exchange in case I ever want to do a painting?"

"Okay. Just one."

She looked up at him and, raising his phone, he clicked it.

"Let me see it."

He clicked on the photo and held up his phone. She studied the image.

"Okay," she said.

Jake smiled at her, then asked, "That American woman with you at the lecture, so you like her okay?

"Do you have a fantasy about her?"

He laughed. "But of course. Not because she reminds me of anyone. But because she'd make a good model, too. So the three of them ... even though they're American ... they agree with Boucher's message?"

"*Oui.*"

"Didn't I see one of them go backstage while I was waiting to follow you? Are they friends of Boucher?"

"Yes, they do some work for him."

"Work? Like what?"

"I don't know. *Pourquoi?*"

"It's just nice to know there are other Americans besides *moi* who care about issues. They'll be staying with you a while?"

"No, they left."

Jake had a hard time hiding his reaction to that.

"Left Canada? For where?"

"New York, I suppose. What do I care? They're Raphael's friends. Our apartment is too small. I'm glad they're gone ... even if they are the less stupid Americans."

She was getting impatient with the subject. He had to let it rest if he wanted to get more out of her.

"What are you doing now?"

"*Pourquoi?*"

"I'm the stupid American tourist, remember? Rather than steal from one, why not teach one all about Montreal ... educate him?"

She held his gaze in her typically confrontational way.

She finally spoke: "*D'accord.*"

~

Raven seemed to enjoy talking about the city. Although she put down tourists, she suggested doing the most touristy thing she could think of – going to the top of the Tower of Montreal, the equivalent of going to the top of the Eiffel Tower in Paris, or to the top of the Empire State Building in Manhattan.

Jake again found himself on the Orange Line from the Mont-Royal station. This time, however, he was next to Raven, not at the opposite end of the car, and, this time, at Berri-UQUAM they transferred east on the Green Line, not west. She sat next to him. With her special petulance, she stared down anyone who happened to look her way. He wondered if she were seeing wallets as much as faces.

They emerged at Viau. He commented on the fact that different architects had designed stations.

"Let's see if I remember … one small attempt to fight off mall mediocrity and burger tack," she said, using Boucher/Beaubien-speak.

From there they made their way to the Parc Olympique and the tower. They rode to the top on a two-story funicular that ascends the outside of the 575-foot-high structure. The tower leans some forty-five degrees over the stadium and is the tallest inclined structure in the world, Raven told him – a fact that used to impress her as a child, she added. With its large windows, the cable car provided a panoramic view as they climbed. This flat northeastern part of Montreal, with its mostly commercial developments, seemed centuries apart from the historic center city. Even the apartment complexes looked like they'd been built too fast, mutated tentacles growing out from the city's healthy core.

The view from up on high was inspiring nonetheless. From the observatory Jake could see the famous cross at the top of Mont-Royal – the mountain that gave Montreal its name – as well as the winged monument to one of Canada's statesmen whom Raven couldn't identify. He could also see the St. Lawrence River running to the east. On this clear day, he could even discern the outline of the Laurentian Mountains far to the northwest – nature peaking back at the city-dwellers.

Jake looked back at Raven, wanting more info from her. She made him nervous, what with her kleptomania and simmering hostility, and he had to be circumspect. The top of the tower might be an okay location to get back to the subject of the three Americans, or it might not.

"Have you visited your parents in Florida?" he asked.

"The place of old people and Disney? *Oui* … every Christmas."

"There's more to it than that, starting with the ocean. But I understand your take. What about New York?"

"I used to visit a girlfriend there. At least New York is like another country. The three Americans invited me to stay with them if I want."

He wondered if that meant the Brooklyn warehouse.

"I could be your tour guide. But I can't offer you a place except the street."

"I don't mind the street."

He wasn't sure how to take that?

"How serious are you and Raphael?"

"Today I'm serious, but no one owns my tomorrow except me. He's too serious about controlling me."

She'd given him an opening to probe further. "Raven, you'll steal a man's wallet and his heart. I'm trying to understand you. I want to capture something of you … more than on a napkin … maybe on canvas someday … maybe in a sculpture. Help me begin to understand you."

"You spin words well for an *artiste visuel*."

"You inspire them." He was sure putting it on. "You are a *femme fatale*." That he could say in all sincerity.

She nodded and smiled. She seemed to enjoy the game. Jake did, too, in spite of guilt over his ulterior motives.

He continued. "Here's what I think … you have a boyfriend … a *Québécois*, right?"

"*Oui*."

"Like so many boyfriends, he's possessive of you."

"*Oui, la jalousie*. Always jealousy with men."

"With women as well."

"*D'accord … la condition humaine*. But some more than others. I fight that stupidity."

"So do I. You are a francophone who resents America and Americans and will steal from them, but you will let them in your life. You probably even dated an American college boy."

She smiled. "*Ah oui. Tu es très intelligent.* He turned out to be a *cul* ... he only dreamed of making money. He wanted to take me to Chicago, bragging about his apartment and his computer job for some financial corporation."

"You said you liked the American couple who stayed with you?"

"They were okay. They cleaned up after themselves. She acted *un peu arrogante*, the American way."

"And the one with the shaved head?"

"Marcus. An ass ... so self-important. He used Raphael for a place to stay but wouldn't tell me what he was doing for Boucher."

"Where did Raphael meet him?" Jake asked.

"In New York."

"What does Raphael do?"

"*Tu sais.* He plays chess."

"That's all?"

"He's a master," she said with some pride. "He travels for tournaments."

"Does he take you with him?"

"I don't want to go."

"Does he know Boucher?"

"*Oui*, from Paris. Boucher saw Raphael play ... and win!"

"Boucher also plays?"

"No, he recruits. Chess is a metaphor for *les politiques globales,* he told Raphael. He applies chess strategy to his own work in *la sociologie.* He also told Raphael he should help him with a new book. But the great sociologist had little time for Raphael this trip. He said he was too busy with all his talks around Quebec. Only Marcus met with him and not for very long after the lecture. Raphael was annoyed with him. *Moi aussi.*"

She'd opened up. Was that it for now?

Jake tried for more: "What's Boucher recruit for?"

"He has some project with Marcus and the others."

"A project?"

"Something in the U.S. on American Thanksgiving."

Thanksgiving? Jake tried to hide his eagerness for more. "Really? Where?"

"Raphael knows nothing more about it. He thinks it might be a music festival since Boucher gave them instruments."

"Maybe he does know more and won't tell you."

Had Jake probed too deeply?

She frowned slightly, quickly shrugging it off. "*Peut-être* ... who cares? *Les hommes sont les culs.*"

He collected his thoughts. One thing he'd learned – if the Thanksgiving thing were true – whatever Boucher and his lackeys were up to, it wasn't imminent.

"You opened up some. *Merci*. I now see you just as you, not anyone else. And I like what I see. I'll try to be less of a *cul* than most men."

She smiled, then put her arm through his.

"Okay, you try."

They rode the Green Line back to Saint-Laurent. Just before they exited the metro, he asked Raven, who hung on his arm affectionately much of the time now, if she wanted to come back to his hotel.

"*Nous verrons,*" she'd replied.

He'd asked her for a translation.

"We'll see. I'll get off at your stop. *J'ai faim. J'ai soif.* I'm hungry and thirsty."

Over Indian food and beer on Saint-Laurent, she told Jake about her childhood outside Quebec City and he told her about his in upstate New York. He still didn't know what the rest of the evening held.

Outside the restaurant she suddenly looked concerned.

"Anything wrong?" he asked.

"*Non.* I don't care."

"About what?"

She pointed down the street. "A chess player who knows Raphael. I think she fucked him."

"Did she see you?"

"I don't know. I don't care." She turned to Jake. "*Écoutes* ... I'll come back to your hotel. I can give you a massage. You can give me one, too, if you want. But even if she fucked him, you can't fuck me."

"*D'accord*," he replied. He'd picked up that much French.

~

It had been quite a while since he'd been under a roof this close to a woman. Aki had kept an odor-safe distance in her apartment. Raven was another story. She had no reservations about getting naked, telling him she wanted to show him her tattoos and piercings and wanted him naked, too. She also suggested he snort some of the cocaine she produced from inside one of her black leather boots. Jake wondered how much a part coke played in her thievery – steal to rationalize paying for it, or snort it to have bravado enough to steal? Probably both. He told her he was a recovering fiend and he'd better not. The new Jake. Sort of. His oncoming cold helped him maintain his new self-discipline. He had the additional incentive of wanting to keep his head clear and not admit too much. Cocaine could act like a truth serum.

All she said on his declining the offer was, "*C'est bien. Plus pour moi.*"

She stayed late. Not a problem, she reassured him. Raphael often played chess into the night and she often went to clubs, so her returning at that hour was no big deal. She said she knew where he was when he went out – playing chess or talking about it and about politics. Raphael couldn't say the same about her, although he trusted her to be faithful. And she was if he considered massages faithful. His mistress was the game of chess, she contended, which was fine with her since it made him less clingy than the previous boyfriend. She deserved some of the same intensity Raphael got from chess, she reasoned, and Jake was providing that. But it was a good thing he was leaving Montreal, she added with her disarming smile.

It all felt comfortable. He even teased her that he wanted her to steal his wallet so she wouldn't steal someone else's.

Still, the last moments with Raven turned dramatic. She'd been texting on and off during their time together. With cellphones was anyone ever one-hundred percent in a room anymore? After reading a message, Raven stood up abruptly – her naked body now tense – and started dressing.

"Anything wrong?" Jake asked.

"*Ce n'est rien*. It's nothing, just *la merde*."

Pulling her sweater over her head, she grabbed up her bag and, with what came off as a pained smile, walked out the door.

Aftereffffects

DESPITE HIS RUNNY NOSE, smells from the evening before lingered in the hotel room and in his brain: cigarette smoke, garlic, perfume, and Raven's natural odors. Jake took a last look at the room – still a novelty for him – and headed for the lobby to check out.

As he walked along Saint-Dominique toward the Honda, a man came up from behind and fell into stride next to him. Glancing over, Jake needed a moment to recognize him without a hat. But no question – it was Raphael, stringy hair and all. And he didn't look happy, his face now red and pinched.

Jake reached the car and turned to face him directly. He met his eyes, then read the button on his lapel. It had white lettering that said *Cha/Che* over a black chess piece – a knight.

"Top of the day," Jake said with a sarcastic edge.

"You fuck my woman?" Raphael asked in a thick French accent.

"No," Jake was happy to announce.

Raphael persisted: "What do you want with her?"

"Company. And a face to paint. What's wrong with that? You should chill out. She's faithful to you."

"That painting shit is bullshit. You just want to fuck her. You Americans are pigs."

Jake felt anger push to the front of his brain, mixed with the pressure from his sinuses. Pig Americans? He wanted to ask if that included Marcus, Ned, and Leandra but refrained of course.

"I'm sure men from around the world would find her interesting. But I repeat, we didn't fuck. So maybe you should trust her and step away from my car."

"Did she talk about me?"

Jake sighed, trying to let the anger vent out. He would love to deck this guy – a typical reaction to such matters during his upstate New York years – but where might that lead? He had no more interest in French jails than American ones.

"She said you're a famous chess player and she loves you. Good enough?"

Raphael tapped the black-and-white button. "I also know how to make *chaos*." He used the French pronunciation for that word. "You leave her alone."

Jake felt achy and that only made his fuse shorter. He stepped around him, purposely bumping him, then quoting a line from a song: "If you cling too tightly, you're going to lose control."

He didn't know if the concept registered in Raphael's brain, but the words distracted him long enough for Jake to unlock the car door and slip into the driver's seat.

Before closing the door, he added, "This pig American who didn't fuck your girlfriend is leaving Montreal, so you can relax."

Raphael grabbed the door and held it open. "I wasn't finished."

Jake took his phone out of his jacket pocket as if he were about to make a call. Instead, he activated the camera, aimed it at Raphael, and quickly took a photo.

"And now I have a reminder why I don't want to come back. Happy?"

He grabbed the door handle and pulled hard. Raphael released it and the door slammed shut. Jake drove away without looking back. Not that he was running from the self-proclaimed maker of chaos. He was running from his own urge to escalate.

~

Jake drove southward on Route 15. His nose trickled; he sneezed some. Raven would probably pay the price for spending time with him. He'd warned her about a possible cold, but she'd shown her typical insouciance, waving off his concern. She was the kind of woman who led to extreme consequences. She would probably pay a price on the relationship level, too. Jealousy – humanity's condition, she'd described it. Raphael had certainly revealed his.

How did the chess player fit in with the Americans? Had Boucher recruited him just to provide them with lodging. What were they up to? Why a drum, a photographer's bag, and a suitcase?

Of everything he knew, the watch repair bit made him wonder if something big was going down. Some kind of timer? Did the drum hide explosives? Some incident on Thanksgiving? Raven had said Raphael thought it was a music festival. Including drugs provided by a new French connection? Jake would search online for music festivals taking place around Thanksgiving. At least pondering the mystery helped dissipate the suppressed anger at Raphael. And at least he had some time to try to solve it with Thanksgiving weeks away. It all seemed so unreal, he thought, pulling in line to cross the border back into the United States.

As he approached the customs booth, he stupidly felt guilty for knowledge of some possible plot. Would he be hassled by the custom agents because he reeked of guilt by association? No, but maybe because he was fighting a cold. In this post-pandemic day and age, a cough or a sneeze might force him to become an expatriate.

Getting back into the States took a lot longer than entering Canada. The line of cars advanced agonizingly slowly, ramping up the suspense. But the glove-handed agent – after looking at Jake's documents and asking him where he was from, what he'd been doing in Canada, and if he had anything to declare – seemed to barely register his answers, crabbily waving him through.

Accepted by his native country once again. He felt like the good little American.

Protector of the peace?

Time would tell.

PART IV: THE OTHER NEW YORK

Lew Archer, P.I.: *"When there's trouble in a family, it tends to show
up in the weakest member. And all the other members of the family
know that. They make allowances for the one in trouble … because they
know they're implicated themselves."*
– Ross Macdonald, *Sleeping Beauty*

Sisterville

JAKE SAW THE LAST supermarket before open road and pulled
into the parking lot. From Route 87 he'd picked up 20 west and
now was well beyond the heavily populated suburbs of Albany.
On getting out of the car, he took a deep breath: country air, so
different from city air, not that pungent odor of chemicals that
sticks to one's insides.

After time in the big cities, shopping in this other New York
prompted culture shock. Less diversity, less fashion attitude.
Jake, reverting to a past self, focused on the task at hand, grocery
shopping. He purchased some items he knew his sister liked,
choosing the pricier brands – organic coffee, Vermont cheddar
cheese, imported crackers, dark chocolate, and kombucha. Also, a
power bar for the ride. And he remembered to get cold medicine.
Not great timing to arrive sick. Caitlyn might see it as further
proof of his not taking proper care of himself.

Back behind the wheel, Jake continued westward, pretty much
a straight shot to his hometown. This road south of the Mohawk
River had been the original route west in wagon days, all the way
from Boston, through Albany, and eventually to Buffalo (formerly
Fort Erie), and beyond to the prairies and plains. He tried to keep
a positive attitude, taking inspiration from pioneers venturing
forth to a new life. But he felt used up, like stretches of this road.
The construction in the 1950s of the Thruway to the north – the
east-west Route 90 section – had meant a decline in the traffic
along this corridor. The remaining homes struck him as modest
and some of the businesses, dingy. Yet behind them he saw the

foothills of the Catskills rising up, with the rich colors of autumn now showing through.

The anxiety about seeing his sister derived in large part from his last visit two summers ago. He'd been strung out and listless. He'd also had a few arguments with her boyfriend Rory. Jake hadn't talked to Caitlyn since her March birthday. He'd been slurring drunk and she'd cried. He'd apologized in a text the next day, saying he would call when he got his new life together. But he'd only texted a few times over the next months and only in response to her increasingly aggravated messages. Stupid asshole failure of a big brother, he'd told himself time and again, which had served as an excuse to self-medicate. His falling out of touch had undoubtedly led her to think the worst. But he was returning to her abstinent, something he'd hadn't been since about age 13 – no longer so glaringly their mother's son.

He sure wasn't looking forward to seeing Rory. At least his sister's significant other made a point of keeping a relatively low profile when her brother was around.

Jake knew he was getting close to his childhood home what with familial thoughts biting incessantly at his mental heels. A red-tailed hawk flew above him. It rode the air currents, gliding gracefully and heartening his own forward motion.

~

"Hello, Sis." Caitlyn stood frozen in her doorway as if in shock. Her face then disintegrated into tears and she came at him, flailing, causing him to drop one of the grocery bags. Nothing broke. Good thing he hadn't bought eggs.

"You fucker! You fucker!" she cried out. "Why? Why? I thought you were dead!"

She fell into his arms.

"I'm sorry, I'm sorry," he offered. "I screwed up bigtime."

She stepped back, wiping her eyes. "You sure did."

Jake looked her over. She'd lost weight, not quite as much as he had, but she had less to lose. Lines around her eyes struck him as deeper. Her wavy dirty blond hair, he saw, still had that lustrous sheen of youth – no doubt at least partly because she'd never messed with perms and dyes.

"You look great," he told her.

She waved that off. "Yeah, right. Always with the bullshit."

Cracker was demanding attention, sniffing at Jake's legs. He was a mutt, mostly cocker spaniel, now with a faded yellowish coat. But he seemed to be doing just fine for his advanced dog years. Jake bent over to rub his ears, then retrieved the groceries.

"I couldn't believe someone was knocking without Cracker barking," Caitlyn said. "He even barks at Rory. Where the hell have you been? You change your phone number to avoid me?"

"I got pretty far down. Lost my phone and didn't bother getting another. I just reactivated my number. Let's settle in and catch up. I brought treats this time. Cracker must think they're for him."

"You better be staying awhile," she said.

"I am." Jake stepped all the way into the small frame house, Cracker still at his feet, and Caitlyn shut the door behind him.

"Is Rory working?" he asked.

"He's gone."

"Gone where?"

"Just gone."

"For good, you mean?"

"Yeah, I threw him out." She was on the verge of crying again. "I've been pretty far down myself. I even canceled all my social media accounts to avoid the world. Became a Luddite like you, ha, ha." She was fighting to keep it together. "Believe me, your disappearance had a lot more to do with feeling down than his being gone."

He hugged her with his one free arm. She went with it, then stepped back, looking him up and down.

"You look like shit, Jake … washed out. Growing a beard doesn't hide that, you know."

Jake was glad to hear her honesty again. "I started feeling under the weather a couple of days ago," he said. "Not a big deal."

"Under the weather? Hasn't that expression gone out of style yet? Don't you mean feeling under one virus or another? You better be telling it like it is and it's nothing worse than that."

"It's all about phlegm, like a good old-fashioned cold. Runny nose. A little achy but no fever yet, I don't think. A tender throat, some sneezing, but certainly no dry coughing. I can even smell, even though I'm clogged up, and I can taste. Anyway, I was in the city all the shutdown months and was pretty sure I'd caught it and recovered, remember?"

"Maybe I did, too, but I've since gotten the vaccine to be sure. I bet you haven't."

"I did!"

"Whattya know. You're full of surprises."

They passed from the tiny vestibule into the living room, where Cracker took his usual spot on his pillow next to the couch, already having accepted Jake's return as a done deal. They continued into the kitchen. So many memories went with this house and the pieces of furniture his sister hadn't replaced. The walls were more worn than the last time he'd been here. He remembered Rory had promised to repaint the house inside and out. That obviously hadn't happened.

While putting the groceries away and happily announcing each item as a good choice, Caitlyn repeatedly looked over at Jake, as if to be certain he wouldn't vanish before her eyes.

"What're you living on? Your sculptures?"

"I just sold the first in a long time, enabling me to get the hell out of New York." He looked down then back up. "When I said I got pretty far down, I meant all the way to the street. I've been living homeless."

She slammed a kitchen cabinet shut. "What!?"

"I got evicted, then ran out of friends to leech off. I was a mess."

"You could've …"

He didn't let her finish. "I know, I know. Sure, you would've taken me in, but I just couldn't face doing that to you. I also realized that the challenge and shame of living on the street helped me stay clean. I've managed to keep off the hard stuff, except for two relapses in three months. No limit on cigarettes and once in a while beer or herb."

After a moment of shaking her head at him, she finally said, "Fuck you for putting me through your vanishing act whatever the reason."

"Keep it up with the 'fucks.' I deserve 'em."

"I'll heat up some soup. You need it. Afterwards, give me the whole damn story."

~

They sat next to each other on the living room's beat-up couch. He told her about his increasingly self-destructive drug use, his alienating people in the art world, his eviction, and his crashing on people's couches. He told her about Aki's purchase of his sculpture … after dumping water on him in a doorway. He told her about Rainy and how she was using one of his sculptures to hang pots and pans. He also told her about going to Montreal but fibbed about why. She would have worried, especially since the whole weird thing he was investigating might be drug related. He fabricated going to an exhibit at a Montreal gallery – a show including a friend he'd met in New York, who might be able to help him get a show. She expressed how exciting that would be and that he'd better let her know in time for the opening if he got a show there. She could be such a forgiving sweetheart, making him feel extra bad about the lie.

It was her turn now. She told Jake about her repeated breakups with Rory because of his moods and drinking, something she knew about all too well. She'd taken him back lots of times and felt the abused woman in a recurring cycle even though he'd never laid a finger on her. Her getting pregnant and feeling trapped, then losing the baby, had made her realize she couldn't face building a life with him.

"You were pregnant?!" he exclaimed.

"Damn straight, a-hole."

"I'm so sorry, Caitlyn."

She waved it off, but her deep hurt was obvious. She went on to say she'd put all of Rory's stuff on the street. Since she lived in a village where people paid close attention to a neighbor's drama, her doing that was the finality they both needed. Her pregnancy, miscarriage, and going it alone during the period Jake was off the radar had made everything that much harder for her. Jake repeated how he knew if he called her and told her his situation, she would have felt obliged to take him on, something she didn't need when he was so strung out.

"At least goddamn let me know you're alive. I was packed more than once to go search for you."

"Did you toss my stuff out as well for being such an asshole?"

"Real funny. It's all still in the garage … just where you left it forever ago."

He broached another troubling subject: "And Mom? Any word? She still in Oklahoma?"

Caitlyn let out an enormous sigh, rubbed her slender fingers through her hair, then spoke deliberately. "I guess so. After I called to tell her about the miscarriage and kicking Rory out, she told me she was leaving her latest guy but staying there. She said she again had no permanent address or number, meaning she stopped paying her rent or phone bill or lost her phone. Hmmm, all this sounds familiar. It's been just great, not being able to call either of you."

"Hell," Jake said with a sigh of remorse. "Was she drunk when she called, like I was the last time you and I talked?"

"Surprisingly, no. Or so it seemed." She clenched her teeth, her gaze inward, then relaxed somewhat. "I hope I can stop worrying about you. I hope you do well here on out, Jake. I hope you've beaten your bad habits once and for all. It's great to see you sober like this. But whatever happens in your life, you have one thing you can't let slide … and that's staying in touch with me."

Jake hated himself all over again. "Yes, yes, I promise. No crossies." He held up his open fingers.

She sighed.

"I'm serious," he insisted. "Never again like that."

"I want to believe."

"Believe!"

She gave a nod that seemed to indicate she did.

"Is Hughie still in Alaska?" Jake asked.

She was a half-sister. She knew her father, Hugh Edmonds, and had his last name unlike Jake who had grown up with his mother's maiden name. Hughie had left the family when Caitlyn was six. She'd reconnected with him as teenager through a lot of effort on her part. He'd eventually sent her a chunk of money – twenty-eight thousand – which she'd used to pay off their mother's mortgage and buy the house outright from her, with a payoff of some thou to Jake toward what might have someday been his share. That was the money he'd used to move to New York City. For her it had been like a payoff from a deadbeat dad for not having to deal with a daughter he seemed to care little about knowing.

Caitlyn was blinking her eyes hard – blue eyes like her father's, unlike Jake's – a nervous tic she'd had since childhood.

"Yeah, he's in Anchorage. Works in a cannery. Says he earns a lot less money than when he went out on boats, as if I'd ask for more. For a while, I thought I'd visit him there. I even bought a van that Rory was going to fix up as a camper. Thing is … I don't know if I want to see him."

"Maybe he's finally a responsible adult," Jake offered.

She shook her head. "Oh, I don't know. I might visit him someday. The van's for sale regardless. I don't care about it now. If you buy it, maybe I could hit you up for a ride out there. Interested?"

"Wow, that's a thought. Uh … give me five minutes to decide, okay? What're you doing for money?"

"I've been temping. Mostly office work … some housekeeping when necessary. It's tough getting by like that. But I'm going to keep it that way. I need an open schedule. I've decided to go back to school."

"What? Really?"

"I want to teach."

"Teach what? Music?"

"Not just music. I want to teach little kids, so some music."

"Great, great! Back to Oneonta?"

"No, Herkimer. For now. I need to get the rest of my credits for my sophomore year."

"New love interest yet?"

"They're already sniffing around. But I don't want to deal with men for a while. It's about me!" She pointed her thumbs at herself.

"Right on, sis. I'm taking my love life slow, too. I got to hang with some great women while in the city. I'm still not over any of them even though they're sure over me."

"Hell, you're still not over Francesca."

Francesca had been the last of his high-school girlfriends.

"Hey, some happy memories. How many kids does she have now?"

"Three and counting."

"Whoa."

"She still looks good."

"Don't tell me that," he joked.

"The new Jake, you say. Just beer and pot. You sure you can handle them without wanting something else?"

"Yes, yes. I'm sticking to just them. You still smoke?"

"A little. I have some. It was Rory's. Want to for old time's sake? I don't want it around much longer being a wannabe teacher."

They used to smoke together as teens. Those were the times they would sneak away and do a lot of the talking about their mother. Now, they could openly smoke and talk in the living room.

"Let's do it," Jake said. "I'll just take a hit or two. Pass it to me when you're done with it so you don't catch my cold."

"Showing restraint. That's a good sign and, speaking of that, you should give up cigarettes. Didn't you tell me last Christmas that was the plan?"

"Yeah, one of those best laid plans."

She stood up and retrieved a Mason jar holding bud remnants and rolling papers from the bottom of the stereo cabinet.

"You roll," he told her. "You were always better at it."

"That's because you were always too impatient for the next high."

"Good one."

After smoking up, their conversation danced about from small-town gossip to big-city oddities. She filled him in on some of his old pals – how they often asked about him and acted like his going to New York City was like he'd relocated to some other universe. He told her about the friends he'd made on the street – Manic Mary, Ricky Rad, Tenor, and Mackerel.

"There are many paths to homelessness and many outcomes," he finished.

"And the big sleep is an all-too-common outcome, I bet."

Their mother had adopted that term for death from a movie of that name she'd obsessed over. It had a lineup for the ages, she'd insisted: based on a Raymond Chandler story, directed by Howard Hawks, and starring Humphrey Bogart as P.I. Philip Marlowe and Lauren Bacall as his femme fatale love interest.

"I'm afraid it is."

"You're freaking me out!"

"Jake Soho is one of the lucky ones. I have you."

"Yes, you do! What's with the Jake Soho? After the neighborhood?"

"Right. That's what my street friends called me, starting with Ricky. It's like the graffiti thing … you know, tags … with a first name and location."

"To hell with that. I prefer Jake Shaleville or Jake Elm Street as your tag."

"I'm also fine with Jake, Caitlyn's brother."

Cracker half-slept, brown eyes on them. Seeing his sister on her own like this, without the simmering tension between her and Rory, he got a clear take on how great she'd turned out. Knowing that at least some of her wonderful traits had to come from their mother – their alcoholic, man-dependent, man-eating, underachieving, smart-as-a-whip mother, who taught them classic movies, classic mysteries, and classic rock – helped him forgive her dysfunction and neglect.

"You should go to bed. You look like shit," Caitlyn said.

"You told me that already."

"Well?"

"Show me the way."

"You know the way," she said, smiling, but got up to show him to his old bedroom nonetheless.

~

Jake woke up. He'd pushed all his blankets aside but still felt hot all over. Fever?

He reached for his phone on the nightstand and checked the time. 3:31 a.m. He held the cell in his hand a while, thinking back over the day that had taken him from Montreal to Shaleville, from Raphael to Caitlyn.

He started to put his phone back down but angled it back up to do a search for "Cha/Che." A listing for Chaos/Chess appeared and he clicked on it. The site came up with a black background and white block lettering.

"Cha/Che …
Where chaos and chess meet.
Where chess is logic.

107

Where chess is art.
Where chess is meditation.
Where chaos is a statement.
Where chaos is a tactic.
Move with chaos.
Win with chaos.
In the game of chess, occupy chaos ...
Cha/Che."

That was it. No further explanation. No names or contact info. A splinter activist group? When Jake did a search on Raphael and chess, a lot of names came up – with Raphael appearing as both a first name and last. None of them seemed to fit a Raphael chess player in Montreal.

Cha/Che? What a stupid name for a movement, like a bastardized dance, Jake thought in his cold-pressurized head. And what a stupid manifesto, one that pathetically appropriates the concept of the classic game.

Brotherdom

LEANDRA AND RAVEN look down at him, laughing. Smiles melt into scowls. What's bothering them? Or, rather, what's bothering her because now the two have become one. Caitlyn's hovering now and, after crying out in fear, she runs away from him. He follows her along a New York City street. She leads him to Port Authority and a bus ... no, a van ... and their mother is driving them home after Caitlyn's softball game. Where's Cracker? They'd left Cracker behind and have to go back for him. No, Cracker is already in the van ... sitting in whose lap? Caitlyn's. No, Natalie Beaubien's. He has an urge to sit next to her. But he's a little boy and his mother will interfere. He can tell his mother that Natalie is teaching him French. His mother won't care. The van becomes Rainy's apartment. She's telling him to grow up and take responsibility ... that if he doesn't, he'll go through one relationship after another and end up on the street. She's right, he knows at the time, also knowing that in hindsight. She can't stay. He can't stay. She has to get to class. He has to get to class. There's a test that day. He might make it in time if he doesn't have to hide the sheets of his bed. They're wet. Wet with what? He's not a bedwetter. He doesn't want Caitlyn to know he drinks so much he can't hold his bladder. She'll understand his sweat. That's what it is … sweat. In newfound clarity, he knows he's in a dream and he's breaking a fever. He struggles to open his eyes …

Had that dream been seconds or minutes or even hours? Dreamtime was impossible to determine; moments seemed to move infinitely sideways, not forward.

Jake rolled over and out from under sweat-soaked sheets. He looked at his phone. 7:24 a.m. He felt better on this third day in his hometown. He'd succumbed to a full-fledged flu – at least it was only that – but it seemed the fever had finally broken and he could function. His sister had turned down temp jobs to care for him and had set him up in his old bedroom with everything he might need – aspirin, tissues, fluids, soup, reading materials.

Jake looked at the dirty off-white ceiling and the now-motionless battered white ceiling fan. When this had been his bedroom, the ceiling had been sky-blue and the walls, yellow. He'd hated both colors. Off-white everywhere was much better, even though the room needed painting again. Jake had the thought that the true nature of a haunted house is one haunted with memories. All the familiar stuff around him had aged as he had, but the recollections were timeless.

It still felt weird, even after the hotel in Montreal, to sleep indoors at all. A room, even this modest, seemed swank to him, despite the worn paint, the somewhat warped dresser, the bedstand with cup rings on the finish, and one shabby chair in need of upholstering.

Jake had caused a lot of trouble when young, typically in motion as a toddler, hard on teachers from pre-K through high school, rebellious to his mother – for one, in addition to his drinking starting as preteen, also a pill thief by age fifteen, raiding her prescriptions – and angry at much of the world. His moods had swung rapidly from dark to elated. It was sure hard not to hear echoes of his feral self when in this room.

The one window faced east and sunlight was streaming through the gauzy curtain, announcing this day as promising. Jake pulled himself up and sat on the edge of the bed. He felt mild dizziness and an urge to cough. He let the cough out, then stood up. He waited on his feet until another cough came. He would cut back on the cigarettes, he resolved yet again, despite knowing how easy it was to make resolutions from a vantage point of recovery. Ignoring excuses to light up would be the real test. Recalling Caitlyn's voice telling him to quit would help.

Jake slowly got dressed and moved through the door toward the bathroom at the end of the hall. His sister had taken over the bedroom that had been their mother's, turning her original, much smaller bedroom into an office. He heard quiet singing through the cracked door.

"You awake, sis?"

"Just reading. Come on in."

He entered. She was still in bed, sitting upright with a book in hand and a pile of papers next to her.

"I heard singing," he said. "What was that?"

"Something I made up."

"Great to hear your voice again besides in my head. It's been a while. Starting a new band?"

She'd started one her junior year in high school.

"I'll save my singing for first graders." She closed the book, then looked him over. "You sure look and sound better."

"Broke my fever. Time for a cleansing shower. You don't need to babysit me today."

"You sure?"

"Yes! You healed me."

"I was worried. When you got feverish, I thought about calling the health clinic, but your temperature never got scary high. Amazing, considering how you've been living."

"We must come from good stock. Mom rarely got sick if you don't count all the mornings-after. She even ignored the shutdown, you told me?"

"Or so she bragged. Did some good even. Remember? She worked in a soup kitchen in Houston some of those months."

"She does have a heart."

"Somewhere in there." Caitlyn picked up her phone. "I'll see if I'm needed elsewhere."

~

After showering and dressing, Jake walked outside and, standing on the small porch, took a deep breath of crisp air. Here he was in Shaleville again – so named because of the ledge of shale beneath it, making any kind of digging a foot or two below the surface more about a pickaxe than a shovel.

Early morning, a peaceful time of day to reacquaint himself with Elm Street. Not one elm tree represented the name anymore, since Dutch Elm Disease had long ago taken that genus out. Maples now flanked the street, their leaves autumn red and yellow from the cold nights. Many leaves had already fallen to the ground, with many more to follow.

The fact that Caitlyn had never moved out of their mother's house, or even traveled more, used to bother Jake. Maybe she would decide to seek out a teaching job in some other school district and sell this house. Or maybe her way was better. Forget about physically fleeing, instead embracing the geography of the past to achieve emotional liberation. Could it work for him?

A truck – a silver Ford pickup – turned the corner from Main Street toward Jake. He stepped back into the shadows of the doorway, not feeling small-town sociable just yet. The vehicle, hauling several full black trash bags in back, turned into the driveway of the small white ranch house standing kitty-corner across Elm. From where Jake stood, he could see the driver get out and hurriedly unload the bags, carrying them in a side door – three of them. He was beefy with longish hair, wearing jeans and a camouflage sweatshirt. He looked like one of the town's good old boys, but Jake didn't recognize him.

Jake used to get reports from Caitlyn about who in Shaleville had moved away or died, or if a house had changed hands. She hadn't mentioned anything about the widow who had long lived in this ranch house or about a new tenant. A relative perhaps? In any case, Jake understood no former close friends still lived on this block. It made it easier slipping in and out of town without having to catch up.

He walked around his childhood home, looking at the dark green peeling paint on the clapboard. The saltbox house, built in the 19th century, had endured. But it was crying out for attention.

His sister's small Nissan was parked in front of the garage where their mother's junker station wagon had normally sat. The garage door opener had never worked properly; their mother hated backing inside the garage anyway. Jake had sure put in a lot of time shoveling snow or raking leaves from this macadam driveway. He walked to the garage's side door, entered, and flicked on the naked bulb dangling from the ceiling.

Memories kept washing through him. This had been a teen hangout where he and Caitlyn would get stoned together. It now housed the van she'd mentioned – a GMC, more than a decade old, Jake guessed. The vehicle, facing outward, was white as so many cargo vans seemed to be. It had two windows in the back and two flanking the front seats, but no others on its sides, allowing contractors to hide their tools or materials. Minimal rust on the body, he was glad to see. He opened the door and looked inside. Funky, yes, but Rory, being a body shop repairman as well as a freelance car detailer, could have made a nice camper out of it. The front passenger's seat had come off its track and was at an awkward angle. The back curtains looked new, however. Caitlyn probably had made those. Cross-country dreams, now dashed. Unless with her brother, she'd said.

Jake moved to the back of the garage past the shelves filled with odds and ends – hardware, old cans of paint, rags, and some old housewares. He located his boxes in the corner, taped and labeled "Misc Papers," "Books," "Music," and "Clothing." He'd forgotten he'd organized them before moving away. The books were mostly those his mother had given him. He could have used some of them on his many park benches. What remained of his tools were in three plastic milk crates and a big canvas duffel bag. Rory had no doubt picked through them. Jake's stored past life was unsettling. He would have to face up to it and finally sort through it all.

On exiting the garage, Jake saw the man across the street walking toward his pickup. He now was wearing an international orange vest over the sweatshirt and carried a shotgun. This early? Maybe turkey hunting. Small-game hunting season came a lot earlier than big-game seasons. The invasion of the redcoats for deer season, as Jake used to think of it, when hunters in bright colors came from far and wide to hunt these hills, took place around Thanksgiving. Jake himself had never gotten into hunting. Maybe if he'd had a father who had gone out annually, he would have found it a natural thing to do. Their mother used to rant about cruel hunters and "Bambiburgers" – not a concept conducive to blasting deer and eating their meat. The Disney movie *Bambi*, although made in 1942, more than three decades before she was born, had been one of her favorite childhood films and she'd mentioned it at least once every deer season.

The neighbor got into his truck and drove off too fast for the quiet side street. Jake reentered the house and headed for the kitchen. Caitlyn, dressed for work, was making coffee.

"You already look like a teacher!" he said.

"Just an office clerk today. I'll be doing inventory before restocking. They'll need me another couple of weeks probably. You sure you're okay here alone?"

"For sure. But I need some activity. Any suggestions for light work?"

"You still better take it easy."

"I promise."

"Nothing beyond dripping faucets today, okay? Both bathrooms, okay?"

"I can handle that. What else you got? I mean for me to do over the next days. Come on. Give it up."

"There's a leak under the kitchen sink. I keep emptying a bucket. And one drawer in my dresser doesn't slide anymore."

"And?"

"A cracked window upstairs." She smiled mischievously. "I missed Rory's thick skull. It was only a cup I threw and I wasn't really aiming at him. You'd think the window could've withstood that. His skull would have."

"I'm glad you're going solo for now, Caitlyn. You gotta find a guy worthy enough for the likes of you. I can also caulk some of the cracks and paint."

"I can pay you."

"No way."

"I tell you what. Do work for me and the van is yours. I want it out of here. I planned to use the money I got from selling it to pay for some work on the house anyway. It only has about a hundred-and-thirty thousand miles on it. Rory said what really matters is in decent shape. I bought it for twenty-five hundred. We figured it wouldn't cost too much if Rory did the repair work."

"You should be in sales. This is looking possible … make it easier for me to come and go."

"Good. I'll see more of you."

"You'll see more of me one way or the other," he reassured her. "We can go camping together. Settle for the Adirondacks if not Alaska?"

"I want that in writing. In blood."

"Get me a knife, sis. You own the van outright … not Rory, too?"

"I bought it all by myself. It was for my trip. I was waiting on him to fix it up before getting plates."

"What the hell. It's a deal. Consider the van off your hands. Come springtime, I repaint the whole damn house inside and out for the van. And I get parking rights forever."

"Really? Really?"

"Yes, really."

She kissed Jake on the cheek. "My big brother finally showed up."

"Keys in it? Does it start?"

"It should. Rory drove it here when we bought it. The keys are on a hook near the back door. It probably needs a jump."

"You have cables?"

"In my trunk. I'll leave them."

She hurried off to get ready, cup of coffee in hand. Jake poured himself a cup and sat down at the kitchen table, sipping and thinking.

~

Jake eased into the rest of the day. It was good he had something to do. But it was also good he could proceed slowly. He drank a lot of fluids and nibbled at food. He wandered about the house, remembering details of his childhood as he checked on the projects – the leaks, the broken window, the problem drawer, and cracks in the walls.

Locating the keys to the van, he went out the back door and across the driveway. Caitlyn had left the jumper cables in front of the garage before departing in her Nissan. Jake entered through the side door and stepped into the van. He inserted the key and tried it. Nothing.

He slid open the front garage door, then drove the rental car from the street part way into the garage opposite the GMC. He opened both hoods, attached the cable ends, and, with the Honda's engine running, tried to start the van. It took several tries. The engine finally turned over and caught enough of a spark to keep the pistons going, then coughed out months of inactivity. He backed the rental out of the way, then eased the van out of the garage. The engine, although loud, ran smoothly enough. The brakes also seemed okay.

Leaving the engine running to charge the battery, he looked the vehicle over. Expenses would of course include registration, insurance, and inspection. He would change the oil and do the tune-up himself. The tires were decent. Hopefully he wouldn't have to pay for a new exhaust system and brakes.

The vehicle was roomy. After what Jake was used to, he could live very comfortably out of it. He checked the radio. It worked – at least AM did. The CD player wouldn't play or eject the previously loaded CD. One less thing to worry about for now – sorting through his old CDs.

He checked through the supplies in the garage and his own tools. What was missing was essential for working on vehicles – his set of socket wrenches. Not surprisingly so, given that Rory worked on cars. He wouldn't mention that to Caitlyn – just buy another set. His plumbing tools were there along with a jar of faucet washers and an assortment of screws and nails. The hardware of his past. There was also a collection of dusty old and new glass panes leaning against the garage's back wall. One would probably fit the broken window in the house. If not, he would cut one of the big ones down to size.

Jake set about changing washers in the leaky faucets. On finishing, he headed back outside to shut off the van's engine. He heard a vehicle approaching and turned to see the silver pickup pulling in across the street. As before, the neighbor carried black plastic garbage bags in the back, this time four of them. Once again, he hurriedly carried them into the house's side door.

Had he been hunting out of season? Hiding deer parts in the garbage bags? Given their size and number, it had to be a big deer.

Granted, a lot of weirdness in the big city. Yet a lot of weirdness in this other New York, too.

Back inside, Jake looked over the leak under the kitchen sink and made a mental list what he would probably need for that job. He would also buy glazing and caulk.

He headed for the hardware store. It was in walking distance but he drove the rental anyway to save energy. The couple who owned the store weren't there. Their daughter was alone behind the counter and didn't seem to recognize Jake, even though he'd been a good customer over the years. He was relieved not to have to answer questions about his life away from Shaleville just yet.

On returning home, he let Cracker out, leading him behind the garage. He was surprised to hear his cellphone chiming. It was Caitlyn, asking him how he was doing. He assured her he was fine and, besides devoting time to Cracker, was managing to get things done on the house.

Jake managed to solve the leak under the sink with a new trap and putty. He then slowly ate a bowl of cereal at the kitchen counter.

Outside again, he devised woodblocks from some pressure-treated lumber pieces stacked behind the garage and drove the van onto them to give himself access underneath. He examined the exhaust system. There were some small holes from all the rust. Patching them might work, but he didn't have the welding equipment to do that himself. He called the one mechanic in walking distance, who told him he could see about a cheap welding fix of the exhaust system early the next week and do the inspection.

Before returning inside for more repairs, Jake moved to the edge of the property and looked down Elm Street. One car passed. Meanwhile, the neighbor's pickup was still in his driveway.

~

Caitlyn returned soon after 6:00 p.m. and entered the kitchen. Jake joined her. She pointed at the pizza box she'd put on the counter.

"I hope pizza's okay. I got lazy. It's loaded with vegetables. Make a salad? I didn't buy any beer, just seltzer and ginger ale."

"Good decision. Eat in here?"

"Yes, like the old days."

"Check under the kitchen sink," he told her.

She did. "You fixed it! Awesome!"

"A happy homeowner. Good for a contractor's psyche."

"Don't get ahead of yourself," she said smiling. "Two bathroom sinks to inspect."

She headed off.

"Fuck yeah!" he heard, as he started the salad. Then, a few moments later from upstairs: "You did both!" And then: "You fixed the dresser drawer!"

Over dinner, Jake asked her, "Who's living across the street in the ranch house?"

"A guy named Al Mohr. Bought the place after the Wilcox widow died. "Why?"

"He's been coming and going lots today. Poaching maybe."

"He sure can act hateful. He and Rory had some nasty words because Cracker left a present on his lawn. He had a wife when he first got here. No sign of her anymore. Hey, so I don't become like him, I need to stop hiding out. You can help me. Want to go bowling tomorrow? Join the Friday evening crowd at the B.A.?"

Bowling was something they used to do as kids. He dreaded running into old acquaintances at the lanes, a popular hangout. But his psychology was irrelevant here. He had to come through for Caitlyn.

"Sign me up," he told her.

Localized

THE FOLLOWING EVENING, after another day of repairs, Jake had already showered and changed and sat on the couch watching TV when Caitlyn returned home. She had cable and channel-surfing made him feel like he was a voyeur in multiple worlds. Reading newspapers on park benches had kept him somewhat informed and often disheartened. Seeing moving images made some things more real – the cruelty, mayhem, and suffering – and some things less real, as in dumbed down.

Caitlyn went off to get ready. She returned after one more depressing news half-hour, dolled up in a casual way. Her effort reminded Jake how important this evening was.

"You look great," he told her.

"I want to feel sexy even though no one's gonna score this bod for a long time."

Like they used to do in past years on bowling nights, they smoked up before heading out. His sister acted keyed up and talkative, telling Jake about being hit on by a married guy that day at work.

She went to the downstairs bathroom to wash up after smoking. He used the kitchen sink and splashed water on his face and rinsed his mouth. Not that the smell of weed would matter to most. Those who didn't partake pretty much ignored the issue – here as in the city – probably even more so nowadays what with the rapidly changing laws.

They set out into the descending darkness. As they stepped onto Elm Street, Jake noticed that the only lights on in the house opposite were in the cellar – with shades drawn, it seemed. Al Mohr butchering deer carcasses?

They reached the corner of Main Street, then headed three blocks east to Maggie's Bowling Alley and Bar. It used to be Joe and Maggie's. To locals it was just the B.A.

A good number of cars were parked in front of the rectangular building and in the side parking lot as well.

Caitlyn spoke: "Damn, lots of cars. I shouldn't have smoked. I'm freaking out."

"You'll calm down when you drink a beer."

Jake was playing the big brother to help her cope with her jitters, which helped him cope with his.

She replied with, "So you say."

They entered. Music was playing on the jukebox: Eric Clapton's "Cocaine." Still current in these parts after how many decades? A reminder of what Jake should continue to avoid as he'd done with Raven.

Heads turned.

Then: "Caitlyn!"

A not-so-natural blond jumped up from a table near the door. Jake had to think hard before recognizing her. Angela Meola, one of his sister's high-school classmates. She'd filled out but in the wrong places. She left her friends at the table and hurried over to Caitlyn, hugging her.

"You gotta tell me all about the breakup," she said, then looked at Jake. "Caitlyn's big brother! Where the hell have you been?"

"There and back" was all he could manage.

She barely seemed to register his words as she led Caitlyn to an empty table, declaring, "Girl talk!"

"Draft ... Dream?" he called after his sister.

She nodded and gave him an apologetic shrug to be abandoning him.

"That's okay," he mouthed, relieved for her that she had a take-charge friend to run interference.

He approached the bar. He didn't see Maggie or recognize anyone else yet. The bartender, a strawberry blond, had a wholesome look, big smile, and an attentive way about her. Jake ordered two beers from a regional brewery. Dream Draft, it was called, and he'd sure had his share of dreams, good and bad, after drinking too much of it.

He carried one over to Caitlyn huddled with Angela and handed it to her with an encouraging smile. He moved to the small hallway at the far end of the bar. It led to the restroom doors, then opened up to the four lanes in back. From the hallway he heard the sounds of balls rolling and pins dropping. He walked on through.

Bodies launched balls down shiny wood lanes toward pins. Same old place. Their mother claimed that, her senior year in high school, she once had "way too much fun" in the back room with one of the employees.

"Holy damn! Jake's back."

He turned. Rodney Peters, a former classmate and an upstate lifer, faced him. He'd aged, crevices now in his face, probably from too much time spent in the sun – he was a stonemason – and probably from too much drinking, too. Jake wondered if he himself came off aged like that. He'd always liked Rodney. He had a sweet, guileless way about him. Being a fast grower, powerful for his years, he'd protected his friends from the older bullies. Although now lined, he still looked fit ... from moving all that stone around no doubt.

"Yup, in the flesh. How you doing, Rodney?"

"Shitty," he said, obviously meaning it.

Another bowler stood up and approached. Jake didn't know him. Not as buff as Rodney, but wiry. Probably a little older, with even more of a used-up look – old eyes, sunken cheeks, and faded, thinning hair.

"Who's this?" the wiry fellow asked, poker-faced.

"I'm Jake."He stuck out his hand.

The fellow didn't take it.

"This is Dirk," Rodney said. "How long you been around, Jake?" he asked, trying to sound casual.

"Arrived four days ago."

"What'd you do yesterday morning?" Dirk asked with an edge.

Jake wasn't about to answer that. Rodney now was visibly uncomfortable as Jake and Dirk faced each other – uncomfortably close. Jake felt anger rising.

"Easy, Dirk," Rodney said, "I'll handle this. We have a good reason for asking, Jake. You staying at your sister's?"

"What's this?" Jake said, telling himself easy, easy.

The sounds of balls hitting pins and pins tumbling added to the drama.

"You want to know what this is?" Dirk said.

Jake's right hand was clenched. It would feel so good to throw a punch. He'd stored up a lot of punches these past months. If he'd already downed a six-pack instead of just one beer, he just might have.

Rodney edged between them. "I know you," he told Jake. "You were always stand-up. But Dirk doesn't." He turned to Dirk. "Let me handle this, okay? You go chill."

"There's no chilling."

Dirk lingered long enough to prove his manhood, then headed back to his group.

Jake turned to Rodney. "What the fuck?"

"He's just sounding off. We got, uh … robbed today. Just tell me what you were doing yesterday and we can drop it."

Jake tried to see Rodney as a kid again to calm himself down. "I worked on my sister's house! I went to the hardware store! Good enough? Was it your tools?"

Rodney shook his head no.

It came to Jake. He looked around to make sure no one was in earshot but lowered his voice anyway. "You got your crop ripped off, didn't you?"

Rodney let out a big sigh, so big that Jake smelled the beer on his breath. "Yeah, yeah. What we hadn't already harvested got wiped out. Most of it actually. Hacked to shit with a goddamn machete or something."

The code was that if you find someone's herb growing in the hills – someone's hard work – you take a taste, a small percentage, then move along.

"And everyone's a suspect, right? Even your friends."

"Yeah, yeah."

"What a time to return to town."

"We had a lousy July but a great fall to make up for it. Just some light frost. No freeze. We were real close to final harvesting and it was great stuff. That's why Dirk's all psycho … seeing a new face in town."

"I don't rip people off."

"I'll tell him you're stand-up."

"You believe it?"

"Yeah, I believe it."

"Well, that's good. You working tomorrow?"

"Probably. We thought we'd be harvesting. Why?"

Jake had a hunch. "In case I hear anything. Like through my sister and her friends. You got a cellphone?"

"Dirk does. He's my boss."

"What's the number?"

Rodney pulled out a beat-up wallet and from that a business card, handing it to Jake. It said *Callahan Masonry*.

"I'll keep an ear out," Jake said. "I've been there and it sucks."

He'd been there all right, his twelve plants ripped off from state land the last year he'd grown, giving him one more reason to want out of Shaleville.

"Okay, Jake." Rodney managed a half-smile and headed for his friend.

A woman stood up from a bench at the head of one of the lanes and approached Jake. Thirty-something, attractive, athletic

121

body, green eyes, and auburn hair. He knew that he knew her but couldn't call up her name.

"Hello, Jake B. Nimble."

Now he remembered. Lisa Bellinger. She'd been four years ahead of him at Shaleville Central when he was in middle school. Some of the pubescent boys used to try to get the older girls' attention by running right at them fast, then veering away at the last moment. With her looks, she'd been a prime target. After graduating, she'd returned as a substitute teacher Jake's senior year. He'd once unintentionally startled her on a staircase, almost knocking her down. Not long after that she'd caught him running over the tops of desks to get to his seat just before a class. She hadn't reported him but had used the Jake B. Nimble nickname to remind him she had something on him.

"Hello, Ms. Bellinger. You haven't told on me yet, have you?"

She smiled. It was a sweet smile, although masking a certain tension.

"Don't call me that. Just Lisa. No … no report yet. But I never forget." She tapped her brow teasingly. "You back in town for a while or just visiting? I see your sister around."

"Just visiting, leading up to Thanksgiving."

"I hear you've been pursuing an art career in New York City. I'm the full-fledged art teacher now. Perhaps you'd want to come talk to my students sometime this semester."

He would have quite a story to tell. "What a concept. Back at Shaleville Central School. I'll have to think about that. You paint?" he asked.

"Sporadically. More lately. Art as therapy." She glanced over her shoulder at the lanes; another woman was looking at her. "I'm up," she said. "Stay there, will you?"

She went back to the game, grabbing up a purple ball while the machine reset the pins. She crouched, focusing, then spryly moved forward, letting the ball go. It rumbled down the lanes and knocked down all the pins. She glanced over at Jake to see if he'd watched her bowl the strike. He had and let her know it with a nod. She went to the bench and, taking a pen and small notebook out of her pocketbook, wrote something and tore out the page. She came back over to him and handed him the notepaper.

"Here's my number. Feel free to call anytime about coming in to give a talk." She hesitated briefly, then added, "Or feel free to call me to just have lunch or dinner and talk about art." Smiling that masking smile once again, she turned to go.

She turned back and looked up at him one more time, her eyes holding his.

"Truth be told, I just got divorced and I'm bored silly. I'd love to spend some time with someone who moved on from Shaleville. No strings attached of course." She gave a non-teacher smile. " I did get the vaccination by the way. You?"

"Uh-huh."

"Good. Jake B. Nimble, Jake B. Quick, hurry up and phone, okay?"

~

Quite a reentry into local society, Jake reflected while walking Cracker. Following his encounters at the lanes, he'd gotten a seat at the bar for another beer and made small talk with first the bartender, then with Maggie, the creatively grumpy sixty-something owner, who had recognized him and jokingly had bitched about all the rowdy boys who had made her life miserable way too many years.

After Rodney and Dirk had finished bowling and Lisa's group had departed, Jake and Caitlyn had bowled. Despite being a little tipsy by then, she'd easily beaten him what with his tendency to hook left into the gutter. On their walk home, she'd expressed being happy about the whole excursion – her first night out since her breakup – and had headed off to bed, proclaiming with a big smile that she had to sleep off the three Dream Drafts. Jake had stopped himself at two. He'd told her he would walk Cracker. Watching her climb the stairs, he'd wondered to himself what was with all these breakups. His own, Caitlyn's, Lisa's, and even Al Mohr's.

Energized to be on a new case, disguised as a dogwalker, Jake led Cracker along Elm to the corner of Main, then crossed Elm and worked his way back along the block. He passed the first four houses, then came to Al Mohr's. The lights were still on in the cellar, the shades drawn.

Continuing along the sidewalk adjacent to the far end of the little ranch house, Jake took a couple of dog biscuits from his pocket and tossed them into the small front yard. Cracker didn't respond. Jake tossed a third biscuit and the dog got the scent, pulling him. Good old Cracker. Still youthful enough to have a hearty appetite.

Jake was hidden in the shadows, light from the nearest streetlamp blocked by the much larger house to the north. If anyone did spot him, they would see a dog pulling a man onto private property. Al Mohr would be incensed about a dog on his lawn but wouldn't have reason to suspect Jake's real purpose.

On nearing a window just around the house's northern front corner, Jake saw that the window had no shade. A piece of cardboard had been inserted behind the glass. He leaned over as if to pet Cracker and took a deep breath. He knew that odor well.

Neighborhood Watch

CAITLYN OVERSLEPT after their night out and rushed to get ready for work. Jake could have used more sleep but woke up because he had a phone call on his mind. He asked his sister over coffee if she knew whether Al Mohr worked regular hours, fibbing that Cracker may have left him a surprise on his lawn in the dark last night and, if so, he should clean it up. She scolded him for his carelessness, then told him that as far as she knew Mohr worked for a roofing company in Cobleskill and typically left home before she did.

When Jake saw her to her car, he spotted the silver pickup in the driveway. Mohr was home, it seemed. So much for an early departure today. Still busy in his cellar?

Back inside, Jake got out the business card Rodney had given him and punched in the number. Dirk answered.

"Is Rodney around?" he asked.

"Who wants to know?"

"Jake here … the guy you tried to interrogate last night at the B.A. I have some information that I'll tell him, not you."

"Whatever."

He heard traffic sounds, then Rodney's voice.

"Jake?"

"Hey, Rodney. Listen, you said your materials were ripped off yesterday, right?"

"Right."

"You're sure it was yesterday and not the day before."

"Why?"

"Just answer the question."

"Yeah, we checked on them real early. When we looked again after work, it'd already happened."

"What'll you do if I come up with someone who might've done it? How would you know what he had wasn't his?"

A muffled pause followed, probably Rodney covering the phone while he talked to Dirk. Then: "Our stuff's unique around here. Dirk got seeds in Canada. If we're not sure by looking at it, we'll make him show us where he grew his stuff."

"But no rough stuff if I lead you to the thief. You'd just take your stuff back, right?" Jake asked.

"We'll keep it cool."

"Promise?"

"Yeah."

"I mean it," Jake insisted. "You could make things a lot worse for yourself if things turn violent."

"Yeah, I know."

"You in town now?"

"Just leaving it."

"Meet me at Darrell Supply," Jake instructed. "I'm heading right over there from my sister's. Stay outside until I show up, okay? Old friends meeting up and talking out front. You know what I mean."

"Sure do."

Jake went outside, climbed in the rental, and drove over to Main Street and the hardware store. He entered and looked for something to buy. He chose a can of Fix-a-Flat, good to have for the road. Once again, it was the daughter behind the counter and once again no small talk – just as Jake preferred.

When he emerged, Rodney and Dirk sat parked outside in a big red and white Dodge pickup, looking a little agitated. Jake went over to Rodney, who sat on the passenger's side.

"Okay, let's have it," Rodney said skeptically.

"Here's the deal. A certain neighbor of my sister's been acting suspiciously. I saw him rush home yesterday and unload big trash bags into the house. They looked full. He left again dressed for hunting and returned later with more bags. After talking to you last night, I got close to a cellar window and could smell fresh weed in his house. I think he's been trimming down there. The rest of the house was dark."

"Who is it?" Dirk asked.

"You promised no rough stuff? It might be rightfully his."

"Yeah, we agreed."

"You'll make him prove it's not his?"

"I went to Canada for the seeds ... it's called Purple Mash. I know our crop."

"The buds really do look purple," Rodney added.

"You said you'd ask him to show you his patch."

"If it's his stuff, he'll have one and he'll want to take us there to prove it," Dirk said.

"I guess he will at that. This thing makes me nervous. I'm doing it, Rodney, because I remember how you saved my punk ass from older kids more than once. I've been ripped off and I know it sucks. But it could get ugly and I don't want that. If the police show up, you all go down."

"We won't let it get crazy." Rodney turned to Dirk. "Maybe your brother-in-law will go with us."

"Yeah, maybe," Dirk replied, then said to Jake, "No one messes with Mitch. He's a karate teacher."

"Remember, I could have it all wrong," Jake said. "Give me your word no physical stuff. If he takes a swing at you, you hold back."

"You got it," Rodney said.

Jake looked over at smoldering Dirk.

"I'd sure like to deck whoever did this, but, okay, yeah," Dirk said.

Jake still had misgivings. "He's got a shotgun so don't all go to his front door and freak him out. Maybe one of you should just go knock like a Jehovah's Witness or something. Wear a suit."

Rodney gave a quick little laugh. "Not bad."

"So who is it?" Dirk asked.

"Of course my name can't come up however it works out. I'll be leaving town again soon and I don't want my sister involved in any way. I haven't mentioned a thing to her, although she'd sympathize with you guys."

"Better that way," Rodney said. "Who is it?"

"I think he's there now, probably clipping and Caitlyn's at work. A good time to go."

"So who?" Dirk asked.

Jake sighed, still unsure if he should proceed. "You know who Al Mohr is?"

"That new guy in town? The roofer?"

"You know where he lives?"

Dirk nodded. "Oh yeah."

~

Jake watched through the trees from the porch. The red-and-white pickup was parked several houses down, Dirk and Rodney in it. No people were on the street.

Another vehicle – a red Subaru Outback – pulled up along the sidewalk in front of Al Mohr's house. Dirk's brother-in-law Mitch got out. Had to be. They'd taken Jake's suggestion. He wore a suit and carried an attaché case. Very official looking. He could be selling encyclopedias, vacuum cleaners, or religion, or be some kind of official, even a cop. Whatever he might be, he sure looked like someone who worked out, his suit tight on him.

Mitch walked up the front steps onto the open porch and knocked on the door. Nothing happened. He knocked again. The door finally opened. Al Mohr stepped outside. They talked briefly. Jake saw Mitch pointing to his Subaru as if to say come see what I have to offer. The two of them descended the front steps and headed for the vehicle. Mitch scratched his head a little too long. A signal?

Dirk accelerated from down the street and pulled in fast behind the Subaru. He and Rodney jumped out. Al Mohr was surrounded and, it was apparent, not happily so. Those around him were keeping their voices low. Rodney kept looking at nearby houses – to make sure no one was paying attention, Jake assumed.

127

A car approached from Main Street. By the time it had passed, all four were heading up the steps. They disappeared inside.

Jake had created this whole scene. He wished he could be a fly on the wall. All he could do was wait and hope nothing really bad happened. He trusted Rodney to keep his word, but not Dirk. Mitch hopefully would keep the calm since part of the teaching in karate is that you use violence as a last resort. But what was a last resort?

Dirk reappeared at the front door and hurried across the porch, down the steps, and over to his truck. He got in and, starting it, backed it into the driveway right up to Al Mohr's pickup. He headed for the side door. Someone met him there and handed him a loaded garbage bag, which he threw in the back of his truck. He went back for another then another. Rodney exited the house, carrying two more bags and tossed them in with the others. He and Dirk climbed in the pickup's cab and pulled out of the driveway.

As they drove away, Rodney stuck his hand out the window and, keeping it low so the vehicle blocked sight of it from Al Mohr's house, gave a thumbs-up. Meanwhile, Mitch strolled casually down the driveway and entered his car, then did a three-point turn and also headed down Elm for Main Street.

Jake stepped back from the screen door and headed for the kitchen, planning to get something to eat before he started working. His phone sounded out. It was Dirk's number.

Jake answered and heard Rodney's ebullient voice. "Jake! Hey, Jake!"

"Hey there, Rodney. All good?"

"You bet. He folded fast … as soon as we asked him to take us to his patch. When he hesitated, we said someone saw him at ours and he confessed."

"You got everything?"

"We told him he could keep the leaf he trimmed off. We just give it away anyway. Not worth sitting on that. Whoops, enough said. Shouldn't talk about damn clients cheating us out of landscaping supplies."

"Good move to let him keep a share. Make him complicit."

"That's what Mitch said. He told Mohr we forgive him 'cause we understand how he couldn't resist the temptation. I doubt he'd mouth off anyway, knowing we'd then beat the shit out of him."

"So it all worked out?"

"It sure did … and Jake, we'll have a little present for you for your help. Not so little actually. Dirk's idea now that he knows you're a stand-up guy."

"I appreciate it. I'm leaving town soon and don't want anything with me on this trip. How about I give you a call when I come back through?"

"Any time."

"What's your home phone?"

"Three-three-one-one."

"Got it." In this town the landline area code and exchange were always the same six numbers.

Jake felt conflicted. He had the satisfaction of knowing he'd actually solved a case, balanced against the weirdness of getting involved in other people's issues without being asked. He also didn't like the lie of omission to his sister. But it was done and the resolution of this Elm Street affair helped psychologically propel him toward the other case he'd taken on. Thanksgiving was fast approaching.

~

Caitlyn returned from work with concern on her face.

"You know that neighbor of mine … the new guy … Al Mohr?" she asked.

Uh-oh, Jake thought. "Yeah. What about him? He say something to you?"

"I didn't see his truck today but I just saw someone else parked in front of his house. I saw him yesterday, too."

Jake wasn't surprised to hear that Mohr was laying low today. But another car?

"Whoever it is gave me the hairy eyeball when I pulled in," she added. "After I came inside, I looked out the window and saw him leave."

"What'd he look like. How old?"

"I just noticed a fedora, kind of like a gangster would wear."

"What kind of car?"

"I don't know … a small gray sedan. I don't think I've seen it in town."

"You make out the plates?"

"New York ones, I could tell. I should've gotten the number."

"Maybe someone from out of town waiting for Mohr's return. A partner, maybe. Mohr *is* a proven lowlife."

Caitlin looked puzzled. "Why do you say that?"

Jake, tired of his lies, filled her in on the marijuana rip-off. He didn't tell her he'd been making the most of his newly discovered sleuthing chops in getting involved … or that his tailing of random people in New York City had actually led him to Montreal. He just told her he'd tipped off an old friend, kind of payback after all these years for Rodney sticking up for a smaller kid.

She was upset. "You sure took a chance. What if something really bad had happened? Not a great homecoming."

"I trusted Rodney not to let it go too far."

"But now this parked guy on the street?"

"Maybe he got ripped off by Mohr, too. In any case, I'll call Rodney and ask him to keep an eye out."

"It all makes me nervous. I gotta think like a teacher in the making. And you …"

"Right. I gotta think like someone in rehab."

"Wait on calling Rodney. It might lead to some ugliness. Let's see if the guy comes back again."

Jake felt the paranoia of the street pushing out from his kidneys, along his side, and to his neck – the ache of those past blows on Vandam Street. He didn't feel them for himself; now it was for Caitlyn. But how could Mohr or this driver, whoever he was, associate her with what had happened?

He would keep an eye out for the gray sedan and ask Rodney to do the same despite her objections.

Wine and Dine and...

LISA BELLINGER opened her front door.

"Hello, Lisa," Jake said. "I brought some wine."

"Great. Red. Perfect. Come on in."

Jake entered the big Victorian house.

"I'm still cooking. Come join me in the kitchen."

He followed her through the vestibule, down the hall, and into a large kitchen. The 19th-century house had been redone with modern appliances, including a restaurant-grade stainless steel stove. On seeing Jake, a calico cat looked up from a bowl of dried food and exited the room fast.

"That's Dali, as in Salvador. He'll warm up to you. Have a seat."

Jake sat on a stool at the counter in the center of the room.

"I'll let you open the wine," she said, handing him back the bottle along with a corkscrew and some glasses. She went to the stove and stirred some red sauce. "I decided on Italian."

He struggled with the cork. "Sorry I didn't give you much notice."

"I told you to be quick. No problem."

She brought glasses over and he poured the wine.

Standing on the opposite side of the counter, looking at him, she asked, "Like my house?"

"Sure do."

"I'll give you a tour after dinner. Wait a second."

She reached over to a side counter and picked up a tablet and began scrolling. She turned the screen toward him. "I always like to show this photo."

Jake looked. The photo showed the house as it had been, obviously abandoned. The walls had peeling white paint and the windows were gaping black holes.

"This is what we brought it back from," she said.

"Aha. You and …?"

"Yes, my ex. Remember the Phys Ed teacher, Paul Davis?"

"Yes. But wait … the art teacher married the P.E. teacher?"

"He never went to one gallery with me even though I watched a ton of sports with him. He barely even looked at my paintings."

"Is that what did you two in?"

"I guess you could say that. I guess you could say I was so unhappy I drove him to an affair."

"Don't tell me. With the girls' basketball coach."

She looked at Jake questioningly. "It was the soccer coach. Your sister say something about all this?"

He laughed. "No, really, that was a guess."

She laughed as well. "I always sensed you were smart as well as nimble. You probably think I'm too forward. I'm not really. I just took a chance with you. I've been fantasizing taking a chance with someone since my divorce, but I haven't till now. I guess I felt comfortable with you because you haven't been around here and because I heard you're an artist and because you were the adorable little Jake B. Nimble who grew up to be ... well, someone I wondered about after you graduated and before I got married. And now, after my divorce, too. Remember, I am only four years older."

She was letting it all out.

"It's been a two-way fantasy."

"Really? Spell it out!"

"You know ... a crush on teacher."

"Still?" she asked.

"You got your stuff together more than I do," he told her. "To tell you the ugly truth, I've been strung out and not very productive lately. I was even living homeless in the New York while coming back from some nasty habits. The city was like college for me and I flunked out."

She thought about that, then waved it off.

"Yeah, well I've been strung out over my divorce and not productive either. It's been hard keeping it together to teach. I'm sure people would make a huge something about your coming over. Did you tell your sister about my forward behavior?"

"She doesn't even know yet that I'm here. I decided to call you after she told me she was working late, then left a note for her. She plans to go back to school to become a teacher so she'll probably be happy I'm hanging with one."

"I don't worry about my rep other than how it relates to school. As for my ex, he's much better off with a jock. So much so that he was happy to get out of here and leave me this big house we'd put so much into."

"No kids?"

"We tried for a while but then decided because of all the students in our lives we didn't need kids." She moved her head to one side then the other. "I go back and forth on that one. I know now it's a damn good thing he and I didn't go that route."

"So what now?"

"Besides you?" she said teasingly.

"Oh yeah ... reliable me."

"I don't know. I've been enjoying living alone. I like the idea of being a painter on my own. While with Paul, that was my dream ... not someone new to nest with and fight with ... rather to paint, travel to France, have affairs, and keep teaching so I might inspire some kid along the way to become a renowned artist."

"Any candidates so far? I mean the renowned artist part."

"I'm afraid not but I've been all caged in ... as a woman, artist, and teacher. I feel I'm only now discovering myself as all three."

"It makes me want to go back to school."

"And fantasize about a teacher?"

"Uh-huh. I'm glad it's Ms. Bellinger again and not Mrs. Davis."

Her eyes held his, then she began making a salad. Jake watched her, appreciating yet being nervous about the loaded situation.

He let his mind go elsewhere: "Hey, ever hear of Paul-Louis Boucher?"

"No. He an artist?"

"A French sociologist. I heard him talk in Montreal. What he's putting out there relates to art in that he objects to the American commercialization of French esthetics ... you know ... MacDonald's and Disney World, mass media, globalization of culture. All that."

"I'm with him to some degree," Lisa said. "But some of the French are collaborating with the foreign companies, aren't they? They have to take some of the blame."

"I guess it's the cultural equivalent of political Free France and Vichy France, like in the movie *Casablanca*. You've seen it, right?"

"No."

"No?"

"My parents didn't watch movies. TV shows, yes. Paul sure didn't either. He preferred ESPN. Big surprise there, right? I rarely allowed myself the time. You a film buff?"

"My mother was a fiend. Made sure my sister and I saw all the classics, especially film noir, and the newer ones she also decided were classics. She got me reading some of the books, too. Said I should know the originals."

"That's impressive. I read books in spite of my parents. I remember your mom. She's not still living in town, is she?"

"No, out west. Couldn't cope here anymore. She has her demons. I have mine."

Jake was revealing a lot. The wine?

"Yeah, like I don't have demons," Lisa said.

While Lisa finished preparing dinner, Jake went to his phone and searched for music festivals around New York City on Thanksgiving weekend. Lots of gigs, but nothing described as a "festival," as Raven had expressed it. There were some events in the South and Southwest. But what kind of a lead was that?

Dinner was ready. They moved to the dining room. It was all so civilized: candlelight; pasta and salad; and the bottle of wine Jake had brought. The wine – more than Jake had had in a good while – helped make their time feel natural and meaningful. They laughed a lot. They talked about art, his street life, and her battles with the public-school system.

Afterwards, they moved to her living room and couch in front of a fireplace. She'd already stacked the paper, kindling, and logs. She lit the paper and they watched the growing flame. Once she was satisfied that she'd done well with her stack, she leaned over and kissed him. He kissed back.

It was intense and might very well have led to the bedroom. Despite the intensity, they agreed – or it seemed like they agreed – it was best not to go too far too fast. Not to mention ex-husbands, Jake had the thought, who might get as perturbed as Canadian boyfriends. Jake B. Cautious?

Not cautious enough apparently. After their time on the couch, while talking in the kitchen again – over coffee for Jake and herbal tea for Lisa – they heard a crashing sound from outside. Then, a car alarm.

"What the hell?!" Lisa exclaimed.

"That sounds way too close," Jake said, getting up and hurrying toward the front door, Lisa right behind him.

"Be careful," she said.

Jake cracked the door. Lisa pressed up against him to look, too. He stepped onto her porch. In the light of a streetlamp, he could see a broken window on the Honda and streaks of yellow paint.

"It's my rental," he said.

He reached in his pocket for the key and shut off the alarm to deafening silence. He descended the porch steps. He could smell the fresh paint. He approached the car and looked inside. Shards of glass covered the driver's seat.

"Anything missing?" Lisa asked from the porch.

He'd luckily taken all his possessions into his sister's house. He checked the glove compartment. All the papers were there.

"Seems like pure vandalism," Jake calmly said.

But he didn't feel calm. His heart was beating harder. His head was hot. These were the same feelings of anger and frustration he'd experienced all too often in Shaleville on being pushed too hard.

"Fucking A," Lisa, the teacher, said.

Calm the Eff Down

LATE AFTERNOON THE NEXT DAY, Jake rode with Caitlyn back from Albany. She'd followed him in her car to the airport while he'd driven the Honda, plastic taped over the broken window.

Jake had had his worries but, after slogging through car rental bureaucracy, he was informed his insurance would cover the damage. Insurance sucked until a payoff, he had to admit.

He'd told Caitlyn about the vandalism over breakfast just before she went off to work. She'd hypothesized that it could have been Al Mohr who smashed the window and spray-painted it. That sure seemed doubtful to Jake. He'd reminded her that Mohr had no way of knowing who had led Rodney and Dirk to him. She'd also asked about the man in the fedora, returning to the idea that he held some connection to Mohr. He seemed to be long gone, Jake had assured her, his earlier presence on the block probably just a coincidence. He'd also told Caitlyn that he'd asked Lisa if she thought her ex, the P.E. teacher Paul Davis, would have vandalized the car out of jealousy. Lisa couldn't imagine that, she'd told him. Maybe kids doing the coming-of-age vandalism thing? Her students? A jealous stalker student? She couldn't fathom their involvement either, she'd said.

When Caitlyn had returned early after work to make this trip, Jake had commented how, as with most vandalism, they'd

135

probably never identify the culprit. She'd fallen silent. All the drama was obviously wearing thin for her.

On the ride to Albany, Jake had had another matter on his mind – his not telling her about his amateur detecting and his real reason for going to Montreal and what had happened there. His rationalization had been that he didn't want to worry her. That only held up for so long. This was a huge lie of omission with lots of accompanying white lies. He'd decided to admit all on the return ride together.

The moment had come. On reaching open road on Route 20 west, he launched into an explanation of the Boucher case, starting with the morning he was attacked on Vandam Street and the start of his tailing people, which had taken him to Montreal. He'd related what he'd learned there, including about Thanksgiving. He told her he wanted to see the case through to its resolution if possible. His new proclivity to detecting had also led him to the case of the stolen grass, he admitted.

Jake kept his eyes on the road ahead as he talked. From time to time, he heard her emit something between a sigh and a groan.

When he finished, she let out her frustration with, "What the eff you playing at Jake? You might get hurt, just like you might've been helping Rodney."

"He and Dirk sure are happy. They owe me. If anything …"

"Yeah, yeah, I know. They're my new guardians. I feel so safe." Caitlyn sure knew how to lay on the sarcasm. "Look," she continued, "That's over and done with. But now you're going off on some crazy adventure. Why not just tell the police what you've found out and be done with that, too?"

"I will when I have something convincing to report."

"Other than your following this Leandra around? You and all the goddamn women. Even a former teacher!"

Jake hadn't told her about kissing Lisa – just that they'd met to talk about the art world. Nor had he filled her in on everything about Raven, like their massages and his confrontation with Raphael about her. And he'd rarely mentioned New York City girlfriends. But Caitlyn knew him well.

"Listen," he implored, "I know it all seems crazy … my following people to pass the time and then actually coming upon something suspicious ... but it's helped me stay clean. I need something to do to keep cravings at bay."

"What about your sculpting? You said Aki ..."

"That period of my life was tied to my doing drugs. I haven't sorted all that out yet despite the surprise payoff."

"Well, sort it out already and return to Shaleville once and for all and calm the eff down."

"You sound like mom lecturing teenager me, although from you it carries weight. Like I've been saying, mom's influence is part of keeping me on track. That's one of the good memories ... the three of us watching Bogie and all the other P.I.'s together. Remember how much you loved Jack Nicholson as Jake Gittis in *Chinatown?* She actually got namesake me... hyperactive me ... to read novels, starting with the Hardy Boys. And you took to Nancy Drew. And Sherlock Holmes, too. Unlike you, I moved on to many other writers tied into films ... Chandler, Hammett, Cain, Woolrich, Thompson, McCoy, Goodis, Leonard, Ross Macdonald, John T. MacDonald. Her collection of books and movies ... along with others I sought out on my own even when I was a drunken fool ... served as my college education. Something good came from her."

"It doesn't feel so good right now."

"Hey, even when young, you'd watch any movie ... no matter how suspenseful and scary it was ... that had a singer in it. Remember *Black Angel* ... with two singers?"

"How could I forget? How many times did mom mention Cornell Woolrich wrote the novel while we were trying to watch?"

"You didn't even mind that one of the singers gets killed. I remember you thought the old-style phonograph was cool. Admit it. Mom, with her thing for old movies, played a part in your becoming a singer in a band. That was a good thing."

"Which I'm no longer. Nor do I have any plans to become a blackmailer, like the singer who got offed. Okay then, Mr.-College-Honorary-Degree-in-Movie-Life-Studies, I have a movie reference to make my point since you used one on me."

"Go for it."

"Here it is, plain and simple. The title *Kiss Tomorrow Goodbye*. Learn from it."

"Starring James Cagney. I forget who else was in it and who directed and wrote the screenplay. But I know it was based on a novel by Horace McCoy."

"Yeah, yeah. But here's what's important. What happens to Cagney's character? Better know this or your honorary degree gets annulled."

"One of his women shoots him."

"Okay, you pass. It'll also probably be a woman who does you in. You're risking your future. You get the message?"

Jake had no ready response other than that she needn't worry because he was super cautious. Caitlyn scoffed at that and remained in a funk all the way home.

That night, she let her anger go and they surfed television together. He hadn't suggested they get out their mother's old VCR and watch one of her old movies. Rather, they relived the old days after cable had come to Shaleville ... that is, those days when their mother kept up payments on time. While poking fun at whatever show or commercial they landed on, they even managed to laugh a little about their new personas – hers, wannabe teacher, and his, wannabe private eye.

PART V: WHEREABOUTS

Frank Delsa, homicide detective: *"A good investigator knows who
to believe and who not to believe."*
– Elmore Leonard, *Mr. Paradise*

Parking Omens

*A TICKING CAME, time moving inexorably toward some dreaded
consequence. But he couldn't make out the shape of the event to come …*

Jake used the steering wheel to straighten up from his sleeping
slouch. The dream sound of ticking had been a cop's tapping on
the driver's side window. He was small with a narrow face, but
his blue uniform added stature. He gestured that Jake roll down
the window all the way.

"Move this van. You're too close to the hydrant," he
commanded. "What're you doing here anyway … sleeping?"

"Waiting on someone." There was truth in that.

"Well, don't wait here. License, please." His tone negated
the "please."

Jake started to reach in his pants pocket but stopped. Cops
didn't like the unexpected.

"My license is in my pocket, okay?"

"Step out of the vehicle."

Jake did so, then slowly reached under his sweatshirt and
pulled his wallet out of his pocket and his license out of the wallet,
handing it over.

The cop studied it. "Jake … uh … Jakes, where's Shaleville?"

Jake had the urge to tell him to look it up. Yet he knew that
cargo vans, without side windows, were suspect in this age
of terrorism. Stay meek, he told himself. "West of Albany …
Otsego County."

The cop studied the sticker in the van's front window. It was
all legal. Jake had made it so on his final day upstate, catching a

ride with Caitlyn to an insurance agency and the Department of Motor Vehicles in Cooperstown.

"All good, right?" Jake asked.

"Why you here?"

Jake further improvised: "To help a friend move."

"You came a long way."

"He's a good friend."

The cop looked hard at Jake, probably to get a sense of whether he was cracking wise, but then said, "Just move on," moving on himself.

There was nothing on this Brooklyn street relevant to Jake other than parking, so he was fine with moving on … if he could find another spot, that is. He was parked on Knickerbocker Avenue, near the corner with Palmetto Street, opposite Firehouse 227. Yesterday, he'd parked on Palmetto to watch the warehouse from inside the van. He'd seen Marcus come and go twice but had witnessed no activity to expose some plan for Thanksgiving. Jake had left that block about midnight, knowing that parking spot would be illegal the next morning. He'd thought this one would be legal another twenty-four hours. Not so. Too close to the hydrant, the man in blue had told him.

Jake had heard lots of negatives from friends about having a vehicle in the city, other than the escape it offered. A fellow sculptor claimed luck with parking defined the New York City experience on any given day, whether good or bad. A facetious overstatement obviously, yet seeming all-too applicable at the moment.

Jake used his pee jug, then sipped from a half-empty cup of cold coffee. He wondered in hindsight if it made more sense to sleep in the back, where he was away from prying eyes. He also wondered if he should have confided to the cop about possible goings-on in the warehouse. His suspicions probably weren't enough for a judge to issue a search warrant. Still ruminating, he ate an orange and some almonds, good travel food.

In his side mirror he saw an SUV three cars back pulling out from the curb. It moved past him. He quickly pulled out himself, then backed up to the opening in the line of cars. What with only inches to spare and rusty parallel parking skills, he needed several approaches but finally succeeded.

Sure enough, with this bit of parking luck, the day had gone from bad to at least so-so.

~

The same doorway Jake had used before Montreal and Shaleville, when he'd first followed Leandra to the warehouse, again served its purpose, giving him a discreet vantage point when Leandra and Ned approached along Palmetto from that street's intersection with Myrtle and Wyckoff.

A small part of the suspense for Jake had been what color Leandra's hair would be. Red or blue or still the silver-streaked black hair? She'd changed it again: platinum blond. Was this a self-image or a fashion thing … or was it her attempt, like he was doing, to avoid being recognized? Her gray, paint-smattered smock extended below an oversized navy blue peacoat. No sketchpad today. Ned wore an aviator jacket. It looked new. Bought with money from Boucher? Both had backpacks.

Jake clicked a picture and looked at it. At this distance their features were blurred. The duo disappeared inside the warehouse. His adrenaline rush on seeing them subsided. Now, more waiting. The wind picked up and he shuffled his feet and rotated his shoulders to stay warm.

Some two hours later, Leandra and Ned exited the building. Jake let them proceed a distance, then followed.

On reaching the end of Palmetto, he saw that they stood at the Myrtle bus stop from where Ned had taken a bus on Jake's first visit to Bushwick. He stepped into a residential doorway and waited. Should he follow them onto the bus and risk being recognized from before? Undecided, he took several more photos, capturing their profiles.

A bus came. The duo hugged. Ned climbed aboard; Leandra headed back toward the intersection. Jake turned to hide his face as if he were entering the building. After counting off some seconds in his head, he stepped out of the doorway and looked for her. She'd reached the entrance to the Myrtle-Wyckoff subway station.

He hurried along the street and down the station's stairs. On reaching the bottom, he saw her pass through a turnstile to the Manhattan-bound L train platform. He stopped and waited. Other people passed him. Leandra moved out of sight.

Jake was prepared, still having credit on a MetroCard he'd purchased before departing the city. He moved close to the turnstiles and waited again.

He heard a train's approach. Swiping his card, he stepped through a turnstile onto the platform. The train pulled up. He spotted Leandra's platinum hair as she entered the train one car down. He hurried toward it, entering the same car on its opposite end from her, and sat down.

Other passengers made it easier for Jake to keep an eye on her without being noticed. She would exit at First or Third Avenue was his guess. He remembered her asking Ned the day she'd delivered the Mickey Mouse doll – after Jake had followed her on this same subway line in the opposite direction – if he were returning to the East Village. He'd also encountered the two of them in that neighborhood, the day he'd followed them to their meeting across from the United Nations.

Sure enough, Leandra exited at the first stop in Manhattan, First Avenue. On leaving the station, she walked eastward along 14th Street, crossed Avenue A, then continued to Avenue B where she turned right, southward. Just before 9th Street, opposite Tompkins Square Park, she climbed the stoop of a rundown tenement house and used a key to enter.

The park would give Jake a place to sit while keeping an eye on the door. How long? Through evening and the night? That same Brooklyn cop might have an eye out for the van, which by the morning would be illegally parked. It might even be towed. Jake had better retrieve it at some point before morning regardless of Leandra's whereabouts.

When she didn't reappear going on midnight, he did so, taking the subway to Brooklyn, then driving the van back to the East Village. On his return in the early a.m., he fortunately found a parking spot on 7th Street that was good all the next day.

Parking luck again. In order to keep luck going on his second night in his tiny mobile home, he would sleep in the back, his presence hidden from passersby, uniformed or otherwise.

Moot Blues

COFFEE, A SOOTHING THING, even on a park bench with biting winds coming off the East River. The raw weather certainly didn't help Jake's sense of self.

He smoked the first of his now three daily self-allotted cigarettes. He kept a newspaper in his lap as cover but didn't read it, his eyes fixed on Leandra's door. It was glossy black and, like the green warehouse door, it held mystery.

Leandra appeared at 11:47 a.m. This time, she had sketchpad in hand. Jake willed her to cross Avenue B and take a seat in the park to draw. Was it time to try engaging her in casual conversation? What might he achieve? Get information? That had worked with Raven. Manage to get recruited by her for whatever they were up to and go undercover? Or try to talk her out of whatever their plan was – a plan that might ruin her life? Would she betray her boyfriend? Not likely.

Leandra didn't enter the park. Walking briskly, she headed north, then cut west at the first corner. Jake hurried to follow. Back to the subway station at First Avenue and 14th Street? Back to Brooklyn? Back to the warehouse?

So it seemed. She entered the subway station on the south side of 14th, hurrying to catch an eastbound train loudly braking to a stop. At the bottom of the stairs, Jake saw her pass through a turnstile just as the train doors closed. She would have to wait for the next one.

The disembarking passengers passed by him. An elderly couple who had arrived in the station behind Jake pushed through the turnstiles. He followed them, concealing himself behind them as best he could. They walked one way on the platform; Leandra, the other. He followed the couple and positioned himself on their far side. Leandra sat down on a wooden bench to wait. She took a colored pencil from her pocket, opened the sketchpad, and began drawing. Wait … she was doing so righthanded. Jake was certain she'd used her left hand before. Ambidextrous? Left hand injured? Or delusion and/or memory loss on his part?

Jake's thoughts raced beyond this nonessential issue. If she were heading to the warehouse, he faced another day of staking out a building. To do what … follow her back to the East Village? To what end? Should he seize this opportunity to talk to her?

How would he start a conversation? "Oh, hello. I can't help but notice your sketchpad. You an artist?"

What would she reply to that lame come-on … if she replied at all rather than just stand up and move away?

A train approached, making his decision moot. He glanced at the couple as they stepped toward the platform's edge, then back at Leandra as she also stood up. She was looking directly at him. He turned away. The train screeched to a halt and the doors opened. Jake looked again to see Leandra enter two cars down, then followed the couple through the door in front of him.

Was she onto him? Should he follow her now? He was pretty certain he knew where she was going anyway.

At the next stop, the first in Brooklyn, he exited the train and followed staircases up and then down to the westbound platform and a train back to Manhattan. Hopefully he'd offset any suspicions.

Jake rode the subway all the way to Sixth Ave, then caught a southbound train to the West 4th Street Station. Before returning to his van, he would use the Washington Square restroom. That, for now anyway, was a definitive plan.

After surfacing, he walked eastward on West 4th, cutting into the park to the restroom's entrance. Afterwards, memories of the familiar surroundings helped him decompress from his disappointment that Leandra seemingly had caught on to him.

A memory from these whereabouts became a reality. Tenor in the flesh. On a pathway, near the eastern edge of the park, his street friend, using his shopping cart as a recliner, lay on top of his confusing pile of possessions, his mouth open, his teeth stained red from wine. He had a "space bag" as a pillow – an inflated plastic bladder salvaged from boxed wine – and looked comfortable enough despite his deathly pallor. Although he wasn't bothering anyone, how long would the cops allow such beatitude?

"Hey, Tenor, rise and shine," Jake said, poking him gently.

Tenor stirred, looked at Jake warily, then smiled in relief. "Why wake a happily sleeping man?"

"To give you more happiness."

Jake handed him a twenty and a ten.

Tenor looked at the bills, confused.

"Will you remember who gifted you?" Jake asked.

Tenor looked Jake up and down through half-closed eyes. "It be Jake Soho. What, someone adopt you? Give you new duds?"

"No, I collected a debt. That money is for food. Promise?"

"You're a hard-ass."

"Promise?"

Tenor, now wide awake, smiled mischievously. "You want a statement in blood?"

"Just say it. I'll take you at your word. Promise?"

"I promise. Thanks, bro."

~

Jake, just before post-workday rush hour, drove by way of the Manhattan Bridge back to Brooklyn, striving to stay calm in the growing traffic. He found parking on Wilson Street. The spot was good all evening and through the night and – once again, praise the parking gods – through the weekend. He moved to the back of the van and changed his clothes to avoid detection, knowing his efforts might be in vain.

He walked around the corner onto Palmetto, taking up position in a doorway across the street and far down the block from the warehouse. As he stood there, he received some long hard looks from people passing by. Was he being recognized as a neighborhood loiterer? How much longer could he pull this off?

After only a few minutes, as if in response to Jake's inner doubts, Marcus stepped out of the warehouse onto the sidewalk and headed toward Myrtle. Jake followed, clicking some photos of his mark on the way. Marcus crossed that avenue and angled up Wyckoff, entering a business offering Chinese Tui Na massage. Finding relief from the cloak-and-dagger stress at the hands of a beautiful Asian woman?

The idea of waiting around in continuing discomfort while Marcus got all relaxed irked Jake. Luckily, a delicatessen stood opposite, where he could sit at the counter near the window and watch the massage parlor. He used the restroom, then ordered a coffee and a bagel with cream cheese.

Marcus must have paid for forty-five minutes worth of massage since he finally exited the parlor after fifty-six minutes. He crossed Wyckoff and entered the deli. Jake, keeping his head low, concentrated on the brown pool of his half-empty second cup of coffee. Marcus passed behind him and approached the counter.

"The usual," he said loudly. "To go."

Whatever the usual was, it didn't take long to prepare, and Marcus soon exited, heading back toward Myrtle. Jake had paid on ordering and was ready to go himself. He waited a few moments, then set out. As expected, he saw Marcus turn onto Palmetto back toward the warehouse. He kept pace.

After Marcus had disappeared inside, Jake made for what had become his lookout doorway. Better standing in a doorway than sleeping in it, he reminded himself. That thought helped somewhat as daylight transitioned to darkness.

The patience he'd cultivated through all the recent stakeouts had worn thin by mid-evening. He stepped out of the doorway onto the empty sidewalk and returned to the van. He used his pee jug. As he emptied it in the gutter, two figures turned the corner and approached. The light of a streetlamp revealed them as young men, both with facial tattoos and piercings. Should he ask them if they had any drugs for sale? Was that stereotyping? Would they be offended? His absurd train of thought got him past his cravings. Jake entered the van and crawled between the front seats to his sleeping platform in the back. He covered himself in his unzipped sleeping bag and closed his eyes.

Doubts doubled down. Sleep eluded him. Self-pity came one moment; self-anger, the next. Feelings of vulnerability underpinned both. Despite the shelter of the van? Or because of it? What was the threat? Random violence? Cops? If either of the first two, cops would become his friends, whether the villainous bearers of dreaded parking tickets or not.

The threat of relapse? Questions, both sensible and absurd, all related to the persistent question … what next? All his choices felt moot. How much longer could he cope? Toss in the towel of this self-appointed private detection and report to the police of the strange behavior surrounding the warehouse, then rejoin his sister upstate?

Caitlyn would probably be relieved at his latest failure. As she'd made clear, she didn't like this movie in which he'd cast himself.

Eleven Nation Army

JAKE STOOD IN THE FAMILIAR doorway on the same side of the street as the warehouse on an all-too familiar stakeout.

He was snapped out of his inward morass by a piercing shout. It came from a three-story building across the street.

Loud and clear, a man's voice: "Fire!"

A window on the building's second floor crashed outwards, shards sprinkling the sidewalk.

Then, another shout – more of a scream – a woman's voice: "Fire!"

The front door opened and a middle-aged woman came running out. Other people exited the burning house and neighboring homes as well.

Black smoke plumed from the broken window. Jake heard a siren in the distance. Someone had already phoned the FDNY and the response was prompt, the first firetrucks no doubt coming from the station on Knickerbocker.

Two red trucks pulled up on the one-way street. Burly men in helmets and black-and-yellow rubber coats launched into action, blocking off the street and readying a fire hydrant and hoses. Others donned masks and readied axes in preparation for entering. One fireman calmed the first woman who had exited the building. He pointed toward others exiting behind her. He stood beside her as she counted them out loud.

Among the spectators on Jake's side of the street was Marcus. He'd walked in the opposite direction from Jake to a Fire Department SUV blocking the street and stood at the curb, looking up at the smoke, now streaming from another second-story window and a third-story one as well. And Leandra and Ned? If they'd been inside, odds are they also would have exited onto the street.

Jake needed action. On impulse, he walked quickly along the sidewalk toward the warehouse. No one seemed to notice him what with all the activity across the street; not Marcus apparently, who, like everyone else, was fixated on the fire.

Jake moved up the three concrete steps to the green door. Had Marcus left it open in these circumstances? Closed but unlocked, Jake discovered on turning the big door handle. He pulled the heavy metal door open just wide enough to enter. It moaned like a sick animal at his intrusion. Jake remembered that moan from day one outside the warehouse. He scooted inside, closing it behind him.

A small vestibule area with metal wall hooks for coats opened into a giant dimly lit chamber. It was cold and damp and smelled of paint, oil, and fresh garbage. Yellowing white paint covered the cinderblock walls. Old fluorescent lamps hung from metal rafters that supported a flat roof with one skylight. Some of their bulbs flickered and their ballasts hummed. The skylight offered little natural light since its glass had been painted white, this paint glossy and new unlike the wall paint.

It was difficult to make sense of the warehouse's contents. Various building materials – sheetrock, metal studding, plumbing, and electrical supplies – had been piled in the middle of the room. Refuse, including empty and stained pizza boxes, had been tossed about. To Jake's right the metal loading door was bolted in three places. Just inside the door was a platform cart with one wheel missing and an open toolbox sitting on its top.

Moving along the side wall to his left, Jake stepped over an empty white paint can, then past a tall aluminum step ladder propped on its side against some empty crates, then over a dried and hardened paint roller attached to an extension pole. In the corner to the left, where the side wall met the rear wall, a piece of plywood was leaning lengthwise on an oil drum, held in place by cinderblocks. A twin mattress on its far side held a sleeping bag and pillow. Next to it stood an old floor lamp and a metal folding chair strewn with clothes.

What was he looking for? Drug paraphernalia? Bomb parts? No time to wonder. Time to search for anything that would shed light on the occupants' plans. He took a few steps farther into the room and, on looking ahead of him and upward, he stopped.

Graffiti covered the far back wall. Slogans and names had been painted in black and/or red: *the end of the world as they know* it; *Eleven Nation Army*; the acronym *ENA*; *The Three Mousketeers* in black and *Plus One* next to it in red; and Marcus's familiar tag, *M. Palmetto*.

A mural filled a large part of the wall to the right. It consisted of giant surreal figures, outlined in various gloss colors, apparently sprayed on. The figures – eleven of them – seemed to be in a state of confusion. In its lower right corner was a tag: *Leandra, Outer Space*. A sample of her work. An impressive one at that. Were drafts of it in her sketchpad? Below it, on a rusty metal table, were dozens of cans of Rust-Oleum spray paint, used and unused, in varying colors.

Jake took pictures.

He angled past the back wall toward the far corner opposite the door he'd entered. On another folding chair rested the black leather photographer's bag from Montreal. The blue vinyl suitcase was on the floor next to it. On a metal shelf fastened to the far side wall were four giftboxes wrapped in shiny green, red, gold, and silver paper, each with a red ribbon. Next to the shelf were makeshift workbenches, cinderblocks supporting two-by-eight planks. On one of them he saw the djembe, now in pieces. On a second workbench were parts of clocks. On a third were several covered joint compound buckets.

Jake took more pictures.

He didn't see the Mickey Mouse doll anywhere. In one of the giftboxes? He was considering opening one but heard the front door – that distinctive moan. Jake probably hadn't been in the warehouse five minutes. In that short time, Marcus must have lost interest in the fire.

Jake rushed for the nearest cover – the damaged platform cart – and crouched behind it.

He could hear footsteps. Jake remained prone on the cold, oil-stained cement floor, straining to hear Marcus's movements over the hum of flickering lights, the noise from the street, and his own pounding heart. Would Jake have to lie here for hours? What if Marcus ordered in more goddamn pizza?

Maybe Jake just should go off on him, like a crazed person. How could Marcus report him if he were planning some illegal act himself?

Jake inched forward on his knees and peered around the end of the cart. From this angle he could see the corner where the bed and toilet were located. There was movement and a light went on in the toilet area.

This was Jake's chance. He rose up. There was no restroom door and Jake could see Marcus's back.

He darted for the front door, stepping around and over the detritus. He expected to hear a shout. None came. He undid the door's deadbolt that Marcus had slid in place on entering, turned the big knob, pulled the door open – slowly to lessen the moan – and stepped outside. He pulled the door shut behind him, feeling it latch.

The firemen were shooting water from a hose through the now all-broken third-story windows. Jake walked quickly toward the crowd of onlookers. A policeman keeping an eye on the gawkers looked at him harshly. Jake now saw that all of Palmetto Street had been barricaded.

"Where you coming from?" the cop asked.

"Down the block. I just woke up."

"Well, stay out of the way."

Jake stepped past him into the crowd, only then looking back. He saw nothing of Marcus. The apparent leader of the "Eleven Nation Army" might eventually notice that the door's deadbolt had been opened, but Jake would be long gone and nothing would be missing.

Jake pushed through the throng and continued toward Irving and then Myrtle. He had to circle around to reach his van on Wilson. He didn't mind since he needed the walk to burn off adrenaline.

At the van he saw that something had been placed under a windshield wiper. A parking ticket? No, it was an invitation to the nearby church at the corner of Palmetto and Knickerbocker.

No need. His prayers had already been answered.

~

Jake sat in the van with the engine running to charge his phone. The adrenaline from his breaking and entering had worn off and he could think clearly again.

Something big was up. Giftboxes. Clock parts. Bomb parts? Bombs inside the boxes? If only he'd been able to check inside one or carry one out of there. Taking one away would likely have given him the evidence he needed, or at least thrown the trio off their game.

It all seemed so chilling. Really, a bombing? What was that Eleven Nation Army bit? An echo of the song "Seven Nation Army" by the White Stripes? Were there eleven participants from eleven different countries? Were they planning some violent act, dreamed up by Boucher against eleven nations? Something at the United Nations? What was that three plus one Mouseketeers bit? A fourth person involved? The third man among them, if not a second woman? With that thought, Jake was reminded of likeable pulp writer Holly Martins, played by Joseph Cotton, tracking the mystery man Harry Lime, the perfect villain as played by Orson Welles, in *The Third Man*, directed by Carol Reed. Martins had had a hard time with the military police.

Should he himself go to the authorities? Go right back to the cops on Palmetto and lead them to the warehouse? He had good reasons not to – besides bias from movies – didn't he? They had the fire on their minds. They would need a search warrant to go inside. Marcus could just send them away, then dump any evidence.

Jake's mind kept looping back around to Leandra. Marcus, he could see as a domestic terrorist, given his zeal and his marginal living conditions. Ned, maybe. But Leandra? That didn't compute, given her apparent dedication to her art.

Pieces of possible dialogue with her again coursed through his brain: "Is what you're doing really worth the risk? ... This isn't your plan ... You might get off with community service ..." and on and on.

What chance did he have in turning her? If he couldn't, how far would she, Marcus, and Ned go in trying to stop him? If he wanted to help her, shouldn't he just stop this bunch before they carried out whatever they intended?

He'd made up his mind. He would talk to New York's Finest in the morning, when Palmetto Street was back to normal.

What now? He was still too revved up to sleep. Time for some food. Despite all the foul-looking pizza boxes he'd seen in

151

the warehouse, he decided to do what was easy. He'd noticed a pizzeria on Myrtle and set out along Wilson toward it.

Inside the pizzeria two men with shaved heads shared a pie between them. They ate in silence and seemed oblivious to anything other than their food. The fluorescent lights were intense. The two servers looked dirty and exhausted.

Jake ordered three slices and two bottles of water – one each for later. The atmosphere was grim, and the pizza, barely passable. However, eating passable pizza in this setting was better than walking by a pizzeria and wanting a slice without money enough to buy it, so often the situation in his recent past.

Jake finished and headed back to the van with his extra water and slice. On nearing it, he saw that a rear right tire was flat. His head now hot, his teeth grinding, he examined it. This was no slow leak around the rim or even a small puncture. There was a slash along the tire's side, a gaping wound in the rubber skin as if cut by a razor knife.

Sicko punks, he thought while opening the back door to get his jack and his temporary donut spare. He wanted to hold onto that hypothesis. Better that one than the idea his marks were out to get him.

Doubting Cops

JAKE WAITED ON A HARD BENCH at the NYPD's 83rd Precinct on Knickerbocker Avenue, near Myrtle. Police came and went. The man in blue behind the front desk glanced over at him from time to time as if to say that he knew Jake was there and that Jake shouldn't bother him and that his time would come. Jake had told him that he suspected some young people would make trouble on Thanksgiving Day. Maybe he should have used the word "terrorism" instead of "trouble" to get immediate attention.

After more than an hour, an officer finally appeared from a back room and sat down next to Jake. Fair-haired and fit, he looked like he was in his forties, although a tired forties, with lines etched on his face. His name was Hamm.

"Okay, spill it. What's this about?" he asked.

Jake gave him the short version, starting with overhearing Leandra's phone conversation in Union Square. He left out his homelessness and his tailing other people before Leandra. To avoid going into all that and offer a more convincing reason to follow her to Brooklyn, he included some of the stuff he'd heard outside the warehouse on Palmetto as part of her phone conversation in the park.

When Jake described Ned as Leandra's probable boyfriend, Hamm asked, "You have a problem with him personally? You have a thing for this Leandra?"

"I don't know any of them personally. Like I said, I overheard some stuff then saw a bag being passed."

"Who passed it?"

"Someone who works for Paul-Louis Boucher, a French sociologist who spoke at the United Nations."

"United Nations? Go on."

Jake told him about spotting Leandra and Ned in the East Village and following them to the park near the United Nations, where they met Boucher and his assistant, then overhearing the conversation in the diner.

"Say again ... who's this Frenchie?"

"His name's Paul-Louis Boucher. He's written books. I decided to follow them to Montreal to hear him talk."

"You went to Montreal because of your suspicions?"

"Yeah, and a woman I met in Montreal said they were up to something on Thanksgiving Day. But she didn't say what."

"What was her name?"

"I never got her real name. But she and her boyfriend were putting these three up."

"Another boyfriend? You get his name?"

"Just Raphael. He's an accomplished chess player. He met this Boucher in Paris."

Hamm looked at him dubiously. "She told you that, too?"

"Right. She said she didn't know what they were planning. I have pictures of all of them plus the stuff they wrote on the warehouse wall in Brooklyn."

"From before Montreal?"

"After."

"You followed them back here?"

"I heard from the woman in Montreal that they'd left there. I assumed they'd returned here."

"How'd you get pictures? You said you didn't know any of them."

"I snuck into the warehouse during the fire on that block yesterday."

"Breaking and entering?"

"Marcus left the door open."

Hamm frowned suspiciously. "Show me the photos."

Jake held up his phone and scrolled through the relevant photos for the officer to see. Hamm snapped shots of some with his phone.

"Come with me," he said.

Hamm led Jake though another door into the inner sanctum. The busy room with desks was drab and dingy but alive with energy, everyone busy, the feral city outside driving the whole scene. A depressed-looking young couple waited at one desk. A man with a big bruise on his face was being interviewed at another. Hamm had Jake sit down at a particularly messy desk and stepped around to the opposite one, where an older, darker-complexioned, and beefier man sat. Beefy but all muscle from obviously working out – and from steroids? They talked briefly, then Hamm went to his desk chair. The other cop walked over and hovered.

"This is Officer Salvo," Hamm said.

"Whattya got for ID?" Salvo asked.

Jake handed over his license and passport. Salvo looked at them and passed them to Hamm, now at his desk. Hamm started writing the information down.

"Tell me everything you told my partner," Salvo told Jake.

"With more facts," Hamm added. "Start with who the hell are you, then tell us why the hell you're following people out of the country and back?"

Their expressions and body language made Jake feel like he was making everything up, telling some fantastic story because he was a raving druggie who liked to follow women around the continent. He told his tale as calmly and clearly as he could, trying to sound like a real private eye with a nose for facts. But they remained skeptical.

154

Doubting cops, as expected, just like in a movie.

~

The warehouse was empty of anything to do with Marcus or the others, even the pizza boxes. The writing on the walls and even the mural had been painted over, and the makeshift bedroom had been deconstructed.

Hamm and Salvo weren't happy. They'd made it clear how much trouble it had been getting the search warrant. The lease was under the name Kyle Construction, they'd learned from the landlord, who told them a super would let them in. They'd arranged for two uniformed cops in a second car and, by that midafternoon, all five of them had made it to Palmetto Street. But the super had been late so they'd even broken down the door – necessitating more paperwork, they'd bitched.

Salvo looked hard at Jake. "Let's see … you're telling us they cleared out sometime since the fire?"

"Doesn't the fact it's so clean indicate they had something to clean up?" Jake offered.

"This is clean?" Hamm said, looking around at the refuse.

"The paint on the wall is fresh. You can smell it. They wanted to hide their writings."

Salvo sighed in frustration. "That proves nothing like you're claiming."

"You're sure none of them were Arab?" Hamm asked.

"Pretty sure. Would that make a difference how you're investigating?"

Salvo's eyes narrowed. "Don't get smart. You know how many reports we have to check out?"

"Maybe Marcus worked for Kyle Construction," Jake suggested.

"Wanna lay odds he doesn't? But we'll look into it. We gotta. If you really think this isn't all just bullshit, find something to convince us besides your eavesdropping and seeing stuff on a wall probably put there by a bunch of self-important activists spouting their cause of the week."

Hamm insisted on walking Jake to his van. Once there, he asked if he could see inside it. Jake agreed. He had nothing to hide.

Didn't he? He'd in fact hidden some information – Leandra's address. He'd planned to provide it but kept putting off doing so. Becoming irritated with the two cops had led him to further procrastinate. If this were really a movie, he would be the valiant P.I., going it alone despite all odds, and Leandra, the misguided and tragic artist, manipulated into carrying out some life-changing act. Was he in reality just a libidinous and greedy heel, bamboozled by a bewitching woman, like in *Double Indemnity*? Walter Neff, played by Fred MacMurray, sure gets manipulated by femme fatale Phyllis Dietrichson, played by Barbara Stanwyck. How many times had his mother told him how that film project had brought together three noir masters? James M. Cain had written the novel; Raymond Chandler and Billy Wilder, the screenplay; and Wilder had directed. Looking back on her behavior, Jake admired her for making him aware of writers and directors and not just actors.

Hamm, on finishing his poking around the van, reminded Jake to be on the lookout for any more relevant information, then departed. Sitting behind the wheel, Jake decided how he would do just that. He would again stake out Leandra's building in the East Village. If he saw evidence of Ned and Marcus staying there, he would contact the cops. He snapped on his seatbelt and pulled away, wondering if he would ever return to Bushwick now that the suspects had evacuated the warehouse.

Sunday driving proved a break from the norm. Sunday parking also kept his parking luck going. He found a spot good till 8:00 the next morning. He walked to his now-regular bench in Tompkins Square Park. The wind was up and the sky was darkening, thunder rumbling in the distance.

The rain came about a half-hour later. Jake crossed Avenue B and chose a doorway to take shelter with a view of Leandra's building. Before long, a middle-aged couple, dressed goth-style and sharing a big black umbrella, descended the stoop and walked past him.

The storm blew on through; the rain tapered to a drizzle, finally stopping altogether. Jake returned to the park. He wiped the wet from the bench with his hand before sitting.

The rain didn't return, and eventually the sun came out. That made the hours leading up to dusk a little more bearable.

Leandra never showed, not even by midnight. Jake was convinced she was staying at Ned's. Marcus, too, probably. He chided himself that, in all his time playing detective, he hadn't discovered where Ned lived. Playing, indeed.

Q.E.D.

JAKE FOUND A METERED parking space not too far from Tompkins Square Park. He had to feed the meter every hour. At least the spot was close enough to the park that it took him only 37 seconds to get there and back if he hustled. On one such excursion, he detoured to get a coffee. On another, he used the park's restroom.

In the early afternoon, he saw the goth couple from the day before exit the tenement building. They walked past him without so much as a glance his way. Soon afterwards, a young African-American woman about Leandra's age appeared through the door and descended the stoop. She headed uptown. She returned after only about twenty minutes with a small bag in her hand.

He should have talked to her. She might know something. She might even be Leandra's roommate. Start ringing doorbells? Not yet. What if Ned responded?

The hours dragged on. At 4:14, the young woman appeared again, this time walking southward.

Jake hurried after her. He dodged traffic, dashing across the avenue. She saw him angling for her and looked away nervously.

"Excuse me," Jake said.

She didn't reply and quickened her pace.

"I'm Jake. I'm a friend of Leandra's. You live in her building?"

The woman slowed her walk. He had her attention.

"You wouldn't be her roommate, would you?" he asked.

"Wouldn't I be? Jake? Jake who? She never mentioned a Jake."

He was walking next to her now. "Jake Jakes."

The woman looked askance at him.

"That's really my name. Blame my mother."

A hint of a smile.

He continued: "I met Leandra recently. She at home?"

"No. Why don't you just call her?"

"Uh … you know … there's Ned, her sort of boyfriend," he adlibbed. "That's how she described him anyway. I don't know if she shares her phone with him. I don't want to cause any trouble. I'd hoped to run into her again. I'm also an artist."

The woman stopped at a red light on 8th Street and turned to face him. She had smart eyes and an equally smart smirk.

"Aren't you the unlucky one," she said. "Leandra's left town … and with her sort of boyfriend."

Jake, surprised, tried to make the next question sound casual. "Oh, where?"

"Why do you want to know? You gonna follow her?"

He faked a laugh. "I can wait. I'll just paint her picture from memory."

She softened a little after that. "I don't know actually. She said Ned planned a surprise vacation for her."

Vacation or escape? "With Marcus and his girlfriend, too?"

She frowned. "Who's Marcus?"

"Leandra mentioned Ned hanging out with him a lot."

"I don't know about that. Ned picked her up and she said he rented the car."

"He probably rented the economy model."

"Sorry, dude, I saw it and you might just be out of luck if you're the competition. A nice big black something or other. Call her in a few weeks after she comes back," the woman offered. "Ned has his own phone. No problem there. To my way of thinking, she needs a break from all the drama with him. Although maybe this trip will fix things. Maybe he'll even propose to her. Maybe she'll even say yes."

Jake gave her a what-me-worry smile and said, "Well, I tried. Thanks, anyway. And your name?"

"Erica."

The light at 8th Street turned green and she started to cross, saying, "I'm off to work. You keep it together, Jake Jakes. Don't fret."

He stayed behind, saying, "Sound advice. Nice to meet you, Erica."

He turned and, fretting, headed back toward the van.

~

Jake sat on the same old bench in the Playground of the Americas, puzzling over all the maybes. Had Marcus figured out someone had been inside the warehouse and followed him to the van and had been the one to slash the tire. Where was he? Maybe he'd fled with Ned and Leandra in the rental. Or maybe he was staying at Ned's while they were away. Maybe they would regroup in the city on Thanksgiving and carry out their plan, then use the car for their getaway. Raven had mentioned a music festival. There were some big concerts in the city on the holiday, Jake had confirmed, but nothing described as a festival. Maybe the United Nations was the target after all. Should he stake out the U.N. on Thanksgiving? Would the NYPD do so, based on what he'd told them?

Undecided on what to do next, he'd returned to the playground in the hope of finding parking good the next day, so at least he wouldn't have to worry about the van. After some searching, he'd found a two-hour meter. As of 7:00 p.m., the spot would be good till the next morning. To do what? While away the hours, spinning his mental wheels?

What else was there to do? He revisited all the events leading to the present. He pictured Leandra – a redhead back then – sitting in Union Square Park. In his mind's eye he saw Boucher's righthand man sit down next to her. He saw Leandra head for the subway with the *I Love New York* bag, the one that held the Mickey Mouse doll.

A realization surfaced in his brain … so manifest that he felt the fool for not arriving at it before. Since being inside the warehouse, he'd been distracted by going to the goddamn cops, as if they could do his thinking for him.

The Mickey Mouse doll. *The Three Mouseketeers Plus One* on the warehouse wall. Boucher's mention of Walt Disney in his lecture. The fact that Disneyland Paris would offend Boucher's sense of French cultural integrity. Thanksgiving, an American-themed holiday.

It all fit.

Retrieving his cellphone from his pocket, Jake searched for Walt Disney World and Epcot Center. Scrolling through the

159

website, he finally located the information he wanted. Epcot had Eleven Pavilions representing eleven different nations.

The Eleven Nation Army wasn't made up of eleven soldiers. And it didn't have the United Nations in its crosshairs. Rather, Jake was certain, the ENA planned a Thanksgiving attack on one or more of Epcot's eleven pavilions. The "end of the world as they know it" was probably a double entendre also referring to Disney World.

Jake had been to the realm of Mickey Mouse. Disney World had been one of the few experiences beyond Shaleville that their mother had provided for him and Caitlyn as kids.

The post-sports-victory advertising slogan echoed in Jake's brain: Yes, he announced to himself, "I'm going to Disney World!"

Peregrinations

ANOTHER ROAD TRIP for peripatetic Jake.

First thing that morning, looking online, he'd found a garage near the Hudson River that repaired or sold tires and limped there on the donut spare. He hadn't expected the slashed tire could be repaired. While waiting for a new one to be mounted on the wheel, he'd sipped the coffee and ate the bagel he'd picked up at the deli on Prince Street before retrieving the van. With a smile on her face Jake had never before seen, the woman at the cash register had complimented him on his new clean look. Aki would be impressed by that, if not by his serendipitous life path.

He drove out of Manhattan under the Hudson River through the Holland Tunnel southward into New Jersey. He picked up Route 95. He pushed on to Pennsylvania, then drove through Delaware and Maryland, bypassing the District of Columbia.

As he drove, part of his brain was on auto-pilot, controlling his now high-speed home; another part meandered through past and future; the remaining part took in sensations of present moments. Gray pavement, white lines. Bumps in the road. Yellow, green, blue road signs. Snaking traffic. Shiny cars, faded cars, SUVs, other vans, pickup trucks, tractor-trailers. Rolling hills. Remnants of blasted rock from the time when the road was built. Broadleaf trees with autumn colors, giving way to dominant evergreens.

Rivers beneath highway bridges. Overpasses, passing like a buzz cut. Gas station signs above the trees. Edges of cities with imagined life. Construction, slowing vehicles into a single lane. Solo birds and flocks of birds. Roadkill. Synthetic roadkill, too – pieces of rubber. The sunny haze of the highway. Warm air striking his face through the open window. Varying winds countering the van's forward motion. State borders, sometimes determined by rivers, but more often arbitrary and not based on geology.

The rest stops, like the borders, were points of reckoning. Should he stop or should he go until the next one? What did he want? Coffee? A sandwich? Chocolate? Gum? A cigar to help pass the time? All of the above? The radio offered some distraction but just limited choices since FM didn't work.

Jake's goal on this first day southward was to cross into North Carolina, about eleven hours total to get there. His timing was good with regard to passing the urban centers and he missed rush hour. He caught some of the afterwork crowd around Richmond, Virginia, although nothing like what he might have encountered near Washington, D.C., when the city gave up its hordes to the suburbs.

Then came some long hours of night driving. Once in North Carolina, Jake kept going until east of Raleigh, exiting onto an Anywhere, USA commercial drive near the highway. He was spent. But it wasn't a comfortable spent; it was raw and edgy. He considered finding a place to pull up and sleep in the van. But he needed to get out of the vehicle. He needed to wash the highway off him. The fancier motels with big bright signs and recognizable names were filled up. Better to find a cheaper place anyway, what with all his recent spending. He was about to give up finding something along this stretch when he saw a "rooms available" sign in front of a small, modest motel. Perfect. He pulled in, stepped out of the van, and headed for the front desk.

A tired-looking elderly South Asian man checked him in and told him where to go. Jake liked that he could park right in front of his room, not a given in the two-story larger motels he'd passed. A green Hyundai was parked in the spot next to his.

As he exited the van and headed to Room 11, carrying a change of clothes and toiletry bag, Jake noticed that the curtain in the neighboring room – number 10, where no car was parked –

had been pulled back slightly and a woman was peeking out. She had a beehive of brown hair. On seeing Jake, she pulled her head backwards and let go the curtain. Moments later, a man appeared from number 12, where the Hyundai was parked. He wore a jacket and tie and held a giftbox. At the sight of Jake, he turned abruptly around, acting like he'd forgotten something, and reentered his room. Jake entered his.

Why the furtive behavior on either side of Jake? Coincidence? Was the ENA crew larger than he'd imagined? Stop it with the paranoia, he told himself. The ENA wasn't everywhere. He waited and peeked through the window as the woman had. The man reappeared and passed Jake's window, giftbox in hand. Jake hurried to his door and cracked it open in time to see the man stepping into number 10.

A rendezvous. What did they think he was – a private eye hired by a suspicious spouse?

Turning on his lights, he headed for the indoor plumbing. After relieving himself, he removed his sneakers and collapsed onto the bed. He would wait on a shower. Turning on the television with the remote, he observed the world as revealed in that little box. He didn't stay awake very long … just a couple of local news stories and weather. Rain in the forecast was the last he heard.

A Smile for a Rain-Soaked Road

JAKE WOKE UP just after 7:00 a.m., with the television still spouting news. He turned it off with the remote and went to the window. The green Hyundai was now in front of number 10, not 12.

After a shower, he gathered up his few things and headed outside. The sky was clouded-over and threatening. He headed for the van to load his two small bags. As he did so, the door to number 10 opened and the man from last night appeared. He didn't do an abrupt about-face this time but gave a friendly nod. Two small suitcases in hand, he casually headed for his vehicle. The woman followed through the same door. Her hair was now pulled back in a ponytail. They were a little older than Jake had figured last evening. Forties probably. But they both still had a youthful bounce. The man opened the trunk and began loading.

"Honey, I'll check out for the both of us," the woman called over to him. "You want coffee for the road?"

"I'll wait," he told her.

One car between them?

It took a moment for it all to make sense in Jake's pre-coffee brain. On donning his detective's hat, he deducted that the lovebirds had arrived together. They weren't cheating on others. The two rooms and the sneaking around and the gift-giving were all part of the love ritual. An extra expense of course but not that much more than a budget dinner and a movie. Case solved.

Jake relocked the van and followed the woman with the bounce down the walkway toward the lobby and the continental breakfast. As he poured his coffee, she even turned and gave him a smile.

A positive start to the morning.

~

The day soon became more challenging. Rain drummed on the van, with wind gusts like cymbal crashes. A radio announcer informed the listening public that November was still hurricane season and that a tropical storm had stalled off coastal North Carolina. As Jake understood it, although inland, this part of Route 95 follows the coastal plain. Storms off the ocean dissipate over land but with less resistance on the eastern flatlands than in the Piedmont country to the west.

To minimize the forces pounding his metal box on wheels, he kept it in the wake of a mid-sized U-Haul. From time to time, a large truck would pass him and the U-Haul ahead, creating an additional wind gust, and he'd clutch the steering wheel even more tightly. It wasn't until after some 150 miles, when he crossed into South Carolina, that the storm let up and he could relax again. In a light drizzle he stopped at a truck stop.

The diner seemed straight out of the fifties. So did his meal – greasy eggs over-easy, grits, sausage, and a muffin. No Egg McMuffin variant here.

South Carolina went by quickly as the sun burned through the clouds, and Jake found himself in Georgia after a couple of hours. The greens of southern yellow pine and the reds of the iron oxides in the soil sparkled with wetness against the blue sky.

The day had turned hot and humid. Without a working air conditioner, he kept both side windows all the way down. At least air on the face and the hum of engine and whine of tires were constant reminders of the high-speed driving task at hand. Even so, he felt more and more entranced as the day wore on. Was there a special brain wave caused by driving?

Jake burned up lots of coffee as well as gas. His eyelids were heavy and he had to blink hard to stay alert. He kept the radio on but, in order to break the sameness, he let auto-search do its thing. Once in a while, if he happened to like a song, he would punch in that station. When it ended, he would reactivate the search.

As darkness fell, he pulled into a rest stop and chose an isolated place to park. He left the window cracked open just slightly in the cooling nighttime air. Cicadas serenaded him to sleep.

Death on the Highway

JAKE WAS BEYOND ROAD-WEARY on finally making it to Florida the next day. But he knew he still had many hours to go before reaching the Orlando area. He thought back to the excitement his sister and he had felt as kids, crossing into the state when his mother had driven them south, only to be overwhelmed with anticipation the rest of the way to Disney World. He resolved to settle in and experience the remaining drive as a period of decompression.

Any self-induced calm didn't last long because of a sudden slowdown. Progress became no longer about miles, rather about advancing yards and even inches. The heat and humidity were oppressive. When the flow stopped altogether, some people got out of their cars to stretch, including a woman and two kids from an SUV stuck in the passing lane next to him.

"Mom, how long is this gonna last?" the little boy asked.

"How would she know?" a girl, older, replied. "It's a traffic jam, stupid."

164

It could have been Jake and his sister on their trip eons ago but with roles reversed. He'd been the older one, eight at the time of their trip to Florida, and Caitlyn, four.

The woman glanced over at Jake, and he was reminded of his homeless self, a visual threat to women and kids on city streets.

"Okay," the mother told her kids. "That's enough. Get in. We might move soon."

"Awww …" the boy objected.

"Get in!" the dad yelled from the driver's seat. "Watch another damn show!"

Jake caught a glimpse of a screen mounted above the SUV's back seat – a television with a cartoon flickering across it. It seemed wrong somehow, having a TV set inside a vehicle. Perhaps better that than more yelling at the kids as his mother had so often had to do.

After almost an hour and a half of inching forward, Jake saw flashing lights ahead. There had been an accident. An overturned truck with a flattened cab lay close to smashed vehicles, one a pickup completely burned out and still smoking slightly, like a crushed cigar butt. Cops waved gawking drivers past the confusing array of wreckage, police cars, and fire trucks. Any ambulances that had been at this scene had already departed. Rubbernecking himself, Jake saw some blood on the closed lane. Those people still standing around the accident scene seemed shaken. Death had apparently come to this highway.

The Sunshine State now felt like the Mortuary State, and Jake couldn't help but think about the hardware in the Brooklyn warehouse and the Mickey Mouse dolls and what a deadly combination they might be in a theme park filled with families.

Did Marcus, Ned, and Leandra really have it in them to cause smoldering destruction similar to what he'd just witnessed on a highway? If so, could Jake stop them?

Big questions.

PART VI: PARALLEL DIMENSION

"Consciousness peeled all the way back to its outermost limits like
the tattered paper opening up on some circus-hoop that has just been
jumped through."
– Cornell Woolrich, *Too Nice a Day to Die*

Cartography

WHAT IS IT ABOUT A MAP? So loaded and filled with possibilities. The eyes move over it, the mind travels within it. Jake would have preferred a paper map spread out over a table, his fingers touching it. Or better yet, a parchment map. A digital screen is as sterile a medium as it gets. But it showed a map and Jake's imagination was projecting into it and beyond it to what might be. He had the thought the Disney experience might not get any better than this untainted version without crowds, relentless commercialism, and, from his perspective anyway, potential violence.

After sleeping just south of Orlando – in his van parked in a Best Western parking lot off Route 4 – Jake had driven a few more miles southwest and pulled into a Starbucks. Now, drinking coffee and eating a Danish, he was brushing up on his phone about all things Walt Disney World. The names excited him. Epcot Center, the focus of his visit, comprises World Showcase, where the eleven Nations are located, and what was once Future World has evolved into three separate "lands" – World Discovery, World Celebration, and World Nature. It occurred to Jake in his heightened state of nostalgia mixed with concern that what seemed timeless to him as a preadolescent – the realm of Disney – is transient and ever-evolving.

Jake learned or relearned that the other three theme parks are Magic Kingdom, Disney's Hollywood Studios, and Animal Kingdom. Other smaller entities include the Blizzard Beach Water Park, the Typhoon Lagoon Water Park, the Disney Springs

166

shopping and dining areas, the Wide World of Sports Complex, and more than twenty resorts and six golf courses.

All these enterprises take up 25,000 acres, making Disney World nearly twice the size of Manhattan and the largest and most visited recreational resort in the world. Regardless, calling it a "world" was hubris, Jake believed. "Land," as in Disneyland, fit better. In any case, it sure took a lot of studying to get his mind around the sprawling Disney World since he was about to travel to a unique place with kingdoms, centers, and parks. And eleven "nations."

Intrepid explorer or not, Jake had to deal with the mundane, like figuring out what kind of ticket he would purchase. With almost a week until Thanksgiving, he would buy a seven-day ticket. Although he would be focusing on Epcot, he wanted easy access to all the theme parks just in case. By taking advantage of the Park-Hopper add-on to the normal seven-day pass, he could go to any of the four parks on any day rather than be limited to one a day, as was the case during the pandemic.

Through it all he would have to pay a daily parking fee. This expedition was going to be expensive. What would Aki say? Blowing through her money like this? First a visit to another country – Canada – now to another "world"? At least Jake didn't need to purchase camping gear. Disney World empties at night and he would be returning regularly to his home-on-wheels.

He did an online search on how to best pay for all the Disney costs – cash or credit – and learned that he could download the Walt Disney World app on his phone and purchase his ticket virtually. He could also order food through it. And he read that Disney theme parks had been phasing in a virtual queue tab for rides even before the pandemic. Now it was a standard thing. He downloaded the app and, for the moment anyway, felt emotionally sanitized.

Disney Theory

JAKE AGAIN SLEPT in a motel parking lot. No one hassled him and he woke up rested. He used the motel lobby restroom to clean up, now being an old hand at this sort of thing. He then bought gas and breakfast at one of the ubiquitous gas stations/convenience stores dotting the landscape.

Driving south again on Route 4. He felt anxious, as if he were close to a phantasmagorical place he might miss if he blinked too long, then end up forever lost in Florida swamps.

Highly unlikely. No way to miss the growing number of signs showing him the way to his destination across the overdeveloped yet sterile flatlands of central Florida. Exit 67, there it was, leading him west by northwest along Epcot Center Drive.

He soon passed under the Walt Disney welcome arch. He'd arrived. Into the heart of supposed light, but perhaps into darkness, ENA style. The road signs now had a purple background, indicating he was in a place apart. Their white lettering showed him the way to the Epcot parking area. Come one, come all.

Come openly like this? Would they recognize him? Had he in fact prompted the ENA trio's (or quartet's?) sudden departure? There was that slashed tire. Coincidence? If they were present and spotted him, how far would they go to deal with him? He would stay ever alert. In any case, he was on his own for now, no cops in tow. This time, he wouldn't approach the authorities until he had undeniable evidence.

Onward into Epcot – originally referred to as E.P.C.O.T. for Experimental Prototype Community of Tomorrow, then as Epcot Center. It had been Walt Disney's pet project over all others in WDW, the increasingly used acronym for Walt Disney World. He'd conceptualized it as a working city and demonstration community, using state-of-the-art materials and technologies and fostering new ideas in urban planning. He'd died in 1966 and, by the time Epcot had opened in 1982 under the guidance of corporate Disney, the team of Imagineers (from the company name Walt Disney Imagineering, or WDI) had shaped it into a theme park with rides, albeit mostly educational ones. Education, science, and the future had become the dominant themes at Epcot. Walt Disney, the Creator, was very likely appeased enough not to rain down fire and destruction on Epcot but rather look after it. Perhaps Jake was Walt's earthly agent, doing his bidding, from the first encounter with Leandra in Union Square Park to the present.

As he approached his target, Jake could see Spaceship Earth ahead on Epcot's northern end, the immense eighteen-story geodesic dome and icon of this particular theme park. It looked like an enormous golf ball, showing the way to a golf course for giants. Where was the beanstalk? Wait ... the Jack of the popular European fairytale isn't a Disney character. Or is he? The Imagineers surely had adopted him as theirs at some point ever since Disney Inc. began producing animated films in the 1920s.

Jake bet his mother would know. She loved the early Disney animated films from her pre-noir phase. Her favorites were *Bambi*, *Pinocchio, Dumbo, Cinderella, Peter Pan,* and especially *Fantasia,* and she'd made sure her kids appreciated them as well, exclaiming often about the fluidity of their animation ... "unlike the modern shit," as she'd put it. It was her nostalgia for those movies that motivated her to undertake the grand family expedition.

He parked the van and stepped out onto the hallowed ground. A caterpillar-like tram hummed by, carrying people to Epcot's entrance. He could have flagged it down but decided to hike the rest of the way. He made a mental note of where he'd parked since the sea of cars was quickly becoming an ocean. His beat-up van did stand out though. He looked extra hard at any black cars, remembering Erica's description of the vehicle Ned had rented. One did go by, seeking out parking, although without recognizable faces inside it.

The temperature seemed to climb with every blink. At least the semitropical moisture in the air felt healthy, offering hydration by osmosis. Being a weather-minded Northeasterner, Jake was overdressed in his sweatshirt. But he had his small backpack in which to carry the garment on shedding it. He also carried a pen and notebook.

After passing through a series of metal gates displaying Epcot themes, he had to stand in line at the entrance. Lines at Disney World were an indelible memory from his childhood. This one had painted markers for social distancing. Once it was his turn, the process was streamlined. A facial recognition scanner proved he was who he said he was, and his phone proved he had pre-paid. He also had to enter a walk-in booth that looked like a metal detector but served as a temperature checkpoint.

The first staffer he encountered was so over-the-top cheerful that his mood was infectious, even through the plexiglass. Jake couldn't help but smile. That was his Happy experience. Grumpy came next; the stern security guard who checked his backpack lacked even the hint of a smile. The two employees weren't dressed as two of the seven dwarfs, but they might as well have been. Snow White and her dwarfs was another European fairytale appropriated by Disney, and for many the Disney film was the only frame of reference. Jake's mother, to her credit, had mentioned the Brothers Grimm to her kids. Come to think of it, Jake mused, whether amiable or stern, whether costumed or not, all onsite Disney employees were reportedly referred to as "cast members."

Jake envisioned the giftboxes he'd seen in the Brooklyn warehouse. The boxes would be opened like any bags. Why carry wrapped presents into a theme park?

Leandra, Ned, and Marcus … were they fantasy characters as well? Had Jake imagined them in the torpor of Big Apple homelessness? Had he really traveled all the way to this otherworldly place because of their behavior on the streets of New York City and Montreal?

He was allowed to enter. A triumph, he couldn't help but feel.

A gift shop soon presented itself and Jake entered it, as had many others, the feeding frenzy well underway. Disney products surrounded the shoppers: stuffed toys, hats, T-shirts, sweatshirts, sandals, backpacks, towels, straws, postcards, pens, books, CDs, DVDs and more. Natalie Beaubien had used the phrase "the peddlers of kitsch" to translate one of Boucher's takes on Disney.

Near the counter Jake found a detailed map, easier to use and more tactile-pleasing than the ones he'd studied online the day before, and he waited in his second Disney line to purchase it. He also grabbed up a freebie brochure that explained the WDW transit system.

The spirit of Walt and his earthly disciples must have been happy with Jake since he was already spending money on top of the hefty admission cost. Focus on the mission, he told himself; worry about the rest of his life later. The map rounded out his gear. He was ready to take on this new world.

As he walked through the first half of Epcot – past the various attractions relating to the land, the seas, energy, space, and imagination – and as the sun warmed him to a reptilian stupor, he began to feel as if he'd crossed over to an existence apart, where the laws of nature as he knew them no longer applied. Not "World." Rather, some kind of "Parallel Universe" or "Dimension." That worked, alliteration and all … Disney Dimension.

Were the other visitors actually parallel beings wearing the bodies of humans? Jake looked deep into their faces to try to discern the answer. But that made him feel even more removed, as if he were projecting astrally.

"Look out!"

"Watch where you're going!"

"Bitch!"

Two mothers with strollers and children passengers had collided, like two planetary bodies.

One of the kids, a little boy, started crying. The child in the opposite stroller, a girl, stared bug-eyed at the boy. The boy's mother, a wiry brunette, pointed her finger in accusation.

"You hurt him!"

The little girl let forth a squeal in delight. The little boy, responding to the girl, now laughed.

"He's laughing … must be okay," the girl's mother, a heavyset blond, retorted. She wore a black Disney T-shirt with white lettering announcing, *The 21st Century Began October 1982.*

"What do you think this is?" the brunette challenged, while pushing her boy away. "A stroller derby?"

A pun in the midst of the confrontation. Not a bad one at that.

Jake had his answer: These were unquestionably human beings surrounding him.

He headed for the Showcase Plaza, the meeting point of the first three Epcot lands and World Showcase. Glancing at the map, Jake saw Epcot as a figure 8, with World Discovery, World Celebration, and World Nature comprising the northern circle, and World Showcase, the southern one. In addition to being a transition point between the two defined parts of Epcot, the Showcase Plaza serves as a refreshment port, where one can spend the coin of the realm on McDonald's fries, McNuggets, and McFlurries. Boucher's lecture had been called "Beyond Big Mac and Mickey Mouse."

Nearby, talking and gesturing to a group of kids, their parents behind them, stood Mickey Mouse himself, in this instance more than five-feet tall. The big rodent was pointing across the lagoon, probably telling the boys and girls about all the fun over thataway. Had Boucher visited a similar spot at Disneyland Paris where Mac and Mick intersected?

Jake walked to the edge of the Plaza and looked over and around the lagoon at the three small islands and the Friendship Boats coming and going to a series of T-shaped landing docks, two servicing the Plaza itself east and west of him. A tranquil and inviting scene.

Too tranquil and inviting, not consistent with his former sense of self at large on the Big Apple's mean streets. Hold on, Jake's brain prompted. Travis McGee works out of a Florida houseboat on blue water under sunny skies, doesn't he? Los Angeles-based Philip Marlowe and Lew Archer traverse more sunny streets than rain-slicked ones. Not Sam Spade in San Francisco, however, who experiences a lot of damp fog in his bones.

The fantasy of this place was contagious, Jake mused. What else was? With that unsettling additional thought, he detoured to a hand sanitizer station before crossing over into the southern half of Epcot, with its ring of eleven nations. He moved counterclockwise along the World Showcase Promenade, where "everyone is a world traveler." He passed the first of the eleven pavilions, this one representing Canada – with Native totem poles towering above it. Would there be a Quebec corner somewhere here with francophones? If Raven could keep her sticky fingers to herself, she could work a concession.

He now walked past the United Kingdom and its Hampton Court Palace. Like a World's Fair, this oval of nations is, he thought. Done with panache by Imagineers around some wonderful themes. Yet ruled by one corporate authority. Borderless, slumless, no risk travel.

No risk? The ENA seemed to have something to say about that.

Jake crossed the bridge spanning the canal between the United Kingdom and France pavilions. Known as the International Gateway, he saw on the map, the canal serves as a second entrance to Epcot, with access from five resorts on the adjoining smaller Crescent Lake to the west by footpath or by Friendship Boat.

He reached France. Many adults seemed genuinely engaged, as if they were standing beneath the real Eiffel Tower in Paris. He wondered what Boucher would make of that. Doubtful he would visit unless he had an onsite role in the mission. More likely a typical general, stationed far away at no risk to himself.

Jake walked on and passed other wonders: Morocco's minaret, Japan's pagoda, the American Adventure's colonial mansion, Italy's belltower, Germany's St. George's statue, China's ceremonial gate, Norway's stave church, and Mexico's Mayan pyramid. Quite the array of sample architecture and cultures – "The historical simulacra of Walt Disney," Natalie Beaubien had translated Boucher's description.

Was all this confusing and even unsettling to the kids in attendance? Any confused children would no doubt quickly come upon something awe-inspiring to them, like a Chinese dragon or French acrobats or the Kidcot Fun Stops with various hands-on activities, or characters milling about. Jake saw Aladdin in front of Morocco, Snow White across from Germany, and Donald Duck near Mexico. These Tadilsweny characters – the fictional anagram of the name Walt Disney from the Astérix series – could be interpreted as a threat to the little Gaul, the French symbol of resistance against foreign invasion.

Jake knew from the internet that other attractions at World Showcase had been designed to please kids, such as dioramas with audio-animatronics, Circle-Vision films, and even some rides, including Norway's Maelstrom Viking ship ride through a village and mythical forest. At most attractions one would come upon stores, offering lots of kid stuff. There also had been plans for other rides and even other pavilions that had fallen through due to lack of funding from nations themselves or other investors. It might have resulted in a Two Dozen Nation Army, or even more.

The pleasure of kids aside, the idea that some Americans would be satisfied with what was here and never go abroad had to upset Boucher. Jake also had some Astérix in him, emotionally resisting the Toon Empire. He saw all these sights from a past self, caught up in the myths of childhood, but also through the eyes of Boucher and his minions – ever globally expanding commercialism. Walt Disney's vision of fantasy characters and technological progress commingled with that of his accountants of the holy dollar. Mickey Mouse and his cartoon pals might be heroes but they are also brands.

Jake found himself detouring to Goofy's side. The big dog stopped to greet him, flopping his ears in a big nod.

What now? Where to take this? Jake thought back to an issue little sister Caitlyn had once broached to him and his mom, and he went with it.

"I'm really stumped," he said. "Maybe you, a celebrity dog, can explain."

"Uh, maybe," the man inside the costume replied in a fairly convincing Goofy-like voice.

"My sister and I were wondering … there's Tigger, a tiger, in *Winnie the Pooh*. Disney has its version of that story, right? And there's the Lion King. Admit it though, there's no famous house cat, is there? Where's the Disney Tom to the Hanna-Barbera mouse Jerry? Who gets to chase Mickey and Minnie? There's the Aristocats, but how many folks can cite one by name? Oh yeah, there's Figaro, the naughty cat in *Pinocchio*, and Lucifer, the wicked cat in *Cinderella*, but they are just supporting characters. My sister sure likes Figaro and even Lucifer a lot but wonders why they never got their own movies. I don't even see them walking around here. What Disney cat has the fame of Mickey Mouse and Minnie Mouse or of Mickey's dog companion Pluto or, pray tell, of famous you? Where's a Disney cat with, say, the stature of a Garfield?"

"That's a very good question," Goofy replied a little tentatively.

Jake gave Goofy a friendly pat on the back and moved on, wondering what the hell he was trying to accomplish with his fantasy character inquisition. Impress the Leandra of his own imaginings, who in reality probably wouldn't give a dog's ass about him?

~

After completing the 1.3 mile walk around the lagoon, Jake headed back in the other direction, clockwise around the loop, lingering somewhat longer at each pavilion, getting a better sense of the layout of each and where explosive devices might be hidden. The possibilities for the latter were mind-boggling, given the motley architecture. An altered Mickey Mouse doll could even be hidden in plain sight.

Jake had already done a lot of walking today in this second largest of the WDW theme parks. He needed refreshment and opted for fish and chips and a beer at the Rose & Crown Pub in the United Kingdom – that is, he corrected himself, at the imitation UK pavilion.

Faux UK or not, it was pretty damn convincing, from the atmosphere to the wait staff, as if he were really on the British Isles. The waitress in her apron costume had a touch of cockney to her British accent and a touch of naughtiness beneath.

Where was he anyway? Easy to slip into illusion on these streets. Exhaustion and one pint of ale facilitated the mental crossing over. Make that two.

After the second pint, Jake, although energized, walked slowly and carefully, keeping an eye out, searching for the three ENA faces and for Mickey Mouse dolls. At least almost no litter at all soiled the Disney Dimension, making it easier to notice anything out of place.

He had an ongoing inner debate about presenting his suspicions to security that something dire might be looming, as he'd done with New York cops. He wasn't even sure the three he'd been tracking were here. Thanksgiving, the scheduled date for Boucher's project as revealed by Raven, was five days away. Would the sci-fi-looking security forces in black and blue – and in street clothes as well – believe Jake and round up every twenty-something with a Mickey Mouse doll on his advisement, or would they consider him the lunatic? He had those photos in his phone. But they proved nothing, he'd learned on dealing with the NYPD. He would bide his time, he resolved yet again, hoping for more information before reporting anything else.

Dusk had come and along with it an easy coolness. Jake stood on the International Gateway bridge between the UK and France and watched darkness fall the rest of the way as artificial light took over, the buildings outlined in different colors. People were gathering, gazing out over the lagoon. There was a buzz of expectancy for the grand finale to the Epcot day – the show over the water known as HarmonioUS.

Jake had read that this was a new production, introduced since the pandemic. It featured lights, lasers, pyrotechnics, and fountains – staged from massive moving barges – celebrating the global influence of Disney music, with international participation. Even though the show had been years in the planning, the reportedly uplifting extravaganza was now associated with the pandemic recovery.

While waiting, Jake could hear the man next to him at the railing saying: "I've seen it three times. It's spectacular, that's for sure. And the music's good. But I still like IllumiNations better with its three parts ... Chaos, Order, and Meaning."

Jake glanced over. The man was speaking to a woman to his right. She nodded in response but kept her eyes on the lagoon. They both looked scrubbed and groomed. On a date? Jake projected that at the moment she resented his messing with her expectations. She said something back but Jake couldn't hear her.

That word again coincidentally . . . "chaos." Jake envisioned Raphael's angry face thrust at him on a Montreal street.

A voice sounded out over speakers situated around the oval. The show was announced. Some people applauded that it was finally starting.

It erupted. Spectacular indeed. Special effects galore. The multinational theme – songs performed in multiple languages – gave it meaning beyond the visual experience. Jake knew a lot of the songs, especially those from his adolescence, associated with the movies his mother had chosen for him, as well as those that had become favorite pop hits of pre-teen Caitlyn.

So much was going on and with such a dramatic ebb and flow that Jake went with it all for a spell, forgetting momentarily the why of this particular Disney trip. But the intensity of the show brought him back to the concept of chaos, and, with that thought, he returned his attention to those around him. Most people were still focused on the lagoon and the sky above. Many vocalized their excitement. Some parkgoers, however, paid only half-attention, progressing along the promenade, even during the climax that mixed wonder with sentimentality.

And then it was over, and more applause sounded out. Epcot would soon be closing. It was time to go.

Jake moved with the flow of people crossing from World Showcase into Future World and toward the parking lot. He broke free to stop at a stand for another beer. Sipping, he kept questioning his presence in this strange place, but even as he did so he kept an eye out for the faces of the ENA trio. Wouldn't it be nice if they didn't show and he could relax on a Disney vacation, a repeat visitor from upstate who had an art sponsor and who had again made it back here to this dimension against all odds?

Jake was three beers along with that thought. He remembered when he needed a twelve-pack to feel anything. He vowed after succumbing to a third beer that he wouldn't drink any more than one or two beers at a time. Certainly not while on the job, hired by the fates. After purchasing a big and pricey bottle of water to sober up, he proceeded toward the Epcot exit, scrutinizing faces on the way. Reflected light shimmered on the silver-colored tiles of Spaceship Earth.

In the Ridley Scott movie *Blade Runner*, set in a futuristic but ever-so-noir L.A., the character Roy Batty, a replicant creepily played by Rutger Hauer, expresses to the cynical ex-cop Rick Deckard, played by Harrison Ford, "I've seen things you people wouldn't believe … Attack ships on fire off the shoulder of Orion … I watched C-beams glitter in the dark near the Tannhäuser Gate … All those moments will be lost in time, like tears in rain … Time to die."

Jake had seen flashing pyrotechnics and glittering lights over the World Showcase Lagoon, his own moments lost in time. But it wasn't time to die, just to sleep.

After using a restroom, he crossed through the park's gates and managed to locate his van. What a welcome sight. With all the walking necessary at Epcot, the park's name is reputed – or so it was claimed online – to be an acronym for "Every Person Comes Out Tired." Another fabricated acronym was "Every Pocketbook Comes Out Trashed."

Once in his van headquarters, Jake sat and watched cars filing past. He wanted to stay where he was and fade into sleep, but this would certainly be one of the best patrolled parking lots in the world of entertainment. After about ten minutes, he fired up the van's engine and followed the flow of traffic to regions beyond.

He pulled the van to the back end of a motel parking lot – one situated not too far from central Lake Buena Vista – and established a temporary camp on the outer perimeter of the Disney Dimension under siege.

The Big Lady

JAKE WOKE UP EARLY with a minor hangover and major guilt for having one at all. To allay the headache and the guilt, he would take refuge in action. Map in hand, he would reconnoiter other parts of WDW until darkness surrounded Epcot. He wanted to get the lay of the entire Disney Dimension. He would leave the van at the Epcot parking area and use the transportation system. From the transportation brochure he knew that the monorail offers service between Epcot and the Magic Kingdom, as well as to some of the resorts; other destinations can be reached by bus or boat.

Jake approached Epcot from the same direction as the day before, parked the van near his prior spot, then set out for his planned first transportation link. It was another halcyon Florida day – the type of day that makes Florida such a likely place for huge theme parks.

"Welcome aboard the Walt Disney World Express Monorail ... your highway in the sky to the Magic Kingdom."

The sleek monorail – this one with six cars and a yellow stripe on the white background – once viewed as a futuristic vehicle, was showing its age, even though the original 1971 trains, the Mark IV models, Jake had read, had been replaced by Mark VIs in 1990-91. Despite being more than two decades old, the train offered a smooth, steady, and relatively quiet ride – except for the recorded announcements – as it hugged its single fat track mounted on tall white pillars.

Through the window Jake watched Disney acreage glide by – a beautifully groomed landscape, like a postcard image with no need for Photoshop. He checked his map and saw that the buildings in the current vista are resorts. Beyond them, the fairways and greens of well-groomed golf courses sparkle.

Based on the map, Jake thought of WDW as a Big Lady with a pear shape. The Magic Kingdom at the northern end made up the head. Two connecting lakes represented the shoulders, with the human-made Seven Seas Lagoon siting to the west, and Bay Lake, to the east, the latter a natural formation. The Transportation and Ticket Center, a hub for comings and goings – or TTC to the Disney Worldly-wise – he saw as the chest between the two

178

bodies of water. The Big Lady's waist consisted predominantly of the resorts and golf courses over which Jake presently coursed. Animal Kingdom to the west and Disney Springs to the east formed the Big Lady's hips. Hollywood Studios and Epcot, to the west and east, made up the inner thighs. Two water parks gave shape to the outer thighs. Jake considered the Wide World of Sports Complex, hosting a variety of sporting events, as the Big Lady's butt. The grande dame he'd created in his mind's eye certainly had a lot of exotic physicality and personality.

A train, heading in the opposite direction, swooshed by on a parallel track to the left. Most of Jake's fellow passengers were parents with little kids. Two young men and a woman, talking and laughing loudly, were an exception. In imagining Leandra, Ned, and Marcus in this setting, Jake was certain they would act more composed than this bunch, their nerves on high alert. And one elderly man rode solo. Reliving his past or fulfilling a lifetime dream? Or perhaps he was a regular who lived out his retirement in the Disney Dimension.

The monorail slithered into the TTC. Jake could have caught another train the rest of the way to the entrance of the Magic Kingdom but decided to take the ferryboat across the Seven Seas Lagoon. He wandered about the TTC for a while to get a sense of bus arrivals and departures throughout WDW, keeping an eye out for the ENA trio, who might have a reason to come to this hub. He then made his way to the dock and the double-deck ferryboat, smaller yet similar in boxed shape to the ferry between Manhattan and Staten Island.

As the boat pushed through the calm water toward Magic Kingdom – the most famous theme park in the world and the quintessential Disney experience for the young – Jake looked at the eager faces of the kids near him on the deck. He thought of his mother and the big deal she'd made about taking him and Caitlyn here after she'd gotten a tax return from a cleaning service job. It had been one of the best family times for him and his sister since they'd had their mother's full attention without any of her questionable boyfriends as competition. And since they'd been so distracted by the Disney alchemy, he and Caitlyn had suspended bickering. A trip to a place out of the normal for them had helped them act normally.

Having disembarked from the boat, on solid ground again, Jake moved with the throng to the Magic Kingdom entrance. It sure felt as if, being a solo adult, he garnered extra attention from the gatekeepers. In any case, he had his "letters of transit" in order – a mental nod to his mother and the fictional phrase she'd adopted from the film *Casablanca* – and he was allowed passage. To reach the Magic Kingdom's inner sanctum, he had to pass through a tunnel, adding to the drama of his arrival to the heart of WDW. Jake suddenly felt like a pilgrim returning to Mecca after many moons.

While doing so, he heard a train whistle summoning him. It was the Walt Disney World Railroad. At the center of the tunnel, a stairway leads to the Main Street Railway Station. A good way to start his reconnaissance, traveling up to twelve miles per hour around the kingdom's mile-and-a-half perimeter for about twenty minutes, he gleaned from the displays.

A brightly-colored steam engine, green with red wheels, about half-scale – this one dubbed Roy O. Disney after Walt's big brother and business partner – stood waiting, open-sided cars behind it. Walt Disney had been a railroad buff, Jake had read, and had built a half-mile-long model train in his Los Angeles backyard. The steam trains of Disneyland – and subsequently of Disney World – had been at the top of the Creator's desired list of attractions.

"Now boarding for a scenic trip around the Magic Kingdom. All aboard!"

Jake stepped into the last car and chose a wooden bench to the right in order to have a good view of the park on the clockwise ride. Within minutes, the train was in motion. He caught glimpses through the trees of the structures within the circle of track. The recorded narration, with music appropriate to the various locations, along with announcements by an enthusiastic conductor, kept him informed of where he was.

At one point, Jake reached out (a no-no!) and grabbed a leaf from a tree. Yes, it was real. Not everything here was illusion.

Jake had vivid memories from his childhood visit. In Adventureland he'd visited Swiss Family Treehouse and Pirates of the Caribbean, the latter recently refurbished, he'd read; in Frontierland he'd taken the roller coaster known as Big Thunder

Mountain Railroad and had stepped onto Tom Sawyer Island; in Liberty Square he'd walked through the Haunted Mansion; in Fantasyland he'd experienced Peter Pan's Flight; in Mickey's Toontown Fair he'd entered Mickey's Country House; and in Tomorrowland he'd taken the ride up and down Space Mountain, an even scarier roller coaster than Big Thunder.

He had to suppress the urge to revisit every one of these attractions. How to rationalize such recreation? That maybe Leandra had the same childhood memories as he did and would want to take some rides, or perhaps commit some nefarious deed at Mickey's Toontown Fair in honor of Mickey's nemesis, the Gallic freedom fighter Astérix?

After completing the train ride, Jake left the railway station and followed Main Street, U.S.A., in the direction of Cinderella's Castle, its array of towers the representative image of the Magic Kingdom. He certainly remembered this walk from years ago, his introduction to WDW: shops tempt kids with Disney products; Disney characters roam the street.

Jake saw Goofy approaching. He seemed the same size as the big costumed dog wandering Epcot the day before. The same man inside? He was relieved when Goofy paid no attention to him.

As he pounded the pavement along Main Street, feeling the effects of cloying humidity, Jake thought about what might lie below. Like New York City and Montreal, the Magic Kingdom has extensive underground activity. Legend has it that Walt Disney on a tour of Disneyland saw a cowboy from Frontierland strolling in Tomorrowland, mixing metaphors as it were. As a result, in order that cast members could move about unseen, he ordered that the Magic Kingdom be built fourteen feet above the original ground, making room for a network of tunnels below. These utilidors, as they became known, like the surface walkways, were laid out as the spokes of a wheel – color-coded tunnels leading to the end of Main Street in the distance. An entrance located behind Fantasyland gives cast members access to them, as do various unmarked doors, some of them located inside attractions, shops, and restaurants. Some cast members thus become mole people for part of their workday – less so than before because changes to park policies allow them to walk aboveground in costume under certain circumstances. Jake wondered if Goofy had used the utilidors today. He also wondered what Big Apple mole person Manic Mary would make of them.

Jake reached the end of Main Street, the center of the Magic Kingdom located in the shadow of Cinderella's Castle. A bronze statue known as "Partners" stands there – Walt Disney hand in hand with Mickey Mouse, both of them smiling, and Walt pointing down Main Street. It might also have been dubbed the "Sacred Duo," with Walt representing the Pope, and Mickey, a High Priest. WDW, Vatican-like. Or perhaps Mickey as the Holy Spirit since his presence permeates everything. Grace had taken a picture of her kids standing in front of this statue. Did he remember that actual event, or did he remember viewing the photo later in life? Did the photo still exist? Back then, Jake had witnessed a show from near this location on the stage in front of the castle. What had that been? A revival meeting?

He felt overwhelmed. Mickey's Toontown, this statue, the World Showcase pavilions – all loaded symbols to the Bouchers of the world and their soldiers. Any of them – or any other part of Disney World for that matter – could be targets for militancy. How could he possibly keep watch over all of WDW?

~

Jake returned by monorail to the TTC and from there caught a bus to Animal Kingdom. The white bus – with the big red lettering proclaiming *Disney* in the famous Disney script – cut through the waist of the Big Lady. He was already familiar with these vistas from his earlier monorail ride.

Of the four theme parks, Jake had read, Animal Kingdom is the newest, opening in 1998, and the largest, five-hundred acres. After the failure of Epcot to engage kids fully, Disney planners designed Animal Kingdom as "edutainment" – animal conservation as the central theme but presented in a fun way. The original press on this park had used the phrase "nahtazu," pronounced "not a zoo." Yet with its many flesh-and-bone animals, Animal Kingdom is indeed a zoo with embellishments, among them exhibitions featuring extinct creatures, such as dinosaurs, and mythological ones, such as dragons and yeti. In the center of them all, the walk-through Oasis animal display leads to Discovery Island on the Discovery

River. The Tree of Life, the Animal Kingdom's symbol, visible from afar like Epcot's Spaceship Earth and Magic Kingdom's Cinderella's Castle, rises up from Discovery Island.

Jake had also read that, during Animal Kingdom's planning stages, some animal rights groups had opposed the idea of WDW using captive fauna for their commercial ends. The firework displays from the relatively near Epcot that might upset the animals in their holding compounds had been a major concern. Some animals had even died early on, creating more controversy. But Animal Kingdom had passed all inspections by the United States Department of Agriculture.

Leandra, the vegan, as a PETA advocate? That made sense. Although Jake had no evidence to support the idea of a threat against this particular park, it felt good to sort out his psycho-grid for WDW as he'd done for Montreal.

Had ENA members studied up on the Walt Disney Company? Did they read, as Jake had, that it claimed to be countering threats to ecosystems and biodiversity and supported specific wildlife causes through grants as well as education while doing its part to reduce its various parks' emissions and plastic waste? Weren't there better targets than Disney for outrage?

Upon entering Animal Kingdom, Jake strolled through the Oasis under a canopy of tropical vegetation, passing a waterfall and a pond with flamingoes. From various viewing areas he saw other exotic birds, as well as an anteater, a boar, a sloth, a wallaby, and a tree kangaroo. Lions and tigers roamed the nearby African savannah.

On Discovery Island Jake ate an overpriced "Safari Barbecue" of chicken wings along with some "Safari Coffee." The burnt coffee at least struck him as safari worthy.

He reached the Tree of Life – well, faux life – a human-made structure with some four-hundred animal representations elaborately carved in the simulated trunk. Jake had no childhood memories from this place. But his curiosity was piqued about the mix of fact and fiction as created by the best and brightest of the Imagineers. What other real or artificial creatures might he encounter?

~

Jake saw in the brochure that no direct bus runs from any of the four theme parks to Disney Springs. The only bus routes there connect to the resorts. As commercial as the theme parks are, all the peripheral lodging and dining and entertainment facilities also serve as huge moneymakers for the Disney corporation, making Disney Springs, formerly known as Downtown Disney, a logical place of protest for the disenchanted and disenfranchised, although not an international-themed one like the World Showcase and its eleven nations.

Rather than catch a bus, Jake walked there with one eye on his map. Disney Springs, he soon experienced, offers stores, restaurants, movie theaters, nightclubs, and even Cirque du Soleil. It made sense that some Florida officials had been opposed to the idea of building a center of commercial activity without an admission fee, unlike the rest of Disney, with concerns that it would draw business away from Orlando and other municipalities. Disney Springs's streetscapes – imitation streets, like most are in WDW, but still streets – reminded Jake of his recent past, and he wandered through them as an ever-watchful private eye might, half-expecting to see Leandra here as he had in New York City and Montreal. Her changing hair color made that many more women he spotted appear to be possible Leandras.

Exhaustion took over. From Disney Springs Jake caught a bus to Disney's Yacht Club Resort, from where he walked to the Epcot Parking Area. He located his van and drove far enough away from WDW to find a sheltered stretch of shoulder.

Time to hunker down and sleep.

So What If They Are?

JAKE HADN'T BEEN CERTAIN he would visit the fourth theme park, Disney's Hollywood Studios. Their mother had taken him and his sister there when it was still named Disney-MGM Studios. She'd been disappointed and let her feelings be known to her kids. As a movie buff, she'd had high expectations. At least back then, the sorcerer's hat from *Fantasia* had risen up at its center as a symbol of the park. No longer. Production facilities had been phased out, too. Change after change at WDW from his preadolescence to the present ... and into the future. Once again, this concept of impermanence. Would the ENA carry out some act adding to that concept?

Their mother had enjoyed the drop-down ride in the dark called the Twilight Zone Tower of Terror since she'd been a fan of that TV show. She'd left him tending to his sister at a refreshment stand when she'd gone on it. But Grace had found little else that pleased her besides that and the sorcerer's hat. She'd at first been excited on discovering a street named Sunset Boulevard after the boulevard in Los Angeles, but had been upset she couldn't find any reference to the Billy Wilder film also named after it – a favorite of hers, as was the starring male actor, William Holden, cast as the central character and postmortem narrator Joe Gillis. As a teen, Jake had in fact used Holden's death from an alcohol-related falling accident to try to scare his mother into moderating her drinking. His frustration with his failure in that attempt, he recalled, had been an excuse for his own weekend-long bender. Like mother, like son.

He saw notice of a relatively new ride, located in the towering Chinese Theatre, a replica of the Hollywood movie palace of that name: Mickey & Minnie's Runaway Railway. Another train, undoubtedly making Walt Disney happy from his cosmic perch. Grace would certainly be sentimental enough to appreciate that. Jake read on the promo sign that Goofy serves as the engineer for Mickey and Minnie. Those hard-working mice and that dog sure have many duties at WDW, he mused.

Jake overheard a comment by an adolescent boy, waiting to take the train ride on a crowded switchback line.

"I liked it better here during that Covid thing. We got on rides quick, mom!"

"Hush up," his mother replied.

Jake remembered complaining about long lines to Grace during their trip here ... and who knows what else.

As he walked around the grounds without committing to any attraction other than some food – a burger at Backlot Express – Jake wondered if at least one among Leandra, Ned, and Marcus might be a movie buff. Enough to visit a park evoking Hollywood and forgo a destructive act? Or enough to resent the park's attractions, as his mother had, and carry one out?

He didn't stay long at the surrogate Hollywood Studios. With only three days left until Thanksgiving, he would keep his attention on Epcot's World Showcase and the Eleven Nations.

~

As day turned to night, Jake ate dinner at China's Nine Dragons and drank a draft in Germany's Biergarten, replete with a Bavarian oom-pah band ("Oktoberfest all year round!"). He wanted a second beer but moved outside and made his way to the bridge at the lagoon's eastern side between China and Germany, choosing a railing to lean on and gather himself.

Impressions of his touring through Walt Disney World continued to swirl within his mind, entangled with old memories, as well as Boucher's tenets and the behavior of the sociologist's disciples. Some of what Jake had seen offended him, but some of it enchanted him, as on his first trip here two decades before. There is indeed magic in the Disney Dimension, he reflected. Re-experiencing it helped him recognize the magic of all the locales he'd experienced on this strange journey – Manhattan, Brooklyn, Montreal, Shaleville, and places in between – each and every one, a magic kingdom in its own right.

His trip to WDW had been edifying. He felt protective of this place and the kids enchanted by it and their parents trying to please them, even as he resented relentless corporate conquest of other cultures.

Were the three ENA members – or even more – really coming this way? Wherever you are, he inwardly intoned, activists one and all, do your thing! Go ahead and protest commercial conquest anywhere you so choose. Give talks. Write letters. Write blogs. Create characters like Astérix. Impugn. Satirize. Even occupy. But no bombs!

Jake turned away from the lagoon and looked back along the promenade. A group of Sikhs, as indicated by their turbans – a family, it seemed, a man and woman along with a teenage boy and girl – approached. He wondered if they questioned why no pavilion represents India. They might even be relieved by that fact. The boy and girl conversed, smiling. Knowing that foreigners could find enjoyment at WDW reaffirmed Jake's purpose in being here.

Two young men approached from the other direction. They had closely cropped hair and wore tight T-shirts and the animated expressions and movements of too much drinking. Jake was not under the influence but he was exhausted, impatient, and irritable. One of the two wore the red baseball-style MAGA hat that all-too often had come to indicate racism and bullying.

Sure enough, he and his companion stopped to taunt the Sikhs.

"Hey, coneheads," the hat-wearing one said, "you part of some show?"

The Sikhs, now tense, kept walking. The men turned and started to follow them. "They're not coneheads," the other said. "They're Muslims."

Jake moved toward them. "Wrong!" he proclaimed. "Ever hear of Sikhism? Get your religions straight. And so what if they are?"

The two turned to face him. The Sikhs, slowing down, also turned to look.

"Who the fuck are you?" MAGA-hat asked.

"I'm the asshole who likes to keep the peace but who's also stupid enough to get arrested for kicking a bigot like you in the balls, then elbowing the dimwit in lockstep with you in the jaw."

Jake crouched. He'd never taken karate, being just a freestyle brawler, but he knew enough about martial arts to find a convincing stance.

The men looked at him, then back and forth at each other. A few other people had stopped to watch. MAGA-hat started toward Jake, slowing down enough to wait for his hesitating friend to catch up. Jake crouched even lower. MAGA-hat angled away slightly and bypassed him to one side, his friend to the other.

"Asshole," MAGA-hat commented.

"Asshole," his friend repeated, like an animatronic echo.

"Didn't I already admit that?" Jake called after them.

He turned back toward the Sikhs. The father, still watching, met his eyes, then gave a nod of appreciation and led his family away.

Had Jake just become an activist? Sort of. And one willing to resort to violence if necessary. But protecting innocent victims, not targeting them or risking them as collateral damage.

Hidden Marcus

JAKE SPENT MOST of his time at the lagoon's southern end, walking the promenade in the vicinity of the centrally located American Adventure. With its gardens planted in hues of red, white, and blue, including roses named after all the U.S. Presidents – deserving or not – as well as a Hall of Flags exhibiting the different flags throughout U.S. history, that particular pavilion might very well be targeted, singled out by Boucher because of its celebration of America's patriotic themes.

After the incident with the Sikhs, Jake questioned his self-control and he resolved to keep a low profile, at least until a possible encounter with the ENA. The stakes were too high not to keep his wits about him and stay on task. He couldn't control his emotions but he could strive to stay at no more than a slow burn.

He drank only water, lots of it. No matter how hot the day became, he ate regularly from stands. Although the pavilions offered tempting air-conditioned dining, he was on a dwindling budget and on a mission.

One of his favorite neo-noir films was *Body Heat*, directed by Lawrence Kasden. Matty Walker – a role nailed by Kathleen Turner – is a femme fatale to the extreme, and her patsy, the easily corruptible attorney Ned Racine – played so well by William Hurt – is sympathetic despite letting himself be manipulated by her. The Florida heat is like another character, helping drive the sensual story. Accept the heat as a character in your inner movie, Jake told himself.

Even though he was focused, things still seemed out of kilter for him, as they sure ended up for Ned Racine. What was bothering him? That he was still shadow boxing an unknown entity?

During his rounds at Epcot, Jake passed much of the time looking for "Hidden Mickeys," disguised images of Mickey Mouse placed by Imagineers throughout the park, including in the resorts. The only Mickey that actually mattered to him was that doll he'd seen in Brooklyn and any others like it. Since he was on the lookout anyway, locating benign versions helped while away the hours.

A brochure that was available at various visitor centers gave away the locations of the Hidden Mickeys, but Jake was determined to find some on his own. He located two: one carved on a Canadian totem pole and another on a promenade tile across from the Rose & Crown Pub.

Jake found something else hidden in plain sight that was relevant to his purpose: written in Sharpie, on a tree sandwiched by France and Morocco, the tag *M. Palmetto.*

No, it didn't identify the tree itself, a palm. Rather, it told Jake what he needed to know: Marcus had been here and probably still was. Jake now interpreted any uneasiness he'd been carrying as the likelihood he was being followed. Roles had been reversed, his nervous system told him. He now glanced regularly over each shoulder. Each and every face seemed threatening. But none belonged to Marcus.

~

That evening, back in the shelter of his van, beyond the outer edges of the Disney Dimension, Jake had the thought that no one at WDW is considered homeless because you can't stay after closing. For Jake the van counted as a home. But within its metal walls, he maintained his anxious, survival mind, intensified by the latest development of seeing Marcus's tag.

With Mickey Mouse in all his manifestations on his brain, Jake kept returning to the ENA doll version as a threat. Were the dolls really bombs? Fragmentation bombs? Or perhaps specialized ones, as in spreading toxins or viruses? Would the public's new awareness and preoccupation with the threat of ever-mutating viruses make extremists more or less likely to attempt spreading one?

Elia Kazan's movie *Panic in the Streets*, involving a pneumonic plague cause by rats in New Orleans, had first made Jake aware of the scary possibilities of an epidemic and, by implication, a pandemic. He remembered how proud his mother had been to ferret out the tape at a flea market – by that time, it was getting harder for her to add to her VHS collection, what with DVDs becoming the dominant format – and how disappointed she'd been that her thirteen-year-old daughter had refused to watch it because of nightmares.

When Caitlyn had headed to the refuge of her bedroom, Grace had drunkenly yelled after her, "This shit happens, girly! Better face it!"

Caitlyn had turned and shouted back, "Fuck parental consent! This is kid consent and I don't give it!"

Seventeen-year-old Jake, angry at his mother, had almost left the living room himself, but he was curious about the latest find. He did tell her, after watching and enjoying the gripping film with her, that she should lay off Caitlyn.

"Movies prepare you for life," Grace had countered.

After that incident, he and Caitlyn had had a long conversation about their mother's movie fixation. He knew from Grace that her father, a self-employed landscaper in southern New Jersey, where she'd been born, had been an obsessive reader of mysteries and had started collecting videotapes in that genre when VHS technology had reached American homes in the late 1970s. He'd died when Grace was fifteen. By that time, she'd also been watching and reading mysteries. The next year, her mother had followed a man to upstate New York, where Grace had finished high school. Her mother had little interest in the video and book collections. Grace, honoring her father's memory, had made them her own.

Jake's conversation with his sister had given her some filial perspective and had probably helped her keep her tongue some months later, when their mother had chosen the apocalyptic film *Panic in Year Zero* for family entertainment. Grace had made a big deal of the fact that one of her fantasy leading men, Ray Milland, had also directed it, then had repeated to Caitlyn how she should watch it to learn about survival. This time, Caitlyn had given her a hard little smile, then left the room without speaking.

Jake, prepared for what he would say to his mother the next time around, had fired away: "If movies prepare you for life, what the fuck happened to you?"

He'd apologized by pouring a shot of bourbon for her, sneaking some for himself.

Onrushing scenes from movies, apocalyptic or not, and multifarious risks to all the kids and their parents visiting WDW – risks like planted bombs – helped fuel Jake's notion of returning there at once to keep nighttime watch. Could and would the ENA enter the grounds at night? Jake could imagine Marcus appearing out of the lagoon in a wetsuit, commando-style. He couldn't see the same for the more laidback couple, Leandra and Ned. Those two he saw as undercover operatives, posing in tourist disguises behind enemy lines.

Action Figures

JAKE STOOD READY as Epcot's front gate opened, ready to track the scat of the ENA – at least one of them, he now knew with certainty. Security had to be well aware of his own comings and goings by now. They also had to be aware of his aged cargo van. And they must have photos of him in the Disney cloud. They had to be ever vigilant; digital technology made it easier than ever.

Jake, using digital tech himself, had started the day online. Some of what he'd learned in his research was revealing about working at WDW. He'd read about a street called Avenue of the Stars running behind many of the Epcot attractions. Connected to it, outside Epcot, is a road known as Backstage Lane. Along it, on the east side of Epcot, behind Mexico, Norway, and China, are situated the Epcot Center Production Center and Epcot Center Cast Services, each with a parking lot. Could Leandra or the others have landed a job to gain access? Not likely unless Leandra had applied for one some time ago. So many possibilities to keep in mind. Jake had to outthink the ENA trio.

Report to the authorities? Once again, with mere suspicions? He wasn't about to tolerate the dismissiveness he'd gotten in New York to the point of a question like, "You have a thing for this Leandra?" For now, he would wander the mean streets of Epcot, his senses in play.

~

Natural daylight faded into dusk and artificial light. The promenade was more crowded this Wednesday evening than on previous evenings, the lead-in to the four-day Thanksgiving holiday, with more people at Epcot than Jake had yet seen, making looking for someone in particular that much more challenging.

Jake decided on the International Gateway bridge, the second entrance to Epcot, this one by water, for his primary stakeout point. The boat service from Crescent Lake is exclusive, he knew, serving only the resorts and villas as part of a package deal. At the United Nations Plaza back in New York, as Jake had overheard, Boucher had passed an envelope with "five grand." Even after Montreal and a car rental and food these weeks – and bomb-making? – the ENA trio probably had funds enough for Disney lodging and transportation. Also from the bridge, if Jake spotted any of them approaching on foot along the promenade from either direction, he could turn away and look out over the water to conceal his face. Jake headed for the bridge and took up position near the France pavilion.

People streamed past him on foot, myriad couples and families with kids. Jake was tired of envisioning the faces of the trio and was even having a hard time calling up Leandra's features.

A boat passed below coming from Crescent Lake. Another came in the opposite direction from the lagoon, returning to the Crescent Lake resorts. Before very long, another arrived from Crescent Lake, and soon another returned there.

When a fifth arrived, Jake caught a flash of a round shaved head in a side window.

Marcus?

The boat plowed through the water toward the nearest Showcase Plaza dock. Jake moved off the bridge in the same direction for a better view.

As the passengers disembarked, he worked his way close enough to confirm Marcus's presence. Yes, it was the mad tagger. He'd undergone a makeover and looked snappy in a yellow raincoat, new creased Dockers, and brown leather Topsiders. A camera hung from his neck and a black leather photographer's bag from his shoulder, likely the same one Jake had seen at

Boucher's talk and at the Brooklyn warehouse. Marcus looked like he belonged on a yacht. The fact that he'd changed his look to such a degree confirmed Jake's worst fears.

Jake looked away as Marcus approached and walked past him toward the International Gateway bridge. Jake turned back that way and followed. Marcus stopped in front of the France Pavilion to take some photos, or so it seemed. He did the same at Morocco and Japan but lingered longest in front of the huge red brick mansion of the American Adventure. He seemed unconcerned about anyone following him, which facilitated Jake's shadowing him. He even took pictures of Marcus from different angles.

After leaving the U.S. pavilion, Marcus walked a little faster. He stopped on the bridge between Germany and China and took more photos as a tourist might. HarmonioUS began. Marcus didn't take pictures of the light show but just observed while visitors all around him clicked their cameras.

Jake scanned the crowd for the others. They might be following him as he followed Marcus. When the show had ended and visitors were expected to leave the park, Marcus continued around the loop past China, Norway, and Mexico, back to the dock in the Showcase Plaza. He stood in line and waited while people stepped onto the boat.

Jake hung back to watch. The area was well lit and even at this distance he could make out the passengers.

People passed by him toward Future World and the parking lot beyond it. Others headed for the dock as Marcus had, among them a striking well-to-do youngish couple. The man sported a crew cut and wore a tan safari jacket. The woman had brown hair and wore a green smock dress and white sweater. She carried a large blue nylon tote bag.

Even though Jake recognized them, it took an extra beat for it all to register – no dramatic hair color, no blue-frame glasses on the woman, no beanie or dreads on the man, and different styles of clothing on both. The J. Crew versions of Leandra and Ned.

They headed for the line where Marcus waited, also seemingly oblivious to everyone around them. Jake moved a bit closer, keeping other people in front of him. While waiting their turn, Leandra reached in her bag, pulled out a sketchpad, and showed Ned … what? A secret message? A hand-drawn map and a route?

Or was she just proud of a new sketch. Marcus meanwhile had boarded the boat.

More reconnaissance this evening for the trio? It was at least Marcus's second day out, as revealed by his tag on the tree. The others as well probably. Jake hadn't seen any of them before now despite their apparent nonchalance. Behave openly today to be able to return tomorrow on Thanksgiving and be accepted in advance of what might come?

Jake wanted to get a photo of the new-look Leandra and Ned before they boarded, but he would have to risk getting closer and refrained.

The boat, full of passengers, pulled out from the landing and angled toward Crescent Lake. Jake watched until it moved out of sight under the bridge, then walked slowly to his van, reflecting on the encounters, their implications, and what he should do next.

With the growing humidity that day, it had felt like it might rain. It finally did. The sprinkle felt good ... kind of calming.

Jake needed that.

T-Day

TWILIGHT HAD FAITHFULLY come after the bright light of an uneventful day and, before long, so had Marcus. He again arrived by boat and wore the same yellow raincoat and carried the same photographer's bag. And he walked in the same direction along the World Showcase Promenade. Jake followed. When Marcus stopped and sat down on a bench opposite Japan, not far from the American Adventure, Jake hurried back toward the Showcase Plaza dock.

Although Jake hadn't expected to see the ENA trio until late afternoon or early evening, he'd been watching the Friendship Boats arriving all day. They evidently had resort luxury while waiting to do their deed. Relaxation and distraction deluxe: climate control, comfortable furniture, delivered food, and Cable TV with streaming options. What would that bunch watch? Did Leandra have a say in selection? Who held the remote? Did she and Ned defer to Marcus? Absurd but stubborn thoughts. After the rain the night before, the day had been less oppressively humid, and Jake had moved on from recurring thoughts of the weather. But to thoughts of who controlled the remote? Were the high stakes thrust upon him fostering the absurd?

This had all become bigger than his small self. Whenever that thought circled back around, Jake had the urge to go straight to security. He had a pretty good idea of the movements and chosen locations of the uniformed guards and those he identified as plainclothes ones - all of them apparently anointed as "cast members," he mused. They seemed to rotate their spots and he didn't see the same likely candidates every night. Part of his take on them was based on how they looked at him. Some among them must have given consideration to his unorthodox use of the park – his paying all this money to watch boats come and go, for instance. But he had no problem with security keeping an eye on him. That way he could quickly summon help if the time came; that is, he now was certain, when the time came.

Ned and Leandra arrived on the next boat. A tight operation. Like Marcus, they wore the same clothes as the evening before – Leandra, the smock dress, and Ned, the safari jacket. Leandra again carried the blue nylon tote bag. Ned now carried a multicolored one representing the ever-present Goofy's head, black dangling ears and all. They headed the long way around the promenade, passing in front of France, Morocco, and Japan. The tape loop of pre-HarmonioUS songs gave Jake a soundtrack as he tailed them.

Both of them seemed wary. They sometimes stopped and looked around as tourists might. As a result, Jake's own wariness grew. He varied his distance to them. He feigned distraction. He also kept an eye out for security, ever ready to sound the alarm.

Artificial light now won out over encroaching darkness. The duo stopped between the amphitheater on the waterfront and a fountain in the middle of the promenade, opposite the columned porch of the American Adventure's colonial mansion. Marcus had left the bench opposite Japan, but Jake spotted him standing beyond the duo, now peering through his camera.

Leandra, at the fountain, took out her sketchpad and a box of charcoals and began drawing. Ned stood slightly behind her, looking over her right shoulder. At the near side of the U.S. pavilion stood a security guard dressed in blue and black with a white hat.

Minutes ticked by, elongated in this other dimension. The three acted busy, fussing with gear, but they each stayed put. Had Marcus stood in that exact place yesterday? Jake seemed to remember he had. The flow of memories was now mixed with the flow of adrenaline, especially as Marcus moved away, leaving Jake's attention on the duo.

The announcement for HarmonioUS came and the spectacle burst forth. By now, Jake knew the show's dramatic arc and he could anticipate the big moments. The music sounded out. Colors exploded in the Disney sky. People all around the lagoon cheered. His eyes stayed on Leandra and Ned. He raised his phone to take a photograph. It might or might not come out at this distance.

Something slammed into his back and he almost lost his footing. His first split-second irrational thought was that it was one of the small motorized Disney vehicles. But then someone's arm in black slammed down on his right arm, causing him to drop the phone. It bounced along the promenade. Marcus was Jake's next thought. Anger surged as he jerked around, still off-balance.

A figure in a black nylon jacket reached down and grabbed the phone and, sidestepping spectators, moved to the edge of the water. Jake saw the figure's arm lift up and jerk forward, launching the phone into the lagoon. His eyes followed it. It was gone. He turned back. So was the figure in black.

Jake processed the image of whom he'd just seen. Raphael, Raven's boyfriend, the chess player. Here at WDW. The "plus one" Mouseketeer?

Jake tried to sort out his racing thoughts. Raphael had apparently lied to Raven about his involvement. Or Raven had known more and had lied to Jake. Or the two of them had become honest with each other after Jake's time with Raven. Had Raphael's confrontation with him over Raven in Montreal been more about the ENA's plans than about jealousy? Raven had seen Jake's license and address. Had she passed on the information to Raphael? The man in the fedora, parked on his sister's block? The rental car's broken window? The van's slashed tire in New York City? All Raphael? Could it be? And Marcus, Ned, and Leandra evacuating the warehouse? Had Raphael clued them in to Jake's presence?

Whatever, whenever, however. The fourth Mousketeer. That was what mattered now. The proverbial Big Clock was ticking and he, like growingly desperate George Stroud in the film of that name – the complex character played by Ray Milland – had put himself on its timetable.

Raphael disappeared into the crowd. Still mesmerized by the pyrotechnics, nearby parkgoers showed no reaction to the phone toss. Jake looked back toward Leandra at the fountain, just as she was putting the sketchpad and markers back into her bag. Seemingly still unaware of his presence, she slung the bag over her shoulder, then took off toward the far corner of the colonial mansion.

Jake hurried after her, looking for the others. No sign of Marcus. Ned, his back turned, had started along the promenade toward Italy.

Leandra headed toward the restrooms located at the eastern end of the U.S. pavilion. She glanced around, then entered the ladies' room.

Jake heard another kind of yelling farther to the east. Panicked yelling. He looked in that direction and saw smoke rising near the boat landing in front of Germany. A bomb? He'd only heard the show's explosive sound effects. He ran toward the nearby uniformed guard, who obviously had heard the shouting and was starting toward it. The guard caught sight of Jake approaching, stopped and braced his body for contact. Jake stopped just short of him, out of breath.

"A woman … I think with a bomb … she entered the restroom next to the U.S. pavilion," he sputtered. "There're at least four of them part of this, the other three all men. Maybe one of them already set off a bomb near Germany."

Jake sure had his attention. His face showed alarm and doubt all at once. Jake was surprised how young he was, a thin blondish beard making him look like he didn't even shave yet.

"This better not be bullshit. Come with me!"

The guard turned and darted back toward the colonial mansion. Jake followed. The guard slowed a bit to pull out a small transceiver and Jake passed him. People had frozen in place to watch them. Jake neared the mansion's porch.

"Wait, you!"

Jake stopped to let the guard catch up.

"Describe what they look like!" he said, passing his transceiver to Jake.

Jake caught his breath, then spoke into it as clearly as he could. "The woman at the American Adventure is a brunette and she's wearing a white sweater and green dress. Her name is Leandra. One of the three guys ... Ned ... is tall and thin with short dirty blond hair. He's wearing a tan safari jacket and has a Goofy tote bag. Another one ... Marcus ... is stockier with short hair and is wearing a yellow raincoat. He's carrying what looks like photography equipment. I'm not sure what it really is. I think they all have explosives in Mickey Mouse dolls. The third guy ... Raphael ... is French Canadian. Dark hair. Ponytail. Black leather jacket. He grabbed my phone and threw it in the lagoon."

The young guard was staring hard at Jake. Goofy bag. Mickey Mouse bombs. Phone in the Showcase Lagoon. How preposterous did all that sound?

"Stay right here!" the guard instructed, taking back the transceiver.

He again headed toward the ladies' room. Jake started to follow.

"You heard him!"

Someone had grabbed Jake's arm from behind. It was a short, muscular plainclothes guard, older than the other by at least a decade, Jake guessed.

"You stay put, understand?" the older guard said in what sounded like a New York City accent.

Jake started to speak but saw that Leandra had exited the restroom, tote bag still slung from her shoulder, before the young uniformed guard had a chance to enter. He stopped to look at her but was letting her walk by.

"That's Leandra!" Jake yelled, pointing.

The young guard turned and grabbed her. The plainclothes guard left Jake's side and went to join them. Someone else came up behind Jake, a tall woman in uniform.

"Stay where you are," she ordered.

The two male guards had Leandra sandwiched between them. She looked at Jake, then back and forth at them, then at Jake

198

again. He saw the flash of recognition and anger in her eyes, then a look of despair.

Caught. Trapped. Ratted out by Jake.

The plainclothesman grabbed her bag and looked inside it, sticking his hand in and rummaging.

"Just a bunch of art supply stuff," he reported.

Shouts came from another direction, these from the northeast. Smoke billowed up at an angle across the water near the Mayan pyramid of Mexico.

Momentary silence ensued, staff and guests shocked into it.

"Did you set that bomb?" the plainclothesman asked Leandra.

Jake moved closer, straining to hear. The female guard let him advance, moving with him, probably wanting to hear herself.

"No!" Leandra fired back with conviction.

"Is there a bomb in there?" the young uniformed guard asked, pointing to the ladies' room.

She hesitated.

"Tell us!" the plainclothesman snapped. "We have descriptions of the others. We're rounding them up now. Tell us! It'll be better for you."

"We know all your names, Leandra," the young guard added. "The others are Ned, Marcus, and Raphael."

He was young but no dummy.

"Tell them," Jake spoke loudly from where he stood, trying to sound like a friend offering sensible advice.

She looked at him with loathing, then turned back to the guards, broken.

"Yes, it's in there. I left a doll in one of the stalls."

"Is it on a timer?" the plainclothesman asked.

"You have plenty of time," she said calmly, looking at a big plastic watch on her wrist. "Ten and a half minutes."

"What kind of bomb?"

"Just a smoke-bomb. Like the ones that already went off near Germany and Mexico. They won't hurt anybody."

The young guard took off, heading for the ladies' room door. Another uniformed guard had appeared, this one the oldest of the bunch, portly and ruddy-faced, like an Irish cop from a big city beat. He moved next to Leandra. A few park visitors had gathered and were watching, fear in their eyes. The uniformed woman left Jake's side and herded them back a distance.

"There's one more smoke-bomb set to go off," Leandra offered matter-of-factly, her voice, unlike her gaze, without emotion. She glanced down at a big yellow plastic watch. "In about twenty-one minutes."

"Where?"

"Near France. In the trees. Good enough?"

The young uniformed guard exited the restroom and approached them tentatively, holding the Mickey Mouse Doll, eyes wide, jaw clenched.

"How do I disarm it?" he asked.

He was trying to sound calm but his voice cracked.

"Just reach in the back. There're some wires between the clock and the saltpeter," Leandra answered, now sounding like a bored high-school science teacher. "Just pull the wires out of the clock."

The young guard seemed frozen in place.

"Oh, don't worry, it's not booby-trapped." She said impatiently. "Understand? I give up. It's over. It's all ruined." She gave a quick angry glance Jake's way. "Disarm the stupid fucking Dance With Me Mickey Doll already. Or we'll be standing in the middle of a lot of putrid smoke."

The plainclothes guard with the New York accent had been sizing her up. He walked over to the younger guard, took the doll from him, and did as Leandra had instructed.

"It's disarmed," he announced, then moved away and talked into his transceiver.

HarmonioUS remarkably ended at that very moment, as if this unlikely group were all part of the show.

"Good," Leandra announced. "Take me away. Read me my rights. I want a lawyer."

She was silhouetted by lights shining in the U.S. pavilion behind her – backlit, film-noir style. She looked beautiful, worthy of any goddamn movie Jake had ever seen. What hair color worked best on cinematic Leandra? Red, blue, black, blond, or brown? All of the above, he decided, aware with that thought of the irrelevant place his mind was taking him.

Guards kept coming from every which way. Meanwhile, park guests, eyes wild, some clutching kids close to them, were heading toward the exits. Within moments, a calm voice spoke through speakers all around Epcot – from on high, it seemed, as if from Walt Disney himself.

"Ladies and gentlemen, we apologize for problems with the pyrotechnics and the resulting smoke. All is under control and there is no need to panic. There is no danger. Please proceed calmly toward the main Epcot exit. Do not try to take a Friendship boat. Rides to all resorts will be provided by Disney staff-members from the Epcot Parking Lot. Once again, go to the exit located just to the north of Spaceship Earth, where you will be met by Disney staffers. Thank you."

Problem with the pyrotechnics indeed.

After more music was piped through the speakers, the message was repeated. Jake had one last look at Leandra as she was led off by the peach-fuzzed guard, the female one, the Irish-faced one, and two newly arrived plainclothesmen. She walked erect, scowling at everyone else's silliness, it seemed, fiery and unrepentant to the end.

Jake himself was led by the female guard and the New York-sounding plainclothesmen carrying Leandra's bag and the defused smoke-bomb, past Japan to the landing in front of Morocco and onto a Boston Whaler-style fiberglass boat with a big outboard motor. Two men were already aboard: a plainclothes Latino-looking man at the wheel, and an African-American, wearing a blue vest and a holstered gun, at the stern. The New York-sounding plainclothesmen told Jake to board, then followed. He directed Jake toward a seat in the middle of the boat and sat down next to him.

Jake pointed to the disarmed, limp Mickey and, to his own surprise, quoted Bogart as Sam Spade in *The Maltese Falcon*: "The stuff that dreams are made of."

~

Disney dimension? What cosmic ride was Jake on now?

The boat crossed the lagoon, the craft skimming lightly over the water, a big wake behind it. During the crossing, Jake managed to get the name of the guard who had deactivated the smoke-bomb. It was Billy, and he was from the Bronx and had been a fireman up north.

Billy and Jake disembarked at the Showcase Plaza's east landing. They were met there by a tram, driven by yet another uniformed guard. Billy waved Jake onto it. It seemed at first that they were heading to the Mexico pavilion. But they angled toward the Odyssey Center.

Billy used his transceiver as the tram pulled to a halt. He indicated that Jake should get out. They walked around to a side entrance on the multisided building and entered an unmarked metal door. The tram driver didn't follow.

Inside a small, dimly lit room with nothing but some chairs and an empty metal table stood a slender middle-aged man in a suit. A younger, much-taller man, with a closely cropped flattop and wearing a white short-sleeved shirt, leaned against a side wall. The man in the suit looked paler than everyone else as if he never went outside. Jake wondered if he favored the artificial light of utilidors over Florida sunshine. It all seemed fitting to him in his present state of mind, like a scene from a movie with framing and lighting adjusted to create a sense of claustrophobia.

Billy placed the bag and the doll down on the table. Mickey's now sorry face was just an empty collapsed shell. He was also ripped open from behind, the tear revealing electronic innards. He was about fifteen inches in height and sported a red hoodie with the lettering "Mickey Mouse Clubhouse," blue jeans, and white sneakers labeled "R" and "L." Leandra had called it a "Dance With Me Mickey Doll."

"Give me your wallet," Mr. Suit told Jake. He pointed to a chair with pallid fingers. "Have a seat ... catch your breath."

He sat down next to Jake and looked at his license and bankcard and at some old business cards and the cash. He passed them to the taller man who also studied them.

He turned his gaze back on Jake. "You reported this incident and identified the woman, I understand. You can ID the others?"

"Yes."

"You know them personally?" He spoke softly and evenly, which made it more menacing.

"Just by sight."

"How'd you know what they were up to?"

"I first became aware of them in New York City. It's a long story."

"I bet." Mr. Suit bit a bloodless lip, looking skeptical. "They know you?"

"Seems so. One of them grabbed my phone and tossed it in the lagoon."

"This Leandra isn't or never was a girlfriend?"

"No, I don't even know her last name," Jake replied.

"How many men did you say there were?"

"Three, as far as I know … Ned, Marcus, and Raphael. I became suspicious of Ned and Marcus in New York City. I don't know any of their last names either. I saw the first two in Epcot last evening and again tonight. I became aware of Raphael in Montreal."

"Montreal? A minor detour north on the way to Florida?"

"I first followed them there and figured some stuff out."

Mr. Suit nodded knowingly … or was it unknowingly. "This Raphael …"

"He's the one who slammed into me from behind and threw my phone in the lagoon," Jake interrupted. "That's the first I knew he was here. I think maybe he was checking up on me in my hometown."

"Shaleville, New York?"

"That's the place."

"You're sure that's all of them?"

"Like I said, as far as I know."

Tall Man finally spoke: "We found and defused another smoke-bomb doll, just like this one. Two had already discharged. That makes four. We hope you're right and that's all there are."

Jake thought about the four gift-wrapped boxes in Brooklyn. "I only saw four giftboxes when I cased their warehouse. I assume the Mickey Mouse dolls were inside."

"Cased their warehouse? You fancy yourself a private eye or something?" Tall Man asked.

"Hardly," Jake lied. Why even attempt to explain his shamus rehab to this bunch? "After I entered the warehouse," he added, "I reported what I'd seen to the New York Police Department."

Mr. Suit tilted his head upward at that. "Is that a fact? And …?"

"By the time I led them there, all evidence was gone. The NYPD saw my photos though and copied them. Detectives Hamm and Salvo of the eighty-third precinct were the ones I dealt with."

"Did they believe you?"

"I don't know."

Mr. Suit nodded to himself. "Interesting. We'll check with them. We'll check on all of it." He stood up and added, "We have two men in custody here in this building." He pointed to a second metal door on the back wall. "We're going to open this door. Look through it and tell us if they're the ones. They won't be able to see you."

He nodded at Bronx Billy, who stepped forward.

"Stand there," Billy instructed Jake, pointing to the far side of the door frame, the side from where the door swung open.

Jake took up position. Billy opened the door.

In the middle of a larger room stood five men in a circle – two men also wearing suits, one uniformed guard, a man in sweats, and a man in a Donald Duck jacket. They glanced over as the door opened.

Billy spoke into the other room: "Tell them to keep their eyes on that far wall."

"Look straight ahead," the man in sweats added.

Jake couldn't see the culprits yet. But then the security circle parted to give those in the outer room a clear line of vision. Jake inched forward a little more to get a better angle.

There they were – the two he'd tracked for weeks, Ned and Marcus – standing, facing the opposite direction. Their slouched shoulders projected defeat.

Jake, backing away from the doorway, nodded to his interrogator, who nodded to Billy. Billy waited for the other two suits to enter from the second room before he pulled the door shut.

"That's them all right," Jake told all of them. "Ned and Marcus. The tall one in the tan jacket … that's Ned … he's Leandra's boyfriend. The other's Marcus, the leader, I think. Whatever they were doing was paid for by Paul-Louis Boucher, a French sociologist who's spoken out against Disney Paris."

Mr. Suit gave a nod of affirmation. "We know Boucher's views. We also know he's being charged with fraud in France. Describe the fourth one ... Raphael."

Jake, after processing that bit of information about Boucher, did so.

"French Canadian. About my height. Skin a little darker than mine. Black hair in a ponytail. He was wearing a black nylon coat when he grabbed my phone."

The interrogator and the other two suits stepped to one side of the room and conferred softly.

"Okay, that's it," the interrogator announced, then nodded to Tall Man.

Tall Man looked at Jake. "You're going to tell all this again and more ... "to us, to the Sheriff's Department, and to the State Troopers."

Jake nodded his agreement. Time to get some information himself, as all the screen private dicks do when confronted with heavy-handed cops.

"They sure went to a lot of trouble to set off just smoke-bombs," he said. "Why do you think? Just to scare people?"

Mr. Suit nodded to himself before answering.

"It was to keep us distracted while they vandalized the place."

"Vandalized?"

"Show him," Mr. Suit said to Billy and pointed to Leandra's blue tote bag.

Billy held it open for Jake to see. In the bottom, along with the sketchpad and box of charcoals, were dozens of glass vials filled with different-colored paints.

"Paint grenades, you might call 'em," Billy said. "The others carried spray cans in their coats and bags. Enough to deface a lot of buildings ... probably with revolutionary crap."

"Cute, right?" Tall Man said.

Tag, You're It

THE TEST TRACK didn't do it. Nor did the other Future World attractions – Living with the Land and Mission: SPACE. Ditto regarding dinner at Chefs de France in World Showcase. And that was just Epcot. Jake had the three other parks in which to experience distractions galore and escape his thoughts. He hit many of the reported highlights – from Expedition Everest in Animal Kingdom to Star Wars' Rise of the Resistance and the Mickie & Minnie Runaway Railway in Hollywood Studios – and he still felt like he was sleepwalking. Even the Magic Kingdom attractions he remembered from his childhood – like Pirates of the Caribbean and Space Mountain – didn't register as he'd thought they might. When interacting with Mickey at his Country House, he came out of himself a bit with little sister Caitlyn in mind. But he soon returned to his doldrums.

The fact that he knew the Disney powers-that-be were manipulating the situation to keep him at Disney World – and, he assumed, away from the press – made the whole experience weirder.

Jake had been ordered to stay in Orange County for at least a week in case the DA needed to talk to him and perhaps call him as a witness. And he was encouraged to stay at WDA of his own free will rather than possibly a jail cell as a "person of interest." He didn't know if the various authorities had meant the latter, but he'd resigned himself nonetheless to staying over at Disney World for an unspecified amount of time. At the heart of the deal, he had to sign a nondisclosure agreement. The unique arrangement included perks: a free room at the Beach Club Resort on Crescent Lake; access to VIP lounges; the privilege of being led to the front of lines on any ride he requested; and even some expense money in the form of a credit card with a balance of seven-hundred dollars good anywhere. The digital Disney Magic Band also provided was linked to the credit card, facilitating his use of park offerings. He assumed its primary purpose was to monitor him, but so be it. He was indeed coasting on his own personal ride that he's dubbed the Resignation Train.

During the first days of his special guest status, Jake had had two handlers with him most of the time – a man and a woman, Fred Glover and Maria Dos Santos. Even if he wanted to venture forth on just a short walk along Disney's Boardwalk – the entertainment, dining, and shopping complex surrounding Crescent Lake – he had to notify his handlers and they would accompany him. It felt like being under "theme park arrest," with George Orwell's Big Brother as a new Disney character in a futuristic time way beyond the fictional loaded concept of the projected year 1984.

Fred and Maria were nice enough – maybe too nice – and their doting presence had begun to wear on him. His final days at WDW, he'd stayed in his room most of the time, ordering in and reading or watching TV.

The authorities had had a tough time swallowing Jake's strange story, especially the fact that he wasn't directly involved with any of the prisoners and had taken it upon himself to track them with no other motivation. The fact that the NYPD had confirmed his contact with them helped allay suspicion. Moreover, a diver had retrieved his phone from the lagoon and a tech team had managed to download the photos, providing some visual confirmation of what he'd described. The photos included his warehouse shots of the wall writings and giftboxes, and all four members of the ENA – Leandra (Leandra Jespersen), Ned (Ned Hayes), Marcus (Marcus Macik), Raphael (Raphael Savard), as well as Raven (Sophie Durant). He himself never saw the photos again. He'd been promised a new phone by Disney officials and, when he later received it, just before his departure from WDW, his contact info had been loaded but none of the photos, not even the recent ones of Caitlyn.

The first time through his story, Jake had tried to offer just the relevant points, but the various authorities had kept digging deeper. He'd decided to tell them about his homelessness at the start of the entire affair because they'd wanted specific dates, and he could offer no proof of a current address there, only his sister's. He'd thought about putting them in touch with Aki but he'd spare her that phone assault.

Mr. Suit (his name was Wilson Todd), Tall Man (Mark Swaggart), and Bronx Billy (Billy Baresi) had come to believe him, it seemed, and so apparently had the county and state authorities. He'd found that telling the truth again and again made it easier for him to recall it in even greater detail. The statements of the perps themselves, Jake had eventually learned, had also helped convince any doubters of his truthfulness.

Jake had persistently asked questions himself. Billy Baresi and Wilson Todd, as well as the district attorney Michael Smits, had offered up some information. And Fred and Maria were willing to discuss their take on events as long as they weren't revealing something Jake hadn't heard from others.

Jake had gleaned the following: The Florida Highway Patrol had caught Raphael on Route 95 near the Georgia border by early afternoon of the day after Thanksgiving. Unlike the others, who had been caught in the act, Raphael hadn't admitted anything yet, other than staying outside WDW at a Best Western and visiting Epcot briefly one day. He still was claiming that he was a tourist from Quebec who had left WDW because it was too crowded.

The others, not knowing Raphael's fabricated story, had fessed up to all their doings. They'd also confirmed Raphael's role as the "plus one" Mouseketeer and Jake's as an outsider. They'd told the interrogators that Raphael had heard about Jake from his girlfriend in Montreal – Sophie Durant a.k.a. Raven – and on his drive south he'd detoured to and staked out the upstate address she knew from Jake's license. Jake had learned that he'd been arrested in a gray Ford Focus, consistent with Caitlyn's description of the car she'd seen parked on her block – a rental out of Champlain, New York. Raphael had broken the window and spray-painted Jake's rented Honda out of spite because of Jake's time with his girlfriend. On heading to New York City to join the others, Raphael had assumed Jake was staying in his hometown and not a threat to their plan. But Marcus had seen him leaving the warehouse during the neighborhood fire, and Leandra reported that someone looking like Jake had followed her into a subway station. Raphael had gone looking for him while the others had emptied and cleaned the warehouse and had sliced the van's tire. He would have done more, they'd said – like trash the engine – if he hadn't seen Jake returning. Marcus had advised Raphael to distinguish between a time for chess-like strategy as opposed to a time for creating chaos in a confrontation. Chaos would come soon enough, they'd all assured him. And it had.

On clearing out of the warehouse, they'd thought they were rid of Jake. How could he know where they were going? They'd surmised he might just be a stalker anyway – obsessed with both Leandra and Raven/Sophie – some wacko, manipulative artist who used portrait painting to prey on women. Marcus had seen him walk right by a policeman and not say a word after he'd been in the warehouse. Leandra's roommate Erica had told her by phone that while Leandra was on her "vacation," he'd showed up outside the apartment looking for her and acting smitten.

They'd claimed being unaware that Raphael had spotted Jake at Epcot on Thanksgiving and had followed him and had grabbed his phone, throwing it into the lagoon.

The plan had originated in Paris, where Marcus and Raphael had first met Boucher. Along with Ned and Leandra, they'd formed the so-called Eleven Nation Army. The group called Cha/Che was Raphael's creation with some of his chess pals and really nothing more than that bare-boned website, except in Raphael's head – an outcome of his growing activism.

Before entering WDW, Leandra, Ned, and Marcus had stayed at her parents' house. The Jespersens had retired to St. Petersburg from their hometown in upstate New York near Syracuse. Ned was from Minnesota; Marcus, from California.

The potassium nitrate – or saltpeter as Leandra had called it – and clock mechanisms for the smoke-bombs had come from Canada. Leandra had smuggled the former into the U.S. by bus; Ned and Marcus had smuggled the latter in the suitcase and photographer's bag by rental car. The digital players in the legally purchased Dance With Me Mickey dolls, designed to play the "Hokey-Pokey" and other songs, had been replaced with timing mechanisms to set off the potassium nitrate stuffed inside. They'd transported the doctored dolls south in the giftboxes.

Leandra, Ned, and Marcus had been at Disney World three days. From arrival to capture, they'd playacted rich preppy kids who were all about Disney collectibles. That way, it made sense for them to arrive at WDW with matching Mickey Mouse dolls and openly carry them around on Thanksgiving.

The series of smoke-bombs had been timed to go off at varying intervals at the four pavilions – Germany, Mexico, the U.S., and France – thus creating enough chaos for their subsequent vandalism. That night, Marcus and Ned had carried an arsenal of spray cans in their bags and altered coats with inner pockets. Leandra had carried vials of paint in her art supply bag with the intention of throwing them against walls. A package of Sharpie oil-based permanent paint markers – the fat-tipped variety – had been found in Raphael's vehicle. Ned had been caught heading for the France pavilion, a doll still in his possession. Raphael, the others had admitted, had placed the smoke-bomb near Germany that had gone off first. Someone had managed to mark up a number of exterior and interior walls in Italy before leaving the park, with ink consistent with Raphael's markers. After planting the Mexico smoke-bomb that had gone off second, Marcus had been caught spray-painting a slogan at the China pavilion.

They'd had no intention of hurting anyone, the three had claimed. Their actions were in protest to Disney's policies abroad and a way to demonstrate to the world the relevance of graffiti artists.

They were taggers, not terrorists, graffiti artists who set off smoke-bombs as cover for "bombing surfaces" with paint. Like Jake's friend Ricky Rad, the homeless tagger, and the scores of taggers over the decades, they were artists who chose to work on an urban backdrop. These artists and a chess player from Montreal, with inspiration and funding from a French sociologist, had gotten it in their heads to occupy Walt Disney World with their street art.

Out in the non-Disney reality, full-fledged terrorist attacks were happening all too frequently with innocent lives lost. Jake, Billy had told him, had done well to help minimize an incident with possible unintended injury or even loss of life due to crowd panic.

It was Jake's handler Maria Dos Santos who theorized to him that the perpetrators had opened up so thoroughly about their plans and actions because they considered them justified. Jake himself felt conflicted over the whole thing. Boucher's stance on cultural integrity resonated, even though a multitude of French children would probably argue with him over the merits of Disneyland Paris. And Boucher facing a fraud charge? Not a good look for a sociologist and anti-establishment activist organizer. But was that for real? Jake couldn't find any mention of it online.

In any case, Jake had become the foil in Boucher's and the taggers' show, affecting its final outcome. But he'd been a serendipitous participant with a misconception of what was to unfold. If he'd known what was really up, would he have traveled to Florida or, at that moment on the World Showcase Lagoon, even pointed a finger in Leandra's direction? If it hadn't been for Jake, the street artists probably would have successfully carried out their vandalism – all cleaned up in days if not hours – and then triumphantly returned to their haunts in Manhattan, Brooklyn, and Montreal.

If he were still alive, what would Ricky Rad say on learning that Jake had undone such a momentous act of graffiti defiance? Raven must know by now who blew the whistle on Raphael and his friends and despise Jake for it. Or maybe, seemingly resentful of Boucher's hold over Raphael, she would smile on hearing Jake had thrown a wrench into the works. Even Lisa Bellinger – with her yearning to be part of an art scene beyond small-town America and the public-school system – might have some sympathy for the taggers since graffiti had gone from trains, tunnels, walls, and bridges to art galleries and art books. More likely though, big-hearted teacher she seemed to be, she would argue on behalf of Disney-loving kids.

Jake felt fine about having stymied Raphael, following that confrontation with him outside the hotel in Montreal and his vandalism on the rental car and the van. Maybe Marcus too, based on what he'd observed of his behavior. But Ned? Not necessarily. A tagalong tagger? And Leandra? Given their strange cross-purpose connection, Jake thought about her often. He had an urge to visit her in the Orange County Jail and get her side of it all. Try to see something else in her eyes besides the despair, recognition, and loathing he'd seen at Epcot. Talk to her about her art. Discuss her mural in the warehouse. Tease her about her tag, *Leandra, Outer Space.* But he couldn't have any contact with her, he'd been told, since he might be called as a witness against her and the others.

Jake doubted a trial would happen. He would give odds that the Disney apparatchik would offer a plea bargain in order to avoid any more publicity. They'd stuck to the story that the smoke had come from faulty pyrotechnics and that any vandalism witnessed by park visitors was coincidence. The local papers had reported minor fireworks mishaps and a weeklong suspension of HarmonioUS to ensure that nothing like that ever happened again, plus an unrelated vandalism charge against a rowdy group of twenty-somethings.

When free, the taggers might at least get some attention in their own circles and among Boucher's crowd in France. Maybe

Leandra's actions would even help her career as an artist. And maybe, if Jake ever managed to talk to her, she would see all the subtle shades of color in their intertwined story.

His fascination with her lingered. A good part of that, he knew, was because he'd been so involved with her all these weeks, while never really getting to know her. She'd remained a mystery, like a character on the silver screen.

Ocean Purge

ON HIS RETURN to the non-Disney world, Jake drove east to the Atlantic Ocean and found a quiet public beach in Titusville, where he could sit on white sand near the water's edge. Even after the nine days as a pampered guest at WDW, he was spent.

On his departure, the Sheriff's Department had told him that, although he didn't have to stay in Orange County, he was not, as a potential witness, to leave the state until he heard otherwise. He didn't even know if their instructions to him were binding since he saw no documents to that effect. He wanted to see this case through anyway. With the money from Disney and what was left over from Aki's payment, he could stay on the road a while longer.

Today, he'd finally talked to Caitlyn – something he hadn't wanted to do from WDW, given the nondisclosure agreement – and had filled her in on all the events.

"I can't get my head around how and why you got there, but it seems like you're some sort of a hero," she'd teased.

Jake had told her he better remain an anonymous one, given his agreement with WDW, and that she shouldn't mention what had happened to anyone. He'd also promised he would return to Shaleville before too long, soon after he had clearance to do so, hopefully by Christmas. He also said more than once, as he had in person, he wouldn't go incommunicado as a brother ever again.

In this ocean-induced time of reflection and doubt, Jake thought hard about all the other selves he'd lived with besides that of brother: Jake Wild Child, Jake Rebel, Jake Builder, Jake Sculptor, Jake Druggie, Jake Soho, and Jake Homeless.

What about Jake Shamus? He hadn't told Caitlyn what he really wanted now was another case to help him continue progressing in his self-conceived rehab.

Florida had its dark side. How many park benches would he have to sit on here to find something worth detecting? How long, he wondered with some nostalgia, would it take to find something as engaging as the taggers. A paid case with clear parameters would be a nice change. He'd honed his craft on this one. What a notion – to be hired as a private eye by a paying client on the next.

As for the immediate future, Jake decided that, while in Florida, a good option would be to visit some Seminole sites. The concept of Jake Tracker had also come to mind – from another romantic notion fed by movies and by the possibility of his having Native blood.

For now, he would stay on the sand, letting the ocean wind and waves push against his churning thoughts and perhaps purge some of them.

In Travis McGee's words from John D. MacDonald's novel *A Deadly Shade of Gold*, "Waves can wash away the most stubborn stains, and the stars do not care one way or another."

Jake agreed: Waves, cleanse what you can of me, whether the stars care or not.

EPILOGUE

Sherlock Holmes, detective: *"The past and the present are within the field of my inquiry, but what a man may do in the future is a hard question to answer."*
– Sir Arthur Conan Doyle, *The Hound of the Baskervilles.*

WHILE DRIVING to the west of Lake Okeechobee, heading north to Seminole lands and the Brighton Casino after several days of touring, Jake received a call from Michael Smits, the DA. He pulled over to respond. Smits informed him that plea bargains had been reached for all those indicted. Each was to perform six months of community service. During that period, the female was to stay with her parents and the three others in a minimum-security facility. Jake wouldn't be needed as a witness after all and he could leave Florida. Smits also reminded him that Disney representatives had made it clear they would pursue a lawsuit if he violated the nondisclosure agreement. Jake doubted that would happen, since a lawsuit might disclose what Disney wanted non-disclosed.

In any case, the outcome hadn't turned out so bad for the erstwhile ENA activists. There were some advantages to the big Disney broom and rug. A smoke-bomb in a public place and destruction of property would have probably led to a stiffer sentence if WDW officials had wanted to publicize the event as a deterrent. But why give other taggers – and possibly worse than taggers – ideas? And why hurt business?

~

Music was blaring in order to keep people revved up to play. The casino actually reminded Jake of a theme park, something he didn't want to experience again so soon, and he didn't even place one bet. He left the casino's big noisy room and instead

214

wandered the corridors looking at artwork on walls and products in shop windows.

An elderly couple passed him – retirees, he guessed, seeking recreation and, if fate would have it, a windfall from gambling on their pension dollars.

As he walked past two men standing next to a water fountain – Native Americans apparently, given their long black hair and ribbonwork shirts – Jake overheard a bizarre statement: "Fancy Dancers don't commit murders."

Oh, really?

Jake continued on, glancing quickly over his shoulder. The two men followed him with their eyes, then abruptly turned and walked in the opposite direction.

www.ingramcontent.com/pod-product-compliance
Lightning Source LLC
Chambersburg PA
CBHW060431180626
46817CB00007B/2765